A Novel   Elle Rivers

For my husband, Josh, and my son, Kylan. You are my everything.

And for the typos that persisted through all of my edits. I admire your tenacity.

But I hope I won this battle with the help of the beautiful soul, Kasey Kubica.

A Note from Elle

This novel contains topics some readers may be sensitive to. Please note the following themes are present in this novel: discussions of alcohol and alcoholism, emotional manipulation from previous boyfriend and best friend, as well as favoritism and emotional manipulation from the main character's family. Also, at one point, it is mentioned the child in this book is pushed. It is not on page, and the person responsible is instantly reprimanded and told to leave. They are not redeemed in any way.

I want all of my readers to feel comfortable. If these topics trigger you, please consider skipping scenes or reading another one of my books. If I have missed any topics you feel need to be added, please reach out to me personally at @elleswrites on Instagram, and I will do my best to rectify the situation.

Chapter One

Riley

If Riley knew what was coming, maybe she would have stayed at the bar.

But she didn't. So her night started like any other.

Riley worked at a dime-a-dozen bar in downtown Nashville, Tennessee. Country music played loudly, and tourists in cowboy boots and hats came from all over to experience the Nashville scene. It was ironic, considering locals never came around here.

Riley was born and raised in Nashville, so she knew the difference between the downtown scene and the real city, but the bar paid well when it was busy, and she didn't care how trashy the place was as long as she could keep afloat.

It was a Saturday night, the peak of the party scene. Summer meant outdoor weddings and bachelor and bachelorette parties. The bars were always packed around this time.

Riley was in the trenches of making drinks when there was a jolt to the countertop. Cheap whiskey spilled on her shirt and the edge of the bar top caught her stomach.

Her head shot up, face set in a glare.

Two men were fighting, one pinned against the bar, the other attempting to hit him. Fights always broke out when people drank too much, and the manager never set a limit on how much people could be served. Usually, the bouncer would put a stop to it, but tonight's muscle was useless past midnight. He was probably asleep.

Riley, in all of her five-foot-three glory, had to put a stop to it. The other two bartenders were so busy they didn't notice anything was going on, so she would be getting no help.

"Hey!" Riley said, hoisting herself onto the bar to stand taller than the two morons fighting. "Break it up, guys!"

The men ignored her.

Riley rolled her eyes. Men never listened to her.

"I said break it up!" She jumped down, much less elegantly than she wanted to, and shoved her bony elbows in between the two of them. A punch flew and hit her shoulder. She turned and slammed her fist into the guy's face so hard it knocked him down.

He was probably too drunk to even stand up straight, but she was proud of herself anyway. The fight was over, even if her hand was aching.

"Hey!" the other guy snapped. "That's my brother!"

Riley turned to him; her eyes narrowed. "Are you fucking kidding me? Get out of here!"

"You should give me a free drink—"

"Get the fuck out!" Riley yelled. She was wondering if she was going to have to drag them out herself, but the bouncer, half asleep, grabbed the guy and pulled him out of the bar.

"Took you long enough," Riley muttered, shaking out her hand. Everyone was looking at her, which made her want to hide behind her bar. Luckily, her manager rushed out of their office and let Riley go home early for breaking up the fight.

Riley climbed into her car, her boyfriend's old SUV, and began the drive home. Her shoulder ached, and she knew she was going to be sore as hell the next day. She made plans to ice it and sit in a hot bath.

Riley pulled up to her apartment at 3 a.m., which was early for her. Usually she was out all night.

Her spot was taken by a familiar blue car. Riley wondered why Sarah, her best friend, would be at her apartment this late. Maybe Riley had missed a text where Sarah told her she was coming over, but Sarah hated Riley's boyfriend. So why was she here?

Riley peeled herself out of the car, the summer heat sticking to her skin. She groaned and pulled off her flannel.

As she walked up the stairs, she wondered what she would be walking into. David would be playing his video game up until Riley got home, but Sarah was a wild card. Riley hadn't ever known David and Sarah to be in the same room together.

Riley unlocked her door and walked in. The TV was off, and so was the PS5. Maybe David went to bed early—but he was the type of guy who slept during the day and stayed up all night, so he should have been awake.

She tossed her flannel onto the couch and turned to walk down the hallway to their bedroom, wondering where Sarah and David could be hiding.

She heard people talking, which made her pause.

"How are we going to tell her?"

Sarah's voice.

"She's going to be angry," she added.

"Yeah, but we have to let her know eventually," David replied. "It's hard here, babe. I feel bad every time I see her."

Riley blinked, her brain trying, and failing, to make sense of what she just heard.

Why the hell was David calling Sarah *babe*?

"I know, but she's my best friend," Sarah said. "I can't believe I did this to her."

"It's going to be better in the end. We love each other, and she knows she and I aren't going to work out."

Riley opened the door fully. Sarah and David abruptly turned.

"You . . . what?" Riley said, not able to form a complete sentence. She pointed between the two of them. "You guys are together?"

"Riley, what are you doing here?" David asked. "Your shift ends at five."

"No, you don't get to ask me what I'm doing here," Riley said. "I fucking live here. I pay half the rent!"

David looked away. That was a clear sign of guilt. David always made eye contact—except when he was guilty of something.

"Riley," Sarah started. "We didn't want to hurt you, but we just . . . it just . . . *happened* one day."

"One day? Like a one-time thing?" Riley asked.

Silence, and then Sarah spoke up.

"No."

"What the fuck?" Riley asked. "What the absolute fuck?"

"Riley," David said. "You had to have known this was coming. We don't work together. We make each other worse people."

Riley couldn't believe her ears.

She thought they worked.

Riley thought he was the one. Sure, they didn't spend a ton of time together and she hadn't felt a spark in years. That only meant they knew each other and were used to being together; they were comfortable, complacent. That wasn't a bad thing, was it?

"How . . . how did this even happen?" Sarah started to answer, but then Riley shook her head. "No, never mind. I don't want to know."

Riley left the hallway and grabbed her keys.

"Where are you going?" Sarah asked.

"Do you really think I'm going to stay here?" Riley snapped. She grabbed an empty cardboard box and set out to grab her clothes from the bedroom. The bed was a mess and Riley knew she had made it up before she left for work. That implication made her pack up her things faster.

She felt the threat of tears prick her eyes, but she forced herself not to cry, not while she was in their presence.

"Where are you going to go?" Sarah asked. "I'm sure we can make something work. David can come to my place, or we can stay in the guest room."

"Oh no. I cannot even look at the two of you right now," Riley said. "And I'm not telling you where I'm going because I don't want to see either of you."

"Are you going to your mom's house?" David asked.

"Fuck off, David," Riley said. That's exactly where she was planning on going—not that she'd admit it.

"That's a bad idea. You and your mom don't get along."

"Save the lecture." She emptied her two drawers of clothes into the box. "I don't think either of you have the moral high ground right now."

There was an awkward silence while Riley gathered her things. Her rage simmered underneath her skin and she felt like she could explode at any moment.

"I'm also not paying my share of the rent this month," Riley added as she hoisted up the box of her things. It felt good to say it.

"But—" David tried to say.

"Nope!" Riley said. "You can have the furniture in this divorce."

"But we weren't even married. You have to pay your share of the rent!"

Riley set her jaw and stared at David. "Is that all I'm good for? Rent?"

David was quiet.

"I don't have a job," Sarah said, her voice quiet.

"And whose fault is that?"

Sarah looked down.

"I'm not dealing with the guilt-tripping from you two," Riley said, rolling her eyes. "I'm leaving. Have a nice life."

"Riley, wait!" Sarah called, but Riley did not stop to listen. She didn't stop until she was in her car with the doors locked.

No one came after her.

Riley took a moment to make sense of it all, but she felt the threat of tears again, and this time it was worse than the last. Instead of crying, Riley turned on her car and drove to her mom's house, her fingers digging into the steering wheel and knuckles pale from the tight grip she held the entire way there.

When she arrived, no lights were on, as expected. Jane Emerson went to bed at nine on the dot, for she was a woman of habit. Luckily, Riley still had a key. She went in through the back door and tried to be as quiet as possible when she entered the room.

Riley grew up in a townhouse in Franklin, a suburb south of the city. When she was little, it was more of a small town where almost everyone knew each other. Now it was known as the upscale side of town. Riley's mother fit in perfectly.

The house still felt like it did when she was a kid. The granite countertops were sparkling clean, nothing on them. The dining room table was organized as if people were coming over at any given moment. The couch was in pristine condition. When either she or Amanda's kids were over, there was plastic on the furniture.

Riley, who was covered in whiskey and wearing only a tank top and jeans, felt out of place. She felt like she needed plastic on her *life*.

Her childhood bedroom had long since been converted into a guest room, but Riley knew it was still hers. The closet was filled with all of the things she left behind when she moved in with David.

It was in her old room that the thoughts hit her again, but this time, she let the tears spill over. For a moment, Riley was overwhelmed with emotion and cried on the floor. The carpet was comforting, and it felt like she was a teenager again and not a failed adult.

But soon, crying on the floor wasn't enough and she knew she wouldn't survive if she continued to feel the deep, aching pain in her chest.

Riley walked downstairs to the kitchen and found her mom's wine cabinet. Wine wasn't strong enough, but it would do since it's all she had.

She found the cheapest bottle and opened it. Hopefully, when Jane discovered it was gone, she wouldn't be too upset about it. Riley took a long drink, hoping the alcohol would chase away what happened.

The kitchen light flashed on and Riley turned to see her mother, in her fluffy robe, standing in the hallway.

"What are you doing here at 4 a.m.?" Jane asked, her critical voice cutting through Riley like a knife. Her mother eyed her state of dress. "Did you get into a fight?"

"It was at work. It's unrelated." Her voice cracked with emotion.

"Unrelated? Riley, that job is dangerous! I have told you time and time again you need to—"

"David is cheating on me," Riley said, stopping her mother's lecture.

"What?" Jane raised a hand to her chest and her jaw dropped open.

"David is cheating on me," Riley reiterated. And when her mother stared at her with wide eyes, she added tearfully, "with Sarah."

"Oh no," Jane said. "Really? Are you certain?"

"She admitted it," Riley said. "They both did."

Jane walked over to her daughter, arms outstretched for a hug, but she stopped when she got close.

"Oh, you smell awful. Go take a shower." Jane gently pulled the wine bottle out of Riley's hands. "And then we'll talk."

Riley would have taken the hug, but she was happier about the fact Jane wasn't mad about the wine.

"Do you . . . do you think I can stay here for a while? You know how rent around here is, and I can't—"

"It's fine. You can stay here. Now go get cleaned up."

Riley nodded, heading back to the bathroom she had been in a million times before.

She took a long look at herself in the mirror.

God, she really did look awful. Her brown hair was a mess, probably from the fight at work. Her hand and shoulder were already turning yellow against her pale skin.

Riley's face, however, was the worst. Her brown eyes were red and puffy. Her entire face was swollen from crying. Her skin was slightly flushed from the wine. She looked like she had been through the worst night of her life.

And she had.

Still in a daze, she turned on the water, setting the temperature as high as it would go. She ignored the pain in her hand and throughout her body as she stood in silence under the steady stream for a long time. When the hot water finally ran out, she went downstairs where her mom was already making breakfast for her.

Riley didn't know what her future was going to hold. She didn't know how long she was going to be living with her mom or what her life was going to look like without David in it.

They had been together for five years, and all of it was gone after one night.

Riley didn't say anything, but she let her mom feed her breakfast like when she was a kid. Jane asked her questions about how Riley found out, and what happened at her job. She answered in a distant voice, none of it feeling real.

Just a few hours ago, Riley's life was normal. She had her own place to live and a boyfriend who she thought loved her. Now, she found out it was all a lie, and her best friend was the reason why.

It was funny, she thought, how things could change so quickly.

Chapter Two

Oliver

Oliver was having a long day, and for a father of a four-year-old, long days were harder than they used to be.

For one thing, Oliver's daughter, Zoe, hated being away from him. That made going to work difficult. It had gotten so bad he was wishing he didn't need money to support them.

However, working was the only way he could afford to make a living for them. It was the only way they could live in a safe, gated neighborhood, and he could make sure she had the best childcare around.

Oliver worked for a health care company. His father was the CEO, and Oliver has been appointed to be the CFO right before Zoe was born. He had always been good with numbers, and because of his father, he was given a job as an analyst right out of college.

Then his work ethic helped him quickly rise through the ranks to CFO. He was proud of it, and he sometimes had more money than he knew what to do with, but it meant he had to trust his daughter to someone else.

"Just go to sleep!" a sharp voice yelled, breaking the silence of his home. That was Zoe's nanny, who came with a million and one references and qualifications.

Oliver felt a rush of protectiveness over his daughter. He never yelled at Zoe and felt personally responsible to make sure no one else did.

"No!" Zoe's voice said. "I'm not going to sleep until Daddy gets home!"

"Do you know what happens when little girls are bad?" the nanny asked in a threatening tone.

"I don't want the ruler. I want my dad!"

That was the final straw for Oliver, who felt a white-hot surge of anger pierce his chest. That was *his* little girl. No one talked to her like that.

"What is going on here?" Oliver's voice came loudly as he rounded the corner to the living room. Zoe ran over to him and hid her face in his legs. He knelt down to check on her. Her brown eyes were tear stained, but she had no other signs of injury on her.

"Mr. Brian!" the nanny exclaimed, putting on a friendly smile. "I didn't hear you come in."

"Would that have stopped you from threatening to hit my daughter?" he asked.

The nanny paused, obviously not knowing what to say.

"Sir, she was being very difficult and—"

"We agreed no corporal punishment," he reminded her, and before the nanny could even respond, he continued. "This isn't working out. I'm dismissing you from duty."

The nanny went red in the face. "For one mistake?"

Oliver looked at Zoe, who was staring at him with wide eyes. "One is far too many."

"Well—"

"I'm not interested in hearing excuses."

The nanny's cheeks darkened. "Sir, please give me another chance."

"Obviously you and Zoe don't get along. This isn't working out," he repeated.

The nanny stared at him for a long moment.

"I expect my full check for tonight then."

With that, the nanny grabbed her purse and stormed out of his home. Zoe was tense in his arms even after the nanny slammed the front door, a sound that echoed through the house.

"I'm sorry, Daddy," Zoe said quietly.

Oliver sighed. "It's okay. Sometimes things don't work out, and I'm sorry she threatened you with a ruler. Why didn't you tell me?"

Zoe shrugged.

"Is that why you didn't like her?"

"She's not you," Zoe said.

Oliver sighed again. Zoe had been attached to him ever since she could walk. He knew it was because he was the one parent who was consistent in her life.

"Baby," Oliver explained softly, "Daddy has to be able to go and work so we can have a nice house."

"I know," Zoe said sadly.

"Someone has to watch you while I'm gone."

"I know."

Oliver groaned, trying to draw out a plan in his mind for childcare. "Miss Amanda will have to watch you until we figure something out."

"Okay."

Oliver kissed his daughter's hair. "Let's go to bed."

Zoe was quiet as they did their bedtime routine. When he laid her down, she grabbed his arm to stop him from leaving. While she was falling asleep, Oliver checked his calendar and began sending invitations to his assistant to cover for the nanny while he worked.

Amanda had worked for him for a year now. She was professional and thorough, and had two boys of her own, which made her somewhat qualified to watch Zoe. He didn't like to have her do it, since it made his days in the office much busier, but when it came down to it, Amanda was capable, at least until her normal time of 5 p.m.

Amanda began accepting the invitations immediately and Oliver felt relieved she was so responsive. He knew she would be open to watch Zoe, as they got along somewhat well. Zoe still cried when Oliver left and Amanda could never get her to sleep, but he knew he could trust her not to hit his daughter.

Because Amanda had her own kids, she usually couldn't work nights. However, Oliver knew of a big charity gala coming up in a week that he needed to attend, so he took a chance and sent her an invitation for babysitting the night of the event. She sent him a text immediately after she received it.

Amanda: Can we talk about this one?

Oliver looked over to Zoe who was fast asleep. He began setting her down so he could get up. She moved in her sleep, but he was able to sneak away. He called Amanda once Zoe's door was shut.

"Hey," Amanda said.

"So, what's going on?"

"I can't watch Zoe that night, Oliver," Amanda said. "I wouldn't have childcare of my own, and Zoe hates my boys."

"I knew you probably couldn't, but I needed to ask. My dad has to go to the gala with me, so he can't watch her," he told her. He wasn't sure what he was going to do now.

"I'm sorry, Oliver. I know you can't cancel."

"Do you know anyone who could do this?" Oliver asked, going out on a limb. Maybe Amanda had a friend, or someone in her family could watch Zoe for the night. It would be better than a total stranger.

Amanda was silent for a long time. "I do know someone who would probably be free . . . but—"

"Who?"

"My sister, Riley," Amanda said.

"You never mentioned you have a sister."

"I do," Amanda said. "But she does her own thing most of the time. She's . . . sort of a mess, but she does like kids and she's surprisingly good with them."

"Would you trust her with your kids?"

Amanda paused. "Yes, I would. She's irresponsible, but not about kids."

"Is she safe? Would she hurt Zoe?"

"No," Amanda said, and she almost sounded horrified by the thought. "But she's . . . she works in a bar and drinks and is kind of into the party scene."

"I'm out of options," Oliver said, sighing. "Can you ask her? I can pay her."

"I will ask."

"Thank you," Oliver said.

"I'm sure she would be willing to do it. But Oliver, I want to warn you again, I'm only suggesting this because there's no one else. She's not your normal kind of babysitter."

"It's for a few hours," Oliver replied, taking a deep breath. He was going to have to deal with it. He was out of options. "Besides, as long as she's safe, I'm fine with it."

"Let me ask her. Can I come in late tomorrow? She's staying with my mom, and I can stop by there to ask her in person."

"Sure," Oliver said. "Let me know what she says."

"I will," Amanda replied.

"Thank you, Amanda." He hung up the phone.

He turned to poke his head back into Zoe's room. She was still asleep, holding onto the blanket where Oliver had laid. She was his whole world, and while he didn't know Amanda's sister, what other options did he have? He hoped it wouldn't be a total disaster.

He felt a wave of exhaustion hit him. He was so tired of nights like this, where he was scrambling to get childcare figured out, where he was sneaking away from Zoe, who only wanted to be near him.

Oliver had been doing this alone for four years now, and he was tired. He only wished someone else could step in and take over for a bit.

Chapter Three

Riley

Riley was face down in her bed, drool coming out of her mouth. It had only been a few days since she started living with her mom, and it was already rough. Being around her mom too long was something that drove Riley up the wall. And Sarah's betrayal didn't help anything, either.

How could Sarah have done this to her? She had always been on Riley's side, always quick to come to her defense. Plus, Sarah never even liked David and always said he was a bad influence.

It didn't make sense. Sarah and David would never work together. David had to be in control. He wanted things to be clean and organized and to know how everything worked. Sarah was messy and was still figuring out her life.

There was no way they could work, no way they *should* work. Riley and David always worked because she was good at being whatever he wanted. Sarah wasn't going to be able to do the same.

The sound of her door opening, a shrill squeak from the old hinges, caused Riley to blearily look up. The sun pounded against her head.

Riley's sister was standing in the doorframe. Amanda was younger by two years and had her entire life together. She had a stable job working for some executive of a huge medical company and a perfect husband and two amazing kids.

Riley, obviously, was nothing like her.

Amanda didn't talk to Riley much. They hadn't spoken since she broke it off with David.

"Are you here to make your apologies for my shitty ex?" Riley asked.

"Are you hungover?" Amanda retorted, her tone accusatory. Riley felt embarrassment wash over her at her current state, but then she mentally shook it off. She refused to feel guilty for being cheated on.

Riley muttered, "Doesn't matter."

"What happened to your shoulder?" Amanda asked, gesturing to the black and blue bruises showing behind the green tank top.

"Work," Riley said.

"Nice," Amanda replied sarcastically, crossing her arms. "You're dealing with your stress by drinking and you're getting into fights at work. Very mature of you."

Riley rolled her eyes. It was one thing to be told off by her mother, but another to be told off by her *younger* sister.

"Aren't you supposed to be nice to me because I was dumped?"

"Nope, not at all. You're my sister and this is tough love," Amanda said. Riley hated how confident she sounded.

"Why are you even here? Isn't it a weekday? Shouldn't you be working?"

"I got permission from my boss to come and talk to you."

"Why?" Riley sat up. Her head protested the action. She knew she shouldn't have gone for the tequila.

"Can you at least get more ready for the day?"

"Amanda, I got in at 6 a.m."

"Whatever." She rolled her eyes. "I need you to do me a favor."

"And you thought the best way to ask was by coming here and lecturing me?"

"You would get something out of it too," Amanda said. "Trust me, you're not in a position to refuse."

"I will if I want to," Riley replied. "I had the worst night of my life recently, so I get a bit of a pass here."

Amanda sighed, rubbing her forehead. She looked annoyed, but also a little stressed. For the first time, Riley wondered what the favor was.

"For what it's worth," Amanda said, in a softer voice, "I'm sorry this happened to you. David leaving you for Sarah is awful. No one saw it coming."

Riley's defensiveness faded.

"Well, nothing I can do now," she said quietly. "I thought he was the one but . . . maybe not."

"Wasn't he kind of a loser?" Amanda asked.

"I never thought he was," Riley replied, and her immediate response was to defend him. He wasn't a loser; her family didn't understand him. But then she remembered the night from hell, and . . . well, maybe Riley herself never understood him, either.

Amanda rolled her eyes again. "Your taste in men, I swear."

"Okay, enough judgment," Riley snapped bitterly. "What did you come here for? What favor do you need?"

"My boss needs a babysitter."

Riley blinked. "And you're asking me?"

"Yes, I am. He really needs someone. It's at night and you're the only person available."

"Can't mom do it?"

"God, no," Amanda said, shaking her head. "Mom does not have the patience for this kid at all. They would both be screaming by the time the night was over."

Riley had to agree. Jane didn't even really watch Amanda's kids by herself. She knew her mom loved her grandkids, but she had done her time as a parent and didn't want to do it any more than she had to.

"Why are you asking me?"

"I'm asking you because you're patient with my kids, and this one is . . . difficult."

"That bad, huh?"

Amanda sighed. "She's not bad, but she's really attached to her father. So when he's gone, she gets . . . emotional."

That didn't sound *too* terrible. She could probably figure out how to be there emotionally for a little girl. And even if she couldn't—it was only for a few hours, right? "And why can't you watch this kid?" she asked. Riley knew Amanda would rather cut off her own hand than ask for help from her.

"Luke and Landon . . . don't get along with her," Amanda said, and the last part was grounded out, like she hated admitting it.

"They bully her, don't they?" Riley asked. Luke and Landon were more than a handful.

"My kids are not bullies! They roughhouse."

"Yes, and when the other party doesn't like it, it's bullying," Riley reminded her.

"Okay, enough about me and my kids," Amanda said, her tone tense. She hated being criticized. "The point is, he'll pay you, and I know you want your own apartment instead of living with mom forever."

Riley considered it. She did miss her independence. Her mom had already noticed Riley was sneaking bottles of whiskey into the house.

"Okay, I do need the money," Riley admitted.

"Can you appear like a normal human being for a few hours?"

"I *am* a normal human being," Riley defended.

"You dress like you found your clothes in a dumpster."

Riley narrowed her eyes at Amanda. Yeah, Riley's clothes were old and mostly from Goodwill, but she didn't have a job where she needed to dress up every day.

"I'm a bartender. Do you think I'm going to wear my nicest clothes to a place where people try to I have to break up fights and get booze spilled on me?"

"Yes," Amanda said, crossing her arms. "You dress for the job you want, not the job you have."

"It's really obvious you've never worked a service job."

Amanda headed straight to college after high school and began working for the company she was at currently as soon as she graduated.

She was so lucky and didn't even realize it.

Riley was sure Jane wanted the same for her, but that wasn't the path she chose.

Amanda rolled her eyes. "Riley, I'm being serious. This is my job. I need you to do this right."

"Fine, I will dress decently for your rich boss man," Riley said to get Amanda's glare off of her. "I'm not going to do anything that gets you in trouble. I think I can handle watching one little girl for a few hours."

"Thank you, so you're free Thursday night? Mom's been adding your work schedule to our shared calendar."

"Yeah, I'm off," Riley said. It felt weird to have her job listed next to Amanda's on the shared calendar, and even weirder that Jane took it upon herself to add it. But this was how her mom was—she had to know everything.

"Okay, I'll let him know."

"What's his name?" Riley asked. She felt sort of bad she never knew who Amanda's boss was. Then again, she didn't exactly care to know—what would she do with that information anyway? She wasn't their mom. She didn't need to know everything her family was doing.

"Oliver Brian. His daughter's name is Zoe. She's four. And she really is the sweetest thing," Amanda said as she pulled out her phone, presumably to alert her boss.

"Great, so I won't be bringing wine," Riley joked.

Amanda looked up from her phone to glare at her.

"I'm kidding," Riley said, rolling her eyes. No one in her family appreciated her humor.

Amanda returned to texting her boss and Riley sighed. This couldn't be *that* bad, but the pressure was still on. This was her perfect little sister's job at risk, after all.

Thursday came and Riley found herself driving to Oliver Brian's at 5 p.m. She knew he was affluent just by the fact he had an assistant, but it still did not prepare her for the moment she pulled up to his house.

Riley knew she would be going to the fancier side of town. Green Hills didn't come without its huge price tag, so she expected something nice.

But *this*? What company did this guy work for?

Oliver lived in a gated community, and the security guard at the entrance side-eyed her when she pulled up, as if she was too poor to even be entering the area. Oliver's house was in the back, in a cul-de-sac all on its own. It was a large, two-story house with a huge driveway. It was a painted white brick, probably built recently. In fact, the entire neighborhood was definitely new, and came with the recent housing boom Nashville had experienced.

As Riley climbed out of her car, she wondered who she had to kill to get a place as nice as this one, and then knocked on the door.

"Coming!" a man's voice called, and a moment later, the door opened.

Riley was floored when she saw Oliver for the first time. He was the hottest guy she had ever seen—much less talked to.

She tended to stay with guys in her own league. David was probably a solid seven, and she was maybe an eight on her best day. This guy scored off the chart.

He was tall—six foot, dressed in a tailored suit that hugged his shoulders and waist. His black hair was pushed back on his head, and his dark eyebrows were pulled low as he fixed his shirt sleeve. He had a sharp jawline and a lithe figure.

For a second, Riley could only stare at him, and she wondered if she looked lost. Luckily, the guy didn't notice her expression.

Once his shirt sleeve was straight, his eyes met hers, and Riley had to stop herself from either drooling or saying something incredibly stupid.

"Are you Riley?"

His voice was kind, but firm. It held a level of self-assuredness Riley would never be able to have. She swallowed her emotions, determined not to look foolish in front of him. Amanda would kill her if she did anything wrong tonight.

"I'd have to be to get by the front gate," Riley said.

"Oh yeah, I forgot about the gate," he said. "Come on in. I'm Oliver."

"I'm Riley . . . but you already knew that." She cursed her awkwardness. She was still trying to get past how hot he was. "Now where is this Zoe I've heard so much about?"

"She's a little nervous about tonight." He gestured to the arched door of the hallway where a small head was poking around the corner.

"Oh," Riley said. "I'm sure it'll be fine. We'll get along."

"Right . . ." Oliver said. It didn't sound like he believed it, which didn't do much for Riley's confidence. "She can be difficult for people she doesn't know. I also typically don't leave at night."

"If I can survive the terrors that are my sister's kids then I should be fine."

"I don't believe in corporal punishment," Oliver said, and Riley turned back to look at him, confused.

"I . . . don't either?" Riley said, unsure of how to respond.

"I'm making my expectations clear that . . ." He paused, and then added, "No hitting her if anything goes wrong."

"Understood," Riley said. "Just for the record though, I wouldn't do that to my own kids, much less someone else's."

Oliver looked at her as if he was unsure if he believed her. Riley wondered if Amanda had said something, and if her sister really thought she would hit a child.

But that seemed low, much lower than her sister would go.

"Sorry," Oliver said. "I'm not saying that because I don't trust you. There have been issues in the past."

For a moment, Riley wasn't sure what to say. "Oh, uh . . . It won't be any issue with me."

"People do stupid things when stressed, and I plan on tonight being stressful for everyone involved."

"Okay."

"It's not you," Oliver said. "It's the situation. You need to know what you'll be getting into."

Riley nodded, taking a deep breath to calm her nerves. "I get it. I'll deal with whatever happens here so you can do what you need to do without worrying."

"Can I have your number?" Oliver asked. "Just in case either of us needs anything."

Riley really could have let her mind go places. Just in case they needed each other? *For what?* But Riley reminded herself she was here for Zoe and no one else.

"Yeah, of course," Riley said, and she rattled off her number. Oliver was visibly tense—she saw it in his jaw and his posture. She felt for the guy. Riley didn't have kids, but she knew it had to be hard leaving them.

"Zoe, come here and meet your babysitter, please," Oliver called. The little girl slowly came around the corner, looking down at the floor as she did so. She bypassed Riley entirely and hid her face in Oliver's legs. Riley only caught the fact she had dark hair like her dad.

"Do you have to go, Daddy?" she asked, quiet enough Riley almost couldn't hear her.

"I'm sorry, honey, I do," Oliver replied. "But I'm not gone all night. I'll be back before you know it."

"What if she's mean?" Zoe asked, and Riley winced. Yeah, that wasn't a good sign.

"She's not mean. She's nice. She's Miss Amanda's sister," Oliver said, and Riley could see he was trying to make Zoe excited about the new babysitter, but it came out stilted. It was like Oliver knew it wasn't going to work.

"Miss Amanda doesn't have a sister."

"Yes she does, and it's Miss Riley."

"You don't look like her," Zoe said, turning to Riley. Riley finally got a good look at the little girl. She had brown eyes, which were not from Oliver, and chubby cheeks with an innocence about her Riley wished she still had.

But she couldn't think about how cute the tiny girl was, since Zoe was expecting an answer.

And Zoe was right. Amanda and Riley didn't look much alike. Amanda got her curly, dark hair from her mom's side of the family. Riley got lighter brown and straight hair from her dad. She also had brown eyes and a completely different nose than her sister.

"That's right, I'm much better looking," Riley said.

"No you're not," Zoe muttered.

"Zoe, be nice," Oliver said to his daughter before looking at Riley apologetically. "I am so sorry."

"No, it's fine," Riley replied. "But I do have photos to prove I'm better looking than Amanda."

The little girl looked at her skeptically. "Amanda is nice and pretty. You're mean and ugly."

"Zoe!" Oliver snapped, but Riley waved him off.

She pulled out her phone and scrolled to a photo of Amanda she saved from years ago. It was a very unflattering picture Riley had taken at her sister's wedding. "Here's my proof."

Zoe turned to look at the screen and a smile lit up her face. "She's got two chins!"

"See? I think I'm better looking than this photo."

Zoe paused to consider this for a moment.

"Do you have a ruler?" Zoe asked.

"Nope, no ruler," Riley said. "I don't even have a bag. Purses are for losers." To demonstrate, Riley twirled around, showing she just had her phone and wallet on her.

And then, by some miracle, Zoe let go of her father's legs. Riley wanted to cheer.

Oliver's phone jingled and he sighed. "My ride's here. Zoe, will you be good for Riley?"

Zoe nodded, but her timidness returned.

"I'll miss you, kiddo," Oliver said, and he gave Zoe a hug.

"Miss you too."

"Please call me if anything comes up," Oliver said to Riley before he let go of Zoe and walked out the front door. The little girl's eyes never left her father's figure until he was gone, and they stayed at the door for a good minute after.

Riley remained silent, unsure of what to do. Oliver hadn't given her much direction on her bedtime or anything. She guessed she would have to figure it out. Riley knew Amanda would be pissed if anything went wrong, but what could she do if she didn't receive any instructions?

It was at that moment Zoe turned and ran up the stairs too fast for Riley to even react, much less stop her. She heard a door slam and figured the girl had locked herself in her room.

"Great," Riley muttered. "We're off to an awesome start."

Riley followed her, and thankfully, there was a door decorated with posters of movies and pictures of Zoe. At least she knew where the little girl's room was. She gently knocked on the door.

"Go away!" Zoe yelled. "I don't want you here."

Riley took a deep breath, trying not to get angry at the situation.

"It's okay," Riley said. "You don't have to let me in. We all need space sometimes. But when you do need me, I'll be here."

She took a few steps back and sat on the ground, leaning against the opposite wall. She took out her phone and immediately began researching what she could about four-year-olds. Riley was unsure if she had done the right thing, or if Zoe would ever like her.

However, just as Riley was about to knock on the door again, or call Oliver, Zoe's door opened, and the girl crept out.

"Hey," Riley said. "Do you need me?"

"Why did he have to go?"

"Your dad probably told people he would be somewhere, and it's only fair to them that he's there."

"But I don't want him to go."

"I know, and it's okay not to want him to go, as long as you remember he will come back."

"Does he love me?"

"Oh, of course." Riley tried to sound as earnest as she could. "I'm sure he didn't want to go either, and I've only just met him, and I know he loves you."

Zoe seemed to think about something for a second, and then she walked over to where Riley was sitting, and sat down right in her lap. Riley was shocked, but didn't say anything, knowing she had to let the girl do whatever she needed. She was no stranger to the fact that kids sometimes needed someone to simply hug them to make them feel better.

"Daddy is coming home," Zoe said, but she was mostly talking to herself.

"That's right," Riley said.

"Can we watch a movie?"

"What movie?"

"*Moana*," Zoe answered simply. "I don't like *Frozen*. It's boring."

Riley smiled and nodded and let the little girl lead her to wherever she wanted to watch the movie. They sat on the giant sectional in the living room and Riley got the movie running after a few minutes of fumbling with the complicated remote. Zoe sat next to her silently, before she scooted closer to be right next to Riley.

After the movie, Zoe asked for dinner, and Riley had to try to cook something. She was more of a mixer than a chef, but she managed to make a grilled cheese Zoe seemed happy with. After dinner, Zoe wanted to play with her dolls, and Riley did so, wondering when Oliver would be home.

It was obvious Zoe wanted to stay awake to see her dad get back. She kept glancing at the door, but also kept rubbing her eyes. Riley was concerned if she asked about Zoe's bedtime, she would only get a temper tantrum since she was already so exhausted. So, she let Zoe lead.

"When is he coming home?" Zoe finally asked.

"I'm not sure," Riley answered.

Zoe teared up. "He always goes to sleep with me."

"Oh no," Riley said. "Well, if you're tired, I can go to sleep with you for now. I know I'm not your dad, but I'm here."

"Will you cuddle with me?" Zoe asked.

"Of course."

Zoe nodded, and dropped her dolls, marching to her room. Riley pulled off her shoes and followed the little girl. Zoe laid in the middle of her bed and Riley positioned herself next to her on the right side. Zoe instantly curled into her and was asleep in a few minutes. Riley felt herself smile.

This was exactly what she needed after everything that happened. In the few hours since Oliver left, she hadn't even thought about David or Sarah; she was more focused on making sure Zoe was happy.

Riley felt herself drift off after Zoe was in a deep sleep, tired from the night of watching a four-year-old. She didn't think about the messy house, or the fact the TV was still on. It was possibly a mistake, but she was in a comfortable bed with a little girl by her side, so she forgot about everything else.

Chapter Four

Oliver

The charity gala was giving Oliver a headache. He'd had way too many photos of himself taken, talked to far too many people, and ate way too many of those tiny appetizers they were serving.

It was a long night, and it seemed to drag go on and on. His father asked him to stay until the speech was given announcing the donors of the event, but for some reason it was being delayed. Both he and his dad were annoyed, but they needed to stay.

"When is this going to end?" Oliver asked his father, Jack.

Jack Brian was a good man who ran a good company. Oliver was lucky to work with him, and even luckier to have him as a father. He was kind and caring, and always took a gentle hand with parenting. Oliver wanted to do the same thing for Zoe, but his exhaustion from being a single parent with no help other than his busy father was wearing on him.

"I don't know. I heard they were having sound issues," Jack said.

"I need to get back to Zoe. She's probably having a total meltdown by now."

"You left her with Amanda's sister, right?"

"Yeah, she seemed nice, but you know how Zoe is, and I can't get what happened with the last nanny off my mind." Oliver shook his head. He didn't really need to think about the incident from a week ago, not while he had to be out in public for work, not while he was away from his daughter who was in the hands of a stranger. A ton of his employees were here, and he refused to let them see his worried mood.

"I understand. I am sure she is fine, Oliver. Amanda wouldn't have suggested her sister if it were anything but safe."

Oliver sighed. "I know, but that doesn't make me not want to run home."

"Hopefully this will get started soon," Jack reassured him. "Why don't you go get something to drink? Staring at the stage will only make this worse."

Oliver nodded, agreeing he needed to do something else to distract him. He walked over to the bar, but as he approached, he bumped into someone and spilled their drink all over them.

"Oh no, I'm so sorry," Oliver apologized. In the back of his mind, he hoped this wasn't a precursor to worse things that would happen tonight.

"Oh, it's okay." The voice belonged to a petite blonde woman. "I wasn't watching where I was going."

Oliver reached over to the bar and grabbed a handful of napkins. "Here, at least let me help."

"Well, thank you," she said as she looked up at him. In doing so, her eyes lit up. "Oh, you must be Oliver Brian."

"I am."

"I work with your father at the company. I'm in legal. I only started a month ago. It's so nice to finally meet you. I'm Sophie."

Oliver smiled at her. She was quite a beautiful lady, with her long, blonde hair and bright eyes. He normally didn't look at women, especially ones he worked with, for he was too concerned with ensuring Zoe was accounted for and happy while also keeping his work life separate. But his desire to date someone and *finally* give Zoe the maternal figure he knew she needed won out. Sophie had a dazzling, kind smile, one that faintly reminded him of someone he couldn't place.

"Nice to meet you," he said. "How are you liking the event?"

"It's very fancy. I love that the company invited everyone to this kind of thing. Usually it's only reserved for the special people."

"Everyone is special here."

Sophie smiled widely, pleased with his answer. "How are you liking the gala so far?"

"While it's nice, it's taking forever," he said. Usually this was where he would stop, but he continued on anyway. "I have a daughter at home, and I would love to get back to her."

"Oh, you have a little girl? How old is she?"

Oliver smiled. At least she asked about Zoe. That was a good start. For a moment, he imagined a life where he wasn't as lonely as he was now—where he could have someone to lean on when the days were rough.

"Four. Would you like to see photos?" Oliver asked excitedly. Sophie nodded with a smile and Oliver found himself swiping through various photos of the two of them. Sophie seemed interested and pointed out a few she thought were extra adorable.

It felt . . . wrong to share pictures of Zoe at work, but he had to get out of his shell somehow to meet someone.

"Looks like the presentation is starting," Sophie said, motioning to where the lights had come on. "But I'd really like to get your number, if that's okay."

Oliver smiled, despite his gut swirling with unease, and they swapped phone numbers. She thanked him and disappeared into the crowd, presumably to join her own supervisor. Oliver walked over to Jack, who asked, "Picking up someone at work?"

"You always say I need to open up more."

"She seems very lovely," Jack said. Oliver started to reply, but the lights dimmed, and the presentation finally began. He took a deep breath, hoping everything at his house was okay and he wouldn't return to a screaming child.

The presentation dragged on and the moment it was over, Oliver was heading out of the venue. He called Riley, but there was no answer, which did nothing for his frayed nerves. His leg bounced the entire car ride home, and when he finally arrived, he threw the cash at the driver and ran inside.

Oliver opened the door, shrugged off his suit jacket, and looked around. The house was silent, but the living room lights were on. He walked into the room, finding the TV still on, and dolls thrown around the room—as if Zoe had been playing all night.

But the little girl was nowhere to be found.

It was past ten and Oliver knew Zoe would be exhausted. She wouldn't be asleep though—not for someone she only met tonight.

Oliver also found a pair of Converse on the ground that had to be Riley's, and her phone sitting on the coffee table. Oliver turned off the TV, wondering where they could be. He crept upstairs to find Zoe's door wide open. He glanced in, curious if she was in there.

The room was dark, but the light from the hallway illuminated it enough to see Zoe in her bed. She was sound asleep, mouth wide open, and she was cuddled into Riley's side, as if she were Oliver himself.

Riley was asleep too. Oliver knew he could be annoyed, because technically Riley was sleeping on the job, but for Riley to be asleep, Zoe had to be too.

That was more of a miracle than anything else.

How many nights had Oliver come home, hoping and praying his daughter had finally gone to sleep without him? It was too many to count, and he never thought he would see the day she was asleep while he was gone.

Yet the day had come, and it was for a woman Zoe didn't even know.

This was the last thing he expected to see.

He felt like a bucket of ice had been dumped over him. Yes, the house was a mess and the lights were left on.

But Zoe was asleep.

There had been far too many nights where the house was spotless and everything was perfect. But Zoe was unhappy and had been counting the seconds until he got home.

He would take this any day.

As Oliver was deep in his thoughts, Riley woke, and she jumped when she saw him. It didn't seem to stir Zoe, and Riley was able to successfully untangle herself from the little girl without waking her. Oliver wondered how she was so good at that. He had woken Zoe up hundreds of times trying to leave her room.

Riley tiptoed to the door where Oliver was standing, shutting it behind her silently.

"Has anyone ever told you that you look like Slenderman when you're in doorways?" Riley asked.

Oliver blinked, shocked. "No, they haven't."

"Well, I'll be the first to say it," Riley replied as she brushed past him to go down to the living room.

Riley looked different after a night of work. When Oliver first met her, he thought she was exactly what Amanda had said: a bit of a mess and all over the place.

She seemed to like Zoe, and that's what mattered. Plus, he didn't have a lot of options.

But now, Riley looked different. She was tired, for one, but she looked as if she had been studying something all night, her brows pulled low on her forehead and her lips tense. When she was focused on something, she looked a lot like Amanda.

Oliver took this opportunity to really absorb her. When she had arrived, he was trying to get ready for a miserable night and had only let her in to introduce her to Zoe before he left. He figured this would be the first and last time he ever saw her, so it didn't exactly matter.

Now, he wasn't so sure.

He had more time to look at her, and he could see a couple similarities to Amanda. They had the same curve of their brow and chin. But that was where their family resemblance ended.

Riley had straight, long hair, pulled into a bun. She looked shorter than Amanda, but it could have been the fact his assistant always wore heels and Riley was currently barefoot.

With the way Amanda had spoken about her, Oliver assumed Riley was her younger sister, and yet, looking at her now, he was seeing Riley was quite possibly his age, and older than Amanda after all.

"Sorry for falling asleep and leaving the mess," she said as he followed her downstairs. Her voice was tense, as if she was ready for a lecture. "I needed to distract Zoe to keep her happy."

"No, I'm . . . I'm glad she was happy. She's not great for babysitters."

Riley looked at him. "She was shy. Definitely different from Amanda's kids, but I kept distracting her until she mentioned going to bed."

"She mentioned it?"

"She asked when you were coming home as she rubbed her eyes. I put the pieces together. I was wondering when her bedtime was anyway, so it worked out."

"She doesn't go to sleep for anyone but me," Oliver said quietly. "That was the first time."

"Really?" Riley asked. "I guess I got lucky then."

"Are you sure you don't have kids? You did . . . really well tonight."

Riley's cheeks turned pink like she wasn't used to being complimented. "No, I don't. But they're little adults, like us, just mini versions. I guess my philosophy is to treat them like that."

The words flew out of Oliver's mouth before he could stop them. "Do you need a job?"

Riley looked at him, shocked. "I have a job, why? Are you asking me to watch her at night or something?"

Before she even finished her sentence, Oliver had a plan formulating in his mind. "Zoe needs a new nanny during the daytime. You're the only one she's liked so far."

"And you're asking me?"

"I would pay you really well if you agree," he added.

"Wait, hold on. I'm still working past the part where you're asking *me* to be a nanny. Are you sure about this?"

Riley looked at him like he had two heads, and Oliver couldn't blame her. He didn't make it a habit of offering people jobs on the spot, but seeing Zoe asleep had sealed the deal.

"This is the first time I've come home to Zoe actually being asleep. It's been only me for her entire life, and I have been through countless other people. No one did what you did. So, yes, I'm sure."

"Oh," Riley said, her voice quiet. She went silent, obviously lost in thought. "Well, can I think about it? My schedule isn't that busy, so I can make something work, it's just . . ." Riley trailed off. It was obvious she was unsure of how to word what she was trying to say.

"No need for an explanation, but please do think about it. Just so you know, there wouldn't be a further interview. I'd consider this a job well done."

"You came home to a messy house."

"And a happy child. That's more important."

"I don't think I did anything *that* great, but I see your point," Riley said, smiling. "But I will seriously think about it. It was fun hanging out with an adorable four-year-old."

"Well, you have my number," Oliver said. "I hope you give me a call."

"Will do, sir," Riley said, a teasing twinkle in her eyes. Oliver blanched for a moment, unsure if she was flirting or if this was her personality. "Until next time," she said, and he shook her outstretched hand.

She was gone before he could say anything else. And he was left hoping he would see her again.

Chapter Five

Riley

Riley had been offered a job.

That was the last thing she expected to hear when Oliver returned home.

Riley thought she'd done a poor job. Yes, Zoe was happy and seemed to like her, but the house was a mess. Things were left turned on, mostly because Riley was too focused on Zoe to even worry about it. Of course, she cleaned up before she left, but she didn't think she was going to get paid for it. However, when Oliver sent her the money through PayPal, those few extra minutes were included.

Though he was a bit scatterbrained and didn't give much instruction, Riley knew he was a good boss, simply by the fact Amanda never complained about him. That alone made her consider the gig.

But Amanda wouldn't like it. She would think Riley was the worst option for the job. In fact, she told Riley many times that she was the fun aunt, and only asked her to babysit when she didn't have any other options.

At the same time, Zoe was adorable. She felt like she could really get along with the sweet little girl. It also felt like a job she would like—not be something solely to pay the bills.

Then there was the fact Oliver was also really good looking. She would be happy to go to work every day and look at *that* even if she knew it would never go anywhere.

Riley pulled into her mom's driveway and took a deep breath. She supposed she had a lot of thinking to do. As she climbed out of the car, she checked her phone and saw a text from Sarah, which was simply another apology. She frowned and decided not to answer it. Everything was still raw and sore, and it hurt like the moment she walked into her old apartment.

There were reminders of David everywhere. Even the car she drove used to be his, and one of his flannels was still in the back seat. If Riley focused hard enough, she could still remember the smell of his body wash and the feel of his kiss on her lips. She knew so much about him—his schedule, favorite foods, the way he took his coffee, the way he slept with one leg off the side of the bed—and it didn't make sense that all of that was *gone*.

Riley rubbed her face when she shut the door to her car. She was tired of feeling betrayed and hurt. It was getting worse with each passing day because so much of her life had been intertwined with David's. A knife had cut the tendons of her relationship, and that knife was her best friend.

Her family didn't understand, but she never expected them to. According to them, David was a loser from the start, she was better off without him, but their opinions didn't matter. Riley still loved him.

She felt her eyes burn as she walked through the door. She was so tired of crying, but it seemed to keep happening.

"Amanda texted," a voice said, and Riley jumped out of her skin. She turned to see her mother, still dressed, and sitting on the couch.

"Oh," Riley said, feeling her stomach drop. "What did she want?"

"She wanted to make sure you didn't ruin her job for her."

"Well, that's one way to put it," Riley muttered.

"Riley, this was that man's child, and she was very young. Please tell me you didn't have anything to drink."

"Do you really think I would drink while watching a four-year-old?"

"It would not surprise me," her mother said bluntly.

That stung. Riley may have liked drinking, and yes, maybe sometimes she used it instead of dealing with her problems, but she never would do it while watching a child.

"I didn't. Everything went fine. And for your information, he offered me a job as her nanny because he was so impressed."

That was mostly the truth. His house had been a wreck when he came home, but Riley was not dumb enough to tell her mom that. Oliver still wanted her to be Zoe's nanny, despite that, even if she didn't exactly get why.

"You're lying. I can tell when you lie, Riley."

She frowned. "I'm not."

"Riley, this child is not Luke or Landon, who can essentially take care of themselves thanks to Amanda's excellent parenting."

She rolled her eyes. Her mother's favorite thing to do was compliment Amanda and her parenting. In Riley's opinion, Amanda's kids were average, at best.

"The kid is fine. She was happy," Riley said.

"Okay . . . I am sure I will find out the truth from Amanda," her mother said. Normally, when Jane said something like that, Riley felt guilty, because it usually meant she had done something wrong. This time though, she hadn't. Oliver seemed genuinely happy. Maybe this was the time she did something right.

"I'm sure you will," Riley said. "I'm going to go to bed."

"I know you're not. And do not bring anymore alcohol into this house. I threw away what you snuck in."

Riley paused, but she knew she couldn't say anything. This was her mom's house. She was living here for free. However, she missed her freedom. She missed being able to do what she wanted and not be treated like a child. Besides, her mother had wine in the house and always drank two glasses after work. It wasn't fair for Riley to be told not to drink when her mother obviously didn't have the same rule for herself.

As she walked upstairs, she pondered Oliver's offer. He was going to pay her well. That and her money from the bar meant she could save up and be able to afford rent for an apartment on her own.

Riley made the decision before she even got to her room.

She was going to be Oliver's nanny, and she was going to do a damn good job at it.

Riley shut her door and dialed Oliver. It was still late, but she was hoping he was still up.

"I didn't expect you to call so soon." He must have been a straight-to-business kind of guy.

"I make my decisions quick," Riley said. "I'm in, I would love to be Zoe's nanny."

"Really?" Oliver asked.

"Yeah, she's a great kid. But I do have a few things I want to talk to you about before we really agree on it."

"Okay, go ahead," he replied.

"I do want to keep my other job. It shouldn't interfere with anything. I work late and mostly on weekends."

"That's fine with me."

"And I want to remind you, in case Amanda didn't say anything, I'm probably not going to ever fit the traditional description of a nanny."

"I understand. As long as you keep Zoe safe, I really don't care what you do in your free time. That's up to you."

Riley took a deep breath. "Okay. Perfect."

"Is there anything else?"

"Uh, yeah, what did you say the hourly rate was?"

"Twenty an hour."

"*Shit.* I mean, uh . . . that is more than fair," Riley said, catching herself. If she was working full-time, that was way more than the bar paid her, even after tips. She would be out of her mom's house in no time.

"I want Zoe to be happy, but I also want it to be worth your time. When can you start?"

Chapter Six

Oliver

Riley showed up with her hair in a bun and coffee in her hand, but she was on time. She looked exhausted, and Oliver had the good sense not to mention it.

Riley was wearing the same thing as the night before, but in different colors. She had on a dark tank top with a red and yellow flannel layered over it. It wasn't the kind of flannel bought recently. It was an older piece, definitely a man's size.

Oliver barely registered their initial meeting, but after her impressive first night with Zoe, she was committed to his memory. She was small with a bit of chubbiness around her curves that made her look younger than she was. And though he tried not to, he noticed how her jeans hugged her backside when she bent down, and how much of her front the tank top showed off.

It was obvious Riley dressed for comfort. She didn't dress up for work, or in a uniform like some nannies Oliver had employed. She was here as herself, not some better version. He liked that she seemed to be upfront and honest about who she was.

"I normally work nights, so please don't judge my blood's caffeine level by the time today is over," Riley said when she walked in.

"Well, I appreciate you coming in," Oliver said. "It was Amanda's turn to babysit and I'm sure she appreciates the reprieve too."

"She's got two kids, so I don't blame her."

"But if you need more time to acclimate to a day schedule, I can—"

"No, no, it's fine," Riley said, waving him off. "It was easier to do this in my teens than it is now, if you know what I mean."

Oliver made a weak attempt to match her joking tone. "Are you calling me old?"

"Oh yeah," Riley said, laughing. "You're definitely ancient. I'm sure they have pictures of you in museums."

He laughed. "Yeah, yeah. But I get what you're saying. I've had many late nights as a dad, and it is not like it used to be."

"What are you, thirty?" Riley asked.

"Twenty-nine," Oliver said. He wondered if he should ask her for her age, or if she would be annoyed.

"I'm twenty-six, so you're definitely ancient compared to me," Riley said. "How's the almost-thirties club?"

"Awful and boring," Oliver replied. "The dating pool really shrinks."

After he said that, he wanted to smack himself. He prided himself at his skill for keeping his business and personal lives separate. Why was he struggling now?

"I am sure you don't have issues in that department," Riley said, and Oliver felt a little embarrassed. He decided not to overthink it.

"The dating pool for parents isn't great. Most people don't like the person they're dating to have kids."

Riley nodded. "Makes sense. You and Zoe are a package deal. Some people can't deal with a two for one."

"Exactly," Oliver said.

"So, where is the other half of this package?" Riley asked. "Is Zoe still asleep?"

"She is. She actually slept all night."

"She must have been tired."

"She doesn't know you're here," Oliver explained. "I was hoping she would wake up so I could tell her you were coming instead of Amanda, but that didn't work out."

"So, we could be heading for a meltdown if she hates me deep in her four-year-old heart," Riley said.

Oliver truly hoped not, but he also doubted Zoe hated Riley. There was no way Zoe hated someone she would willingly go to sleep for.

It was that moment Zoe walked down the hallway, rubbing her eyes, and sporting messy hair. Oliver saw out of the corner of his eye a genuine smile blooming over Riley's face.

"Daddy?" Zoe asked. "You came home?"

"I did, honey," Oliver said gently. "But now it's morning and I have to go to work."

Zoe looked down. Oliver took a deep breath and prepared himself for the morning tirade.

"Why is Riley here?" Zoe muttered.

"Riley is going to watch you today," Oliver said.

"For how long?"

"For a while. She's your new nanny."

Zoe seemed to consider the fact Riley was going to be there for a long moment. Oliver resisted the urge to check his watch.

"Okay. You can watch me today, but we have to play dolls," Zoe said.

"Of course," Riley replied, as if it were the most obvious thing in the world. "We can do lots of things, because I'm here all day."

"Yay!" Zoe said, a smile finally on her face. Oliver let out a long breath of air. She was okay with Riley staying. That alone was easier than things had been in a long time.

It was at that point Oliver knew he needed to leave; while Zoe seemed sad for him to go, she didn't fight it. She was quiet as he kissed her forehead and walked out the door.

When Oliver pulled into the parking garage for work, he had a text from Riley.

Riley: Am I supposed to feed this child air?

Oliver laughed and replied.

Oliver: Order something, the card is in the top kitchen drawer. It's all on me.

Another text came in moments later.

Riley: Thanks. By the way, she gave me the ugly doll so she might actually hate me.

Attached was a picture of the worst doll Zoe owned. Oliver knew that particular one well. It was actually the one she gave to her favorite people.

Oliver smiled at the photo.

"Hi, Oliver," Amanda greeted as he walked out of the elevator onto his floor. "Any reason you canceled babysitting for me?"

"I found a nanny," Oliver replied.

Finding childcare for a four-year-old was so stressful.

"Oh, really?" Amanda said. "Great! Who is it?"

"It's Riley, actually."

The smile on Amanda's face dropped so fast it shocked him.

"Wait, really?" Amanda said. "You're kidding, right?"

"She got Zoe to sleep last night."

Amanda's eyes widened. Both of them knew what a feat it was.

"But, Oliver, you met her, right?" she added after a moment. "She's totally unqualified."

"I know she doesn't have proven childcare training, but it's fine. I think she'll do great."

"But she drinks!" Amanda said. "Like all the time. In fact, my mom and I think she has a problem."

Oliver was shocked at Amanda's tone. Riley didn't seem to have anything wrong with her, plus she was an adult. Most adults drank.

"I think she will be fine. If Zoe likes her, then I'm all for it."

"I just . . ." Amanda paused, seeming to choose her next words carefully. "She said yes to being a nanny?"

"Yes, she did." Oliver frowned when Amanda opened her mouth, presumably to say something further. "Let's drop this, Amanda."

She immediately did so, and Oliver felt bad for telling her to let it go, but it was irritating him having his assistant pick apart his choice, a choice she had willingly offered up no less.

Deep down, he knew he was nervous about hiring a new nanny, especially someone so different from the norm—but the norm hadn't been working either. He had to trust Riley would have his daughter's best interests at heart. So far, he hadn't been proven wrong.

"If something goes south between Riley and me," Oliver began, and Amanda looked up at him hopefully, "then it won't affect our working relationship." He hoped nothing would go wrong, but he could imagine that was what she was worried about.

"Okay, thank you, Oliver," Amanda said, sighing. He could tell she was relieved. "I do hope it works out."

Oliver nodded and smiled at her before he walked into his office. He sat and began going through emails, as he usually did. He kept his phone on his desk in case Riley texted him. His phone beeped once, and when he picked it up to investigate, he saw a message from Sophie instead.

Sophie: I had a great time last night. Can we meet again soon?

Oliver smiled. He got a good nanny and a date in one day? That was a new record.

Chapter Seven

Riley

Zoe was quiet after Oliver left. Riley gave her the space she needed, and eventually she turned to Riley and asked, "What are you holding?"

"It's coffee."

"Ew!" Zoe exclaimed, adorably scrunching her nose.

"Oh?" Riley said, smiling. "Have you tried it?"

"I took some of Daddy's, but don't tell him."

"Well, I won't say anything," Riley said. "But you can't have any of mine either."

"I don't want any!" Zoe said. "Can we play with dolls?"

"Of course we can," Riley replied.

"Okay. Are you my nanny forever?"

"I am as long as I can be," Riley said with another smile. Zoe seemed happy with that answer and ran to grab her toys. She returned with an armful of dolls and immediately handed a raggedy one with a homemade haircut to Riley.

She sent a message to Oliver asking about lunch and then another to inform him of the terrible doll Zoe gave her. It was a joke, but Riley could only hope Zoe did actually like her.

But after that, Riley was so engrossed in being with Zoe she hardly checked her phone.

They played for a while before moving to LEGO, and then back to dolls. Suddenly, it was lunchtime and Zoe was hungry.

Riley wanted to take the girl out for lunch, but didn't have a car seat to do so, so she ordered in. Trying to find something that delivered to Oliver's address and also coincided with what Zoe liked was nearly impossible, but after thirty minutes of going back and forth, they finally agreed on something.

When the food got there, and Zoe was eating happily, Riley texted Oliver.

Riley: Is there an extra car seat for Zoe? Getting food delivered past your security SUCKS.

He answered back almost immediately.

Oliver: Ordered one.

"What are you doing?" Zoe asked, breaking her train of thought.

"Sorry, kiddo, I was asking your dad a question."

"What question?"

"Oh, just if I could get a car seat for you. When it gets here, maybe we can go out somewhere."

"Really? None of the other nannies ever took me out."

"Well, I'm obviously not other nannies."

"Yay!" Zoe said happily. "I like you, even if you dress weird."

The insult made Riley have to hide a smile so Zoe wouldn't be egged on, but she loved the little girl's smart attitude.

It wasn't like Riley to enjoy being insulted but hearing a four-year-old say it in her innocent voice made her smile every time. Kids were brutal, but honest.

Yet somehow still adorable.

It was silent for a moment, and then Zoe looked up and asked, "Do you have a mommy?"

Riley paused. "Why are you asking?"

"Because everyone has a mommy, but I don't, and I want to know why."

Obviously, Riley didn't know anything about Oliver's situation to know why he was a single dad, but she could relate to living in a one-parent household.

"I do have a mom, but I don't have a dad. He left when I was really little."

"Why did he leave?"

Well, that was a loaded question. "Sometimes . . . people have other priorities than their kids. Sometimes they want to do other things or see other people. So I don't know why he left."

"Well, I don't know why my mommy left. Daddy never talks about her."

"That's normal. My mom doesn't talk about my dad either, but it's probably because he hurt her feelings and it's hard to talk about."

"Do you think she will come back for me?"

Man, the kid had a lot of hard questions for a woman she only knew a day. Riley didn't know if this was some sort of wild test, or if the kid actually liked her enough to ask.

"I don't know. I don't know anything about her."

"Any time I ask, Daddy gets sad."

"He might miss her," Riley said. "Or he might wish she was here. But what's most important is that he is here for you and is a good dad to you. And he is, right?"

"He's the best dad!"

"Then, that's what matters. It's better to have one parent who is the best, than to have two who aren't."

Zoe seemed to consider it, and then she nodded. "Okay. Do you think he will ever tell me about it?"

"I'm sure he will," Riley answered. "Sometimes you have to give people time."

"Time is so boring, though."

Riley paused, unsure of what to say next, but Zoe was already back to eating and dropped the subject. Riley definitely understood where Zoe was coming from, except she knew her father before he left.

It was hard growing up with one parent. There were so many unanswered questions, so many horrible things kids would tell themselves as an explanation for why a person who willingly brought them into this world had left them behind.

Amanda had been too young to remember their father. Riley did not have that luxury.

She had to stop herself from thinking about it. With everything that happened over the last few weeks, her emotions were sensitive, and it only made it worse thinking about ancient trauma.

"Do you wanna go outside?" Riley asked. She needed the distraction as much as Zoe. "I saw a park around here."

Finished with her food, Zoe exclaimed she did want to go to the park. The two walked there, happily talking about anything and everything. Zoe played by herself for a long time before she recruited Riley to join her.

Eventually, Zoe showed signs of needing a nap, and Riley walked her home, carrying what had to be thirty pounds the entire way. Riley hoped she would gain some muscle from this, because when they got back to the house, her arms felt like noodles.

After changing Zoe's clothes, they both laid down in her bed where Zoe instantly fell asleep. Riley wasn't too far behind her, since she was adjusting her sleep schedule, and woke up about two hours later to Zoe shuffling, waking herself up. Once they got up, Riley ordered dinner and they ate together again.

The sun was setting as the front door opened, and in walked Oliver, looking tired after a long day.

"Daddy!" Zoe yelled and ran over to him. He bent down to pick her up and gave her a kiss on the cheek. Riley smiled at the sight and decided to start cleaning up. As she did so, she heard Zoe regale the tale of her day to her father, who listened patiently.

"How about a bath before bed?" Oliver asked. "It's bath day."

"Turn it on to halfway?" Zoe asked.

"That's right, honey."

Zoe agreed, and Riley heard her bound through the house and up the stairs to get to the bathroom. Oliver walked into the living room where Riley was cleaning up.

"That was the easiest day she's ever had with a nanny."

"Good," Riley said. "I tried to keep her happy."

"Were there any issues?"

Riley went through the day in her mind, trying to find anything that stood out, and one thing did.

"Only one," Riley replied. "But it wasn't really an issue. She asked me about her mother."

Oliver's eyes widened. "Really? On the first day?"

"Yeah, it was definitely unexpected," Riley said. "But don't worry, I only gave her generic answers since I don't know the situation."

Oliver sighed. "Thanks."

"I'm guessing she asks about her?"

"Yes, she does. But she only ever asks me, so I am surprised she mentioned it to you."

"Hopefully it was a one-time thing then."

"I'm trying to avoid the topic, if I'm being honest."

"Understandable," Riley said with a curt nod.

"Really?" Oliver asked, raising his eyebrows. "Aren't you going to give me the whole lecture on being honest with my kid?"

"I don't think it's good practice to give lectures to the guy who's paying me." She gave him a half smile and hoped he knew she was joking. "And she's four. If you haven't told her, then it might be something she doesn't understand yet."

"Well, Zoe's mom is dead, so you'd be right about that."

There was a long silence where the words hung in the air. How was she supposed to respond to a bombshell like that? Was she supposed to say anything at all?

"I am so sorry," Riley said, and then added, "you really don't have to tell me."

Oliver looked mournful, but it was an old sadness he must have been carrying around for a while. Riley messed with the cuff of her flannel, unsure of what to do.

"You need to know in case she asks again," Oliver said, his voice soft. "But there truly is no need to apologize. She never wanted kids, and Zoe was included in that. Then she got into a car accident and . . . well, you can guess the rest."

"That's awful," Riley said. "But thank you for sharing."

"Hopefully one day I can find someone else who is good for me and for her," Oliver said. "Oh, that reminds me, I need to add you to my calendar. I'm hoping you can work one night this week. I have a date."

Riley blinked at the sudden change of conversation, and swallowed down a wave of jealousy that hit her.

This was probably for the best, though. Him dating meant he was off limits—as he needed to be.

"Of course," Riley said. "If I do work, I can ask for the day off. I need it anyway."

"Great," Oliver said. "I'm looking forward to it."

"Well, I should get going," Riley added, suddenly feeling awkward. "I have another job calling my name."

"Right—thank you again for watching Zoe."

"It's literally my job," Riley replied. She waved as she left. "See you."

"Bye," Oliver said. Riley called a goodbye to Zoe, who demanded a goodbye in person. Riley went back to the bathroom and did so, and then left with one more smile to Oliver.

Riley climbed into her car and drove to work, which was about twenty minutes away. En route, she received a call from Amanda.

"Hey," Riley said, balancing the phone between her shoulder and ear. "What's up?"

"So, I heard Oliver offered you a job with him."

"Uh, yeah he did," Riley said. She already knew where this was going.

"And you accepted? I can't believe you!"

"What? The little girl and I get along! I really like her." Riley felt defensive over her choice. This was one thing she was doing well and she could already feel an attachment to Zoe growing.

"You are not mature enough to be a nanny, Riley," Amanda said. "You're irresponsible, rude, and a drunk."

She pressed her lips together, trying her best not to snap. Whenever Amanda got like this, she wasn't going to hear anyone else's point of view. "You asked me to watch her last night, Amanda."

"There was literally no one else," Amanda said. "God, if you ruin my job, I will put you in rehab."

"Excuse me? I'm older than you, and I don't have an addiction."

"Tell that to bottles mom threw out!" Amanda replied. "I have enough on my plate for me to worry about without you fucking things up with my boss!"

"Fuck off, Amanda. I don't need my little sister to tell me how to keep a job. I'm doing fine," Riley said, her hand gripping her steering wheel so hard she thought it would break.

"Just keep your shit together for once in your life, okay? Seriously, this job is how I feed my family."

The line went dead, and Riley threw her phone into the passenger's seat, hurt and angry with her sister. Amanda always prided herself on being better than Riley. And sure, Riley drank a lot, and her life wasn't perfect, but Zoe liked her, and that was enough for Oliver.

But still, she couldn't shake the feeling it was all true. She was a mess. She screwed up everything she touched, and eventually, she would screw up this job too. It was why her mom hated her, and her sister thought she was better than her.

Maybe it was why her dad left too.

Riley pulled into work with tears in her eyes. She was hurt, both from her own thoughts and her sister's words. But she was at work, and if she was going to make enough money to move back out on her own, she was going to have to deal with it.

She took a deep breath, wiped her eyes, and pretended it didn't happen.

Chapter Eight

Oliver

It had been far too long since Oliver had been on a date. He almost didn't even know what to do or how to dress. After work, he wasted time trying to figure out what to wear. He wound up staying in something simple and casual, but still nice.

It had been a week since Riley started work. Zoe took a liking to her new nanny, and it was both relieving and a bit concerning how much Zoe liked Riley. Oliver came home a few nights after 8 p.m., and every time he did, Zoe was fast asleep while Riley was cleaning up. And when he left for work, Zoe hadn't thrown a fit once.

Oliver almost didn't know what to do with himself.

"Are you heading out?" Riley asked as she played with Zoe in the living room. Zoe was too entranced by her dolls to even notice Oliver and Riley were talking.

"Yeah, about to. I look okay, right?"

Oliver wasn't sure why he wanted Riley's opinion about his outfit. Maybe it was because she was the only other adult he knew who would be honest with him, and the only other adult present.

"You look like you haven't been on a date in over four years," Riley said, and she gave him that half smile she always did when she was joking. "I'm kidding. You look fine. I'm sure this woman will have her socks knocked off."

"That's the plan," Oliver said. "If all goes well, I might bring her here if Zoe is still awake."

It wasn't what he usually would do, and he wondered if Riley would tell him it was a bad idea. He had always been so careful about who he brought around Zoe, but he had broken that rule with Riley, and it was going better than he could have imagined.

"That sounds good to me."

A little tension melted from his shoulders, but not all of it. He was moving fast. Of course he knew that, but he felt like he was racing against the clock trying to find someone to be there for Zoe.

Sophie had a clean background, especially since she was employed by his company. They ran extensive checks on anyone who worked there. According to her manager, she was sweet and kind at work, never causing a problem. Even his dad had said nice things about her.

He was still nervous, but all of this told him she was trustworthy.

Maybe.

"Is she still sleeping okay?" he asked, changing the subject. "She's a handful if she's tired."

"No kidding. God, yesterday I thought she was going to burst my eardrums at nap time. You're a loud screamer, you know that?"

"It's for if I get kidnapped," Zoe said nonchalantly before returning to playing with her dolls.

"She's hilarious," Riley said, smiling at her.

Oliver tried not to stare at the way Riley looked at Zoe. She didn't look that way toward Oliver, and he could bet she didn't do that for anyone else. It was not the half grin she gave everyone else. Oliver found his eyes drawn to it every time she did it.

"Well, I have to head out. Thank you for watching her this late at night," Oliver said.

"Yeah, yeah. Just do me a favor and have fun," she said.

Oliver nodded and gave Zoe a kiss before leaving. She said goodbye without even looking up, which made Oliver a little sad, but he was grateful for his daughter's growing independence.

It took him a few minutes to get to the restaurant where he was meeting Sophie. He reserved a private outdoor table for them to enjoy. When he arrived, she was already waiting for him at the front door.

"Hi," she greeted him with a bright smile.

"Hey." Oliver gave her a hug. She smelled of a mix of jasmine and rose. "Was the drive here okay?"

"Oh yes, of course! How is your little one?" she asked.

"She's okay. She's finally getting along with her nanny, so that's good."

"Oh, does she not get along with them?"

"Not until this one," Oliver said.

"Sounds like she is a handful," Sophie replied as Oliver opened the door for her.

"Yes, but that's all kids."

"Of course," Sophie said. "Plus I am sure the nanny is getting her used to a schedule."

"As best as she can," he added. He pulled out her chair for her and she accepted gratefully.

"Is her mother in the picture?"

Oliver tensed up. He hated talking about Zoe's mother. "No, and she won't be."

"I'm sorry to hear that."

"It's okay, it is what it is. It's just Zoe and me."

"That's so admirable, being a single dad." Sophie gave him a soft smile.

Oliver opened his mouth to talk more about Zoe, but she changed the topic. Normally, he would be put off, but it was nice to be able to set aside having to be a father for a few hours. He had been in dad mode for four years without a break. Maybe this was what he needed.

They talked about work and changes in the city. They talked about TV, movies, and their parents. It was a great conversation and Oliver couldn't be happier with how it went. He was so glad, he texted Riley to ask if Zoe was still awake and in a good mood. When she answered yes, he asked Sophie, "Do you want to meet my daughter? I know it's fast, but—"

"Oh, I would love to!" Sophie exclaimed, and Oliver leaned back in his seat. Maybe this would go okay after all.

He let her follow him to the house, and when she pulled up, he led her inside by the small of her back. When he opened the door, he heard a little voice loudly announce, "Jump!" and Riley yelling, "Jesus!"

As he and Sophie turned the corner, Riley caught Zoe from behind the couch.

"You cannot jump off of couches," Riley was saying, sounding tired. "I draw the line there."

"Hey, Riley," Oliver said.

"Daddy!" Zoe said, and she wiggled out of Riley's arms to run to Oliver. She stopped, however, when she saw Sophie. "Who are you?"

"I forgot to tell her," Riley said, and Oliver noted how red in the face she was, presumably from chasing Zoe around. "She's been running wild all night."

"That's okay," Oliver said. "Zoe, this is my friend Sophie. I wanted her to meet you."

"Hi," Zoe said quietly.

"Why don't I help Zoe get to bed?" Sophie offered. "Would you like that?"

"Is she nice like Riley?" Zoe asked.

"Yes, of course she is," Oliver said. Zoe regarded Sophie for a long moment and finally nodded.

"Great," Sophie said, and she turned to Riley. "Maybe then you can clean up. It's a bit messy in here."

Oliver almost missed the look on Riley's face at the words.

"It's upstairs, third door on the right," Oliver said, and Sophie took Zoe by the hand and led her out of the living room.

"You're trusting her," Riley said as she turned and began to clean up.

"I have a feeling about her, you know?"

"Right."

"I think she would be a good mother figure for Zoe. Plus, I do like her."

She glanced at him for a moment, pensive. He didn't know what she was thinking—but he almost wanted to.

No. He made it a point to not talk about his personal life with employees—sure, Sophie was one, but he did not oversee her, and she was not as directly involved with his day-to-day like Riley was.

It didn't comfort him as much as he hoped it would.

"In that case," Riley eventually said, "I hope it works out. This doesn't mean I'm out of a job, does it?"

"No, I plan to date her a little longer before she moves in."

"Oh, and *then* I'm out of a job," Riley said in a teasing voice. "I see how you work."

Oliver smiled but didn't say anything else. Sophie did have a job and worked pretty hard at it. He had no idea how much she would be willing to take on, but anything would be helpful. He needed a companion, someone to take at least some of the weight of parenting off of him, but he didn't need to tell Riley that.

"I'm going to go check in on her," Riley said after she cleaned everything up. "Just to see if she really is getting to sleep."

Oliver was about to say he wanted to give Sophie more time to get to know Zoe, but Riley was already gone.

It was a wild card, letting Sophie attempt to put Zoe to sleep, but Riley had done it. He wasn't normally into letting complete strangers spend time with his daughter. However, Sophie had more credentials than Riley did, and if his new nanny could pull it off, he hoped his possible girlfriend could too.

Riley

Riley turned and walked upstairs. She kept her expression passive, but was fuming inside.

Sophie was stuck up.

It probably wasn't a good idea to tell Oliver that, though, since he really seemed to like her.

However, she couldn't help but think how poor of a match they were. Oliver was a nice guy who cared about his daughter. Sophie acted like the kind of woman who was into Oliver for his looks and his money. Riley saw the way Sophie's eyes roamed over the house and everything in it, as if taking inventory. She saw the way she only looked at Oliver and never gave Zoe so much as a second glance.

And if Oliver was into Sophie because of her looks and nothing else, then what did that mean about him?

Objectively, Sophie was gorgeous. She had delicate features and a beautiful figure Riley was never going to have. On paper, they were a perfect match.

He was obviously going to move fast if he already brought her home, and Riley didn't know how she felt about it. She'd only been here a week and there was already someone else in the picture.

And beyond that, Riley could sense something was off.

As Riley walked down the hallway, she heard Sophie speaking to Zoe in a hushed tone, so she pulled open the door to check in. Sophie turned to look at her, as did Zoe. Zoe's eyes were huge, hopefully because she was with a stranger. If it were anything else, Riley wasn't sure what she would do.

But it wouldn't be elegant.

Riley realized she was jumping to conclusions, so she tried to put it behind her.

"How are things going in here?" She tried to sound as friendly as possible.

"Things are going fine," Sophie said. "Right, Zoe?"

"Yeah . . ." Zoe said quietly.

"Well, Zoe does have a bedtime routine, so if you don't mind, I'll do what I'm here to do," Riley said. Zoe looked nowhere near sleepy, so Riley knew she wasn't going to go willingly for Sophie.

Maybe she was a little too protective of Zoe for being only a week into the job, but Riley wanted to be the one to put her to bed.

"Oh, sure," Sophie said, and she got up. As she passed by the door, she said, "Oliver never told me his nanny was so young."

"I don't think he cares as long I keep his daughter safe," Riley retorted. Why would it matter if Riley was young? It wasn't like Oliver was ever going to look at her like that, especially if he was into women like Sophie. And besides, it was only a three-year difference, even if she had joked he was ancient compared to her.

"Right," Sophie said, looking Riley up and down. Riley resisted the urge to stomp on Sophie's feet. "It was lovely to meet you."

"You as well," Riley said, keeping her voice light. Sophie brushed past her and returned to Oliver downstairs. Riley rolled her eyes.

What did Oliver see in her?

It wasn't Sophie's personality Oliver was into. It was her looks, it had to be. A surge of jealousy hit her again, but she did her best to push it down.

She pulled herself out of her thoughts and turned to Zoe, who was staring at her with wide eyes. She walked over, and laid down next to the girl as she had the first night she was here. Zoe instantly threw her arms around Riley, almost uncharacteristically.

"Are you okay?" Riley asked, concerned for her.

"Are you going to leave one day?" Zoe's mouth was muffled by Riley's shoulder.

Riley didn't know how to answer. She hadn't thought too much of the future. She didn't know how long Oliver would need a nanny, nor did she know how long she would even want to stay in this position. Zoe was amazing, and Riley already loved her, so she didn't exactly *want* to leave, but this wasn't going to last forever.

How did she say that to a clingy four-year-old?

"I'll be here as long as I can. Why do you ask?"

"I'm tired of people leaving," Zoe muttered.

"Hey, it's okay," Riley said. "I'll for sure be here until you go to sleep. Does that sound good?"

She felt Zoe nod, and then covered both of them up with a blanket. Riley could hear Sophie and Oliver talking but ignored it. She didn't exactly want to know what they were talking about.

There were two ways to take Zoe's change in mood. It was entirely possible she was shaken at meeting a new person. She didn't seem to have a lot of socialization, with Oliver's busy schedule and the other nannies never taking her out of the house. So, maybe a new person, in combination with how tired she was getting, made her clingier to the people she knew.

Or Sophie had done something.

Riley didn't need to piss off her new boss by fighting with his girlfriend. Besides, she didn't need to jump to conclusions. But if she ever found out Sophie had done something to upset Zoe, she didn't care what Oliver thought, Sophie would be answering to Riley.

Zoe fell asleep after a few minutes. Riley stayed a little bit longer to ensure the girl was okay. Soon, she heard Sophie leaving, and let out a breath. Riley carefully extracted herself from a passed-out Zoe and crept out of the room, shutting the door behind her.

When Riley arrived in the living room, Oliver was drinking a glass of water. When he saw her, he asked. "So I'm guessing Zoe was still awake?"

"Yeah, I don't think she was going to go to sleep for a new person."

"She did with you."

"See, I'm special," Riley said, trying to make a joke to lighten her own mood.

"Yeah, yeah. You must be a kid whisperer or something." Oliver said it lightly, but Riley could tell he was disappointed Sophie couldn't get Zoe down. But why? Zoe had a track record of not liking new people, and a week ago Riley had been the first one to get her to bed with no help.

"Oh no, I think it's just that kid," Riley deflected, trying to put any ill thoughts out of her mind. "When I babysit Amanda's kids, it's a totally different story."

"I can imagine," Oliver said.

"So, I have to get going before I'm late at the bar. But let me know if you want another date night. I don't mind watching Zoe whenever you need me." Riley hoped that was enough to clear her conscience about how much she disliked Sophie.

It wasn't.

"I will. Thanks, Riley."

"Tell Zoe bye for me," Riley said as she walked out of the house. Oliver nodded and waved as she went.

Riley drove straight to work and arrived a few minutes early. She tried to put the events of the night out of her mind by checking Facebook.

That was definitely a mistake. She saw it right when she opened the app.

Sarah and David had changed their relationship status to engaged.

The update was the top story.

Riley's jaw dropped. She stared at the announcement for far longer than she needed to. Sarah and David were engaged? This quickly? David kept Riley at arm's length for years, saying he wasn't ready for marriage, and now all of the sudden he was?

Everything from the night she found out bubbled back to the surface. It hadn't even been a full month, and they were already planning on spending the rest of their lives together. Meanwhile, Riley was working two jobs to try to fix the problems they had created for her.

Riley slammed the car door behind her. She was more than hurt, more than angry. She was *livid*. Damn David and his old car, and damn Sarah for betraying her like she did. Fuck them both.

Riley walked into work, feeling far more furious than she had in a long time. What were they thinking, putting it on Facebook so soon after she found out?

She downed a shot of vodka the moment she could. The liquid burned, but she felt a sense of relief as it pooled in her stomach. She spent the rest of her shift this way, taking shots when no one was looking, and dancing the line of drunk before people would notice. By the middle of the night, she was so busy her sober thoughts couldn't chase her, and she forgot about them both.

A coworker gave her a ride home, and she could easily Uber back to the bar to get her car before she went to work the next day. It would be fine.

There was a sliver of guilt she felt as she fell asleep, but she pushed it back. She probably shouldn't have gotten half-drunk the night before she was set to watch Zoe, but she would be sober by the time she got to Oliver's.

Everything was fine.

Chapter Nine

Oliver

Oliver woke up ten minutes before his alarm.

Normally, Zoe was up before he was, so when he didn't hear her playing on her tablet or with her dolls, he was concerned that maybe she was sick. He left the master bedroom and quietly walked to her room, opening the door to see what was up.

There were many things he expected to see. Maybe she was still asleep, or maybe she was playing with LEGO in her room, but the last thing Oliver expected was to find his daughter silently crying in her bed.

"Zoe," Oliver said, walking in the moment he realized what was going on. "Hey, what's wrong?"

"Riley's not here," Zoe said, sniffling.

"What?" Oliver asked, confused.

"Riley left."

"She went home like she normally does."

"But I want her here!"

"She'll be here soon."

"But she needs to be here now!"

Oliver was shocked. Zoe never mentioned when Riley would lay down with her and then leave. In fact, she was usually so happy to see her dad that she didn't even miss her. This was unusual. But like clockwork, the doorbell rang, and Oliver looked out of Zoe's window to see Riley's old Toyota.

"Okay, okay. She's here," Oliver said. "You can—" But Zoe was not listening. She jumped out of her bed and ran downstairs. Oliver followed her, but she didn't even notice. Zoe opened the door, which she had never done before, and jumped to hug Riley, who had to juggle her coffee.

"You're back!" Zoe yelled.

"Uh, yeah kiddo," Riley said, adjusting her sunglasses. Why was she wearing sunglasses? "Here in the morning, just like always."

"I didn't want you to go. You didn't say goodbye."

"Oh, well . . . I'm sorry, kid," Riley said, and Zoe let go of her so she could come inside. Oliver saw her take her sunglasses off, but she squinted at the light. A cold realization washed over him.

She was hungover.

"Zoe, why don't you go play with your dolls while Riley gets settled in?" Oliver suggested, crossing his arms.

"But—" Zoe tried to argue.

"Now, kid." Zoe pouted and left the room. He felt guilty for telling her so sternly, but there was something else on his mind.

"Are you hungover?" he asked Riley, even though he knew the answer.

Riley sighed and looked away. "Not that bad," she said after a long moment. "I didn't drink enough water last night."

"You can't watch my daughter like that," he said firmly.

"I'm functioning, Oliver."

"No, what if you need to drive?"

"I have a headache. I'm not actively drunk," Riley argued, glaring at him.

"Whatever you do in your personal time is your business, but coming to work hungover, where you are with my child, is crossing a line."

"This isn't a regular thing."

"It better not be."

"Oh my God, get off your high horse. It's a headache and I stopped drinking a long enough time ago to where it's out of my system. You wouldn't be pissed at me if it was a normal headache."

"But it's not," Oliver said.

"It's not going to mess with my job. I didn't even spill my coffee when Zoe jumped me."

Oliver paused—she had him there. Plus, besides the squinting, she didn't seem to be doing anything else odd.

He didn't know why this upset him as much as it did, but it made him not want to leave Zoe with her. Plus, there was the fact Zoe had woken up and specifically asked for her and not him.

"Okay, fine, but do you at least have a good explanation for this? You knew you were working today."

"I had a bad night," Riley said softly. Oliver was still too annoyed with her to care about her change in tone.

"And . . .?"

"And I didn't deal with it in the best way, okay?" Riley said. "But I'm here, and I am fine to watch Zoe."

"This isn't very professional of you."

"Oh, come on, you knew I wasn't professional from the moment you hired me," Riley protested. "And this won't even affect my work, like I said."

"I'm still not happy about it," Oliver said before he took a deep breath. Maybe he was being unfair, since he was so shaken at how Zoe had woken up. Or he could have been letting what other people said about Riley influence him a bit, so he decided to extend an olive branch. "Is everything at least okay at home?"

"Other than the fact my ex is marrying the person he cheated on me with for God knows how long, yeah everything is fine."

Oliver felt his face heat up. He definitely shouldn't have asked. "Oh."

"Did I mention she was my best friend?"

"Oh, uh, I'm sorry to hear that." Oliver really didn't know what to say, and for a second, he thought she might cry. She was frowning, and she put her hand on her forehead, but she held it together, which was a relief. He had no idea what he would have done if the tears had actually started to fall.

A part of him wondered if it would be a good enough excuse to reach out and hug her, but that was a terrible idea—one of the worst he had in a long time.

"Sorry, I'm seriously fine . . . or as fine as I can be," Riley added. "And I found out about it on Facebook so that didn't help."

"I . . . I don't know what to say."

"You shouldn't have to. I didn't mean to unload on you. I just . . . I had a bad night."

"It's okay," Oliver said. "Are you good to take care of Zoe today, though?"

"Of course I am," Riley said, sighing. "I already took some medicine. I'm just waiting for it to kick in and then I'll be fine."

Oliver wasn't sure, but Riley looked at him like she was scared of something. Maybe him yelling at her? Then it occurred to him that maybe she wanted to be here, and she wanted to watch Zoe. He knew more than anyone it was hard to think of anything else while being busy with her, so he realized he had to let it go.

He took a deep breath. "Okay. I need to head out. But before I go, I need you to know something."

"What?"

"When Zoe woke up and you weren't here, she was really upset. That's why she jumped on you when you came in."

"Really?" Riley asked. "Has she ever asked before?"

"No, not really."

"Hm." Riley paused, lost in thought. "Well, I can try to start saying goodbye to her. Maybe that'll help."

"Yeah, it could be a phase, but I wanted you to be aware of it."

Riley nodded. "Okay, yeah. I'll try to say bye to her tonight."

"Thanks. I really have to get running," Oliver said. He went to the living room to give Zoe a kiss, and she barely looked up from her dolls when he did. However, when Riley sat down next to her, she seemed to brighten up instantly.

Riley smiled back at her, and the two of them seemed so lost in their own little world, neither of them noticed him leaving.

Oliver drove in, wondering what was up with his normally attached little girl. He would maybe have to ask his father if he did anything like that when he was a kid. Maybe it *was* a phase. He hoped it was. It didn't sit right with him for Zoe not to want to be around him all the time like she normally did.

He walked into the building, frustrated and tired. Oliver hoped he had an easy day ahead of him. He completely bypassed Amanda as he headed into his office, not stopping to chat like usual. When it was time for lunch, he ordered out, hoping a change of scenery would help him relax a bit, but when he left his office, Amanda stopped him.

"Hey," she said, her voice laced with concern. "Are you okay?"

Oliver sighed and rubbed his face. "Yeah, everything is fine. I had a rough morning."

"Uh oh, trouble with the new nanny?" She leaned forward on her desk. It was very obvious she was interested to hear what her sister was up to. Oliver knew he probably shouldn't say anything, but he couldn't help it.

"She came to work hungover."

Amanda sighed, as if she had heard this story before. "Yeah, that's something she does. Any time something bad happens, she drinks way too much. She has no self-control."

He shouldn't do this. He didn't like how many times he had broken his own rules since meeting Riley. But he couldn't keep his mouth shut, not when it was her he was thinking of.

"Whatever her personal life is, isn't my business. I don't like she brought it near my child."

"It's a problem, and we all know it," Amanda explained. "She's kind of like our dad. I don't remember him, but our mom told me about him. He drank all the time, and unfortunately, Riley is doing the same thing. And then her ex never made it better. He egged it on. He even got her that job at the bar when they moved in together."

Oliver sort of felt for Riley, especially since she never mentioned her dad to him, but he knew from Amanda he wasn't in the picture. However, it wasn't good that she was using substance to help her feel better—no matter what was going on in the background.

"Well, we already had a talk about it," Oliver said, "so hopefully it gets better."

"Good luck."

Discomfort curled low in his belly. Talking to Amanda didn't help him feel better like he'd hoped. Now he had let details of his personal life slip that he wished he could take back.

Nevertheless, he thanked her for the talk before leaving to get his lunch.

He got a text from Riley.

Riley: Zoe is still clingy. We will see how tonight goes.

Upon reading it, Oliver sighed and wondered what in the world could have been going on with his daughter, and why she was so attached to someone who may not even be good for her.

The thoughts plagued him up until he left. Riley texted him that she had fed Zoe, so he grabbed a quick dinner before heading home. Zoe was watching a movie, and at least smiled when he gave her a kiss. He then pulled Riley to the side to see how the day went.

"She wouldn't let me out of her sight." She shook her head. "So, I've been doing some reading on clingy kids. I've been telling her I have to leave, so hopefully things won't be too bad when I do go."

"Thanks," Oliver said. Then he remembered their conversation earlier. "By the way, I do hope things get better for you. What your ex did was terrible."

Riley smiled at him. "Thanks," she said, and then left the room to say goodbye to Zoe. There was a bit of pouting, but it could have gone worse. Riley had definitely stayed true to her word and prepared Zoe for her departure.

After she was gone, Oliver found himself wondering about Riley's ex and how things ended.

He opened Facebook after Zoe went to bed and searched for Riley. He found her pretty quickly, and her profile picture was of her sitting on a couch with the half smile she gave everyone but Zoe plastered on her face.

It was taken a year ago, and she hadn't changed much since then. She had the same pale skin tone with her naturally straight long brown hair. She didn't look like she was carrying the burden of what her ex-boyfriend did, though.

Oliver scrolled through more photos, and he saw a few with a woman named Sarah. That must have been the girl who was now with her ex. He wondered if Riley was still in a state of denial, or if she even used her Facebook all that often, since these photos were still up.

Eventually, Oliver pieced together her ex-boyfriend was David, a guy with an unfortunate receding hairline and green eyes, and he was now engaged to Sarah.

Hell, the guy had already changed his profile picture to him and Sarah three weeks ago. He sighed, wondering how Riley was doing with all of this change. Obviously, the drinking hinted it wasn't going well, but still, was she dealing with what happened at all? Or was it going to hang over her forever?

Oliver already didn't like David if he really had cheated on Riley with Sarah.

He flipped back to Riley's profile and softly smiled as he looked through her albums. Her photos were of her at a few bars, hanging out with friends. Her hair always seemed to be in a bun, or up, and she always gave the camera that patented half smile.

Riley had other ones where it looked like she was in college, where she seemed lighter. A lot of them were with Sarah, and it occurred to him they may have been friends their whole lives before this happened.

The further back he went, he found a few themes. One was that she didn't ever post about her dad, or her family at all.

There were very few photos of Amanda or their mother, and most seemed to be her and Sarah or David. The second was that Riley herself didn't post much, and most of her photos were tagged ones.

Sarah had kept all of her photos up, while David took his down. Oliver didn't exactly know what that meant, but he thought it was odd all the same.

It was then Oliver remembered that he wasn't the kind of boss who looked up his employees' social media pages. He was strictly professional, but he was more than curious about the woman he left his child with every day.

And with what he'd seen, Oliver didn't understand how someone could be with a person like Riley and then leave them. He wasn't blind—Riley was beautiful, and he liked that she showed exactly who she was, never putting up a front. David really had someone way out of his league, so why did he let her go? If it were Oliver, he didn't think he could.

The next day, Riley generously offered to stay late while Oliver went on another date with Sophie, who seemed to be showing a desire to move away from talking about Zoe.

This could have easily bothered Oliver, but he was sure Sophie was wanting to get to know the non-dad version of him, so he let it slide.

The date went well, and they went back to Sophie's place, which was a small apartment she seemed embarrassed of. Oliver didn't care too much, and he listened to her talk about her family and friends, until she seemed more interested in kissing him.

Before things could go too far, Oliver realized it was getting late, and told Sophie he had to go. She tried to get him to stay, but once he reminded her Zoe was probably awake, she let him leave.

Oliver opened the door to his home to see Riley and Zoe were playing. Zoe barely even noticed he was home, but still stopped when he grabbed her to tickle her. He offered to put her to bed, and Zoe glanced at Riley before accepting. It was strange, but Oliver put it behind him, determined not to be jealous of the nanny.

Thirty minutes later, Zoe was out and Riley was still cleaning. He paused as he saw her, wondering if he should reach out in some way after all that he had learned about her.

"So, I'm guessing if you're a bartender you can make a good drink?" Oliver asked.

Riley turned around, her eyebrows raised. "Depends on what you have . . . Are you asking me to make you something?"

"It's been a long day," Oliver said.

"Okay, sure. Just show me where the stuff is."

"Well, it's a good sign you don't know where my liquor is."

He hoped she wouldn't take it the wrong way, and she laughed.

"Yeah, right. I'm not a teenager. I'm not going to steal your shitty wine."

"I paid good money for the things I have," Oliver replied, opening a cabinet above the fridge. Riley pensively looked at what he had. She pointed out what she needed, since he was the only one tall enough to grab it.

"This kitchen wasn't made for short people," Riley muttered as she got to work. She covered the cup with another to shake the drink, not spilling anything. Oliver could tell she was a pro and probably had been bartending for a while.

He took a sip and was pleasantly surprised it was well done. "This is nice. Thank you."

"All a part of a good day's work," Riley said. "And seriously, I am really sorry about yesterday. I didn't deal with the news well."

"And I am sorry all of that is going on. Especially since they didn't tell you."

"You know what the weirdest part is? My best friend hated him. She always said he was a bad influence, and he was ruining my life. So, why would she want to be with him? It doesn't make sense."

"I would say ask, but if it were me, I wouldn't even want to know."

Riley shook her head. "I can't even think about talking to them. Sarah, my friend, keeps messaging me and saying she's sorry, but then she goes and gets engaged to him without even telling me. I can't deal with it right now. I have to live with my mom because I'm obviously not going to live with my ex, and my mom has everyone convinced I'm an alcoholic or something."

"Do you think it has anything to do with your dad's drinking problem?"

"Probably but—" Riley paused. "Wait, how did you know about my dad?"

Oliver considered what he could say. He could lie, but that also felt wrong, especially to someone who had been lied to far too much, so he sighed and said, "Amanda told me when I hired you that you drink, and when I was telling her you came to work hungover, she mentioned your dad."

"So, you and Amanda were talking about me," Riley muttered, and Oliver could tell the change in her demeanor almost instantly. Before, she had been relaxed, leaning on his counter while she talked, but now her arms were crossed, and her face was set into a dark frown. "That's great to know."

"Riley, I'm—"

"Don't apologize. Amanda loves to talk down about me, but I didn't know you did too." She grabbed her phone off the counter. "I guess I should be happy you still let me have a job, since you know how much of a wreck I am."

Oliver didn't know what to say, but Riley was not done talking.

"I'm going home. Don't worry, I won't come in hungover tomorrow. Goodbye, Mr. Brian."

And just like that, she was gone. Oliver set down the drink and sighed. He did sort of deserve that. There was obviously some sore spot between Riley and Amanda, and when he looked back, Amanda never seemed to have anything good to say about her older sister.

But Riley was the person working two jobs so she could watch Zoe. Riley was the one getting his daughter to bed every night and keeping her happier than he had ever seen her.

And Oliver was talking shit behind her back to someone who never had anything good to say about her.

He had screwed up, but he could only hope he hadn't screwed up Zoe's relationship with her new nanny.

"Where's Riley?" Zoe asked the moment she woke up.

Oliver paused. Was Riley even going to come in today? She said she was going to, but what if she was so angry she had turned to drinking, or what if she decided not to come at all?

"She should be in soon."

"She'll be here today, right?"

"She should," Oliver repeated. "Aren't you happy I'm here?"

"You have to go to work and do things. Riley doesn't. I want *her* here."

Oliver sighed. Maybe he should take a day off soon to make sure he spent quality time with Zoe. The only time he had been home was on the weekends since he was also trying to balance his new relationship with Sophie, so Zoe hadn't seen as much of him.

He was paying the price.

As usual, Riley knocked on the door and Oliver let out a sigh of relief when she did. He didn't know what he would do if she didn't come. Zoe jumped up and ran to the door just as she did the day before.

"Riley!" Zoe screamed and hugged her tightly.

"Hey, kid," Riley said. "Can I set my stuff down and then we can play?"

"Yeah! I'm going to get my dolls!"

Zoe ran right past Oliver who had walked to the foyer to follow Zoe. Riley looked at him with a tense expression.

"I'm here, and not hungover. You don't have to report anything to Amanda."

"Thank you for coming in."

"Did you think I wasn't going to?" Riley asked, and when Oliver looked at his feet, she sighed. "That's really good to know you have such a high opinion of me."

"That's not . . . I thought . . ."

"That I was mad, and I would drink so much I wouldn't come in?"

Oliver paused. That was exactly what he thought.

"I'm here for Zoe, and I don't care what you or Amanda think of me. I didn't have anything to drink last night, and I'll be fine all day. Don't worry about me."

"I'm not. I mean, I know you're a capable adult and everything."

"Yeah, well, you worrying about my every move doesn't give me that impression."

"Okay, Riley, I get it. I shouldn't have talked to Amanda about you. But for the record, you make it really hard to apologize."

"Thanks. I accept your apology. You get a gold star for how difficult it was."

"Seriously?"

"What?" Riley said.

"You have to be the most frustrating person I have ever met." Especially when he couldn't seem to keep any sort of distance from her.

"Oh, that's high praise from someone who has a four-year-old," she countered. "I know I'm snarky, but I'm sure Amanda warned you about that when you two were talking about me. I'm sorry I messed up, okay? But talking to my sister about me being my back? Come on, if you're so mature and perfect like you pretend to be, you wouldn't have done that."

"Can you maybe admit this isn't all about me? Maybe you're tired of being told what to do by Amanda and your mom?"

"Wow, that's a great insight. And you're right, but can you go back to being my boss and not being my therapist?"

"Is it wrong for me to care about your well-being?"

"Then, maybe listen to me and not my sister," Riley said. "She's not perfect. Now, I have to go. Zoe is waiting to play with me, and I'm not going to disappoint her too."

Riley turned on her heel and walked away. Oliver watched her go, unsure of how he felt. In a few minutes, he went from feeling guilty, mad, frustrated, and back to guilty. At least one thing he could trust about Riley was that she was honest.

Oliver gave Zoe a goodbye kiss and didn't look at Riley as he did so. Once he left, he thought about the conversation. There was a difference between what Amanda had told Oliver about Riley, and who Riley actually was. It bugged him.

Talking to Amanda hadn't cleared up anything, and he had crossed a line. Even though Riley could be infuriating when wronged, he still did something bad, and he needed to atone for it. So, when he pulled into the parking garage, he sent a simple text to Riley.

Oliver: I'm sorry for crossing the line.

He didn't wait around to see if she sent a response, because he knew he had work to do. He walked in to Amanda sitting at the front desk and when she saw him, she looked up and greeted, "Good morning, Oliver."

"Hey," Oliver said. "We need to talk about the other day."

"Are you firing Riley?" Her smile slowly fell off of her face.

"No, not at all." Oliver decided not to think about how fast she jumped to that conclusion. "I realized if I am employing both of you, I need to be fair to both of you. I don't want to talk about Riley's past or anything to do with her when we are working. I've always been professional with you, and I want to keep it that way."

"Oh," Amanda said. "Okay, I didn't mean to cause a problem, I just—"

"I know, but I think we can both agree that we need to keep work and personal lives separate."

"Is she getting this lecture too?"

"Of course." He knew it was a lie the second it left his lips. Even if he tried to, he'd break his own rule like all of the other ones he'd made the moment he was standing in front of Riley again.

Amanda frowned, but nodded, and Oliver walked into his office without another word. He checked his phone to see if Riley had responded, and a small smile came onto his face when she did.

Riley: Thanks. Sorry for losing my cool.

There was a part of Oliver that wondered what he got into with employing both Amanda and Riley. There was definitely bad blood between the two.

But he needed to let it go. He had been spending far too much time trying to figure Riley out, more so than he ever had Amanda. But he knew Riley was the only nanny Zoe ever liked, so he had to stay out of whatever family drama she had to avoid losing Riley.

The worst part was, he didn't want to. He *wanted* to figure her out. He wanted to know her side of things, and he wanted to deconstruct whatever walls she kept trying to build around herself.

But he was her boss, and she probably wouldn't like him trying to figure her out, so he had to let it go. He needed to think of Sophie, who hopefully could get along with Zoe. Not Riley, who he refused to look at in that way.

Chapter Ten

Riley

Riley hoped that when Oliver got back, it wouldn't be awkward. She was aware she reacted strongly whenever someone hurt her feelings, and she took things way too far when she and Oliver fought. She had to remember he was her boss, nothing else.

But Riley was not the kind of person to lie about who she was. She never wanted to be fake, or act like someone she wasn't. So, when her feelings were hurt, they showed. She only hoped that they could move past it. She could deal with not liking people she worked with, but she didn't want to dislike Oliver since she worked so closely with him. Plus, Oliver could easily fire her, and then she wouldn't get to see Zoe anymore.

Oliver arrived home right after dinner. Riley had cooked something for Zoe, and they were reading a story. Zoe ran over to her father and hugged him, which was nice to see after she had been acting so strange.

"How was she today?" It was said with an even tone, and Riley got the idea this was exactly how he sounded at work.

"She did well," Riley said, trying to mimic his own inflection, but it sounded weird to her own ears. "We played and went to the park."

"Good," Oliver said. An awkward silence hung between them. She wondered if this was how it was going to be from now on.

"Well, I guess I need to get heading out," Riley said.

"No!" Zoe said, her attention back on Riley, who took a deep breath.

"Kid, we talked about this. I have to go."

"But you stay late when Daddy gets home!"

That was true. Normally Riley hung around to clean up, or she talked with Oliver for a bit, but his tone with her got under her skin. She wanted to be anywhere but here. But she also wasn't about to leave Oliver with an angry kid, so she said, "I know, how about I read you one more book and then I go?"

She glanced at Oliver, who looked annoyed, possibly at her for offering to stay, or because Zoe wanted her to stay. But he nodded, and she turned back to Zoe.

Riley was able to put it out of her mind while reading to the little girl, but when she was done, and she was saying goodbye to her, she wondered if she should say goodbye to Oliver too.

She decided against it. She gathered her things and left without another word.

Riley drove home, still feeling conflicted, but she tried to put it past her. When she got home, she hoped to take a calming bath or something to keep her from having far too many glasses of wine which would result in another hangover.

She walked in the door and put down her things, thinking about her possible bath and if she had a bath bomb hidden somewhere.

However, her plans flew out the window when she heard someone clear their throat. Riley turned around, only to take a step backward at seeing Sarah and her mother sitting in the living room.

"What the hell?" Riley was shocked.

"I asked your mom if I could talk to you," Sarah said. "You've been ignoring me."

"And you need to talk this out. She is your oldest friend, and she is good for you. She is also concerned about your drinking."

Riley couldn't believe her ears. A part of her wondered if she was hallucinating.

"Maybe I'm ignoring you because you're engaged to my ex-boyfriend!" Riley shouted before turning to her mother. "Mom, how could you—"

"You need to grow up and confront your problems, or else you'll end up a drunk like your father!" her mother snapped.

Riley's mouth shut. That really hurt. Her mom never mentioned her father, and when she did, it was never directed at her. Riley barely knew her dad, he left a long time ago. How could she be like him if she didn't know him?

"Your mom told me you've been drinking more," Sarah said. "And I know you're upset. I want to tell you why I did what I did."

"I don't want to know right now," Riley said. "I need more time."

"That is an excuse," her mother replied. "And I am so tired of them."

"I think," Sarah started, looking at Jane, "I think you need to hear the story and then you'll feel better."

"You want me to feel better? Then maybe you shouldn't have slept with David, Sarah. Fuck you!"

Sarah looked guilty for a whole second before she said, "I can't take back what I've done, but I can help you now."

"No, no," Riley said. "I'm tired of this already and we haven't even started. Mom, back out of my life. I've got it handled. And Sarah? Just leave me alone. You can apologize all you want, and you can play the victim, but you fucked my boyfriend. I don't care why you did it, because you went behind my back and lied to me. So, I can drink whatever I want, I can do whatever I want, because I am a grown-ass woman."

"You take one drink in this house, and I will kick you out of it," her mother said with a cold tone.

Riley knew what this was. She knew her mother was exercising her authority since she was staying there for free. Riley took a step back and grabbed her keys.

"Fine, then I won't do it here," Riley said, and she turned to walk out the door.

"Do not come back here tonight then!" her mother called after her. Riley didn't care.

She barged outside and soon found herself pulling into the parking lot of an old, grungy bar a few minutes away. She turned off the car and was about to go inside, but something stopped her.

Zoe. She was watching Zoe tomorrow.

That was enough to make Riley pause and think. She and Oliver had just gotten into a fight about this. Was she about to make the same mistake?

It didn't matter, because either way, she wasn't going to be able to go home. Sarah might still be there, and even if she wasn't, her mother would never believe she wasn't drunk.

Riley desperately wished she could talk to Zoe. She wished she could hang out with her so she would be focused on someone else rather than her own problems. But Zoe was probably asleep.

She pulled out her phone, thinking of calling someone and asking to stay over. Her first thought was Sarah, and then she felt physically sick at the thought of calling her. What would she even do? Go to her old apartment where Sarah lived now? Would Sarah bring up the engagement while David stayed silent and played his video game?

Riley could always call Sarah's mom, but it had been years since they talked, and there was no doubt Mrs. Summers would be on her daughter's side.

David was definitely out of the question, and Amanda would be on their mom's side for sure. Plus, she and her husband didn't have an extra bedroom at their house, so it would be the couch. Which, in all honesty, would be better than Riley's car, which was what she was looking at doing.

She wanted to cry. She also felt like getting drunk. What did that say about her?

The urge to drink always hit her at night, but it was much worse when she was upset, so much so that even during the day she sometimes would sip on something to take the edge off.

That wasn't healthy. None of it was. Deep down she knew, but being with David taught her it was cool to drink all the time.

What was Riley thinking ever being with him? She had her life together before she met him. She was in college and almost graduated when they met at a party Sarah had dragged her to. They slept together that night and then started dating right after. Once Riley graduated, she got a job offer and was considering her master's degree, but David insisted she would be bored in an office. At the time, she thought he was right. So, she worked at a fun, lively bar instead.

Why had she ever listened to him? Young Riley had so much going for her, and present-day Riley was a wreck because of it.

She leaned her forehead against the cool steering wheel and tried to simply breathe, to just exist. Maybe then her pain would feel a little less sharp—it didn't work.

Riley sighed. What she needed was a distraction, but other than drinking, she had no ideas.

Then, her phone rang.

She heard the ringtone before she read the name on the screen, and she instantly knew who it was.

Riley answered with a quiet, "Hello?"

"Hey," Oliver said. "I know it's late, but my dad called a meeting early tomorrow morning, at six. Is there any way you can be in at five?"

"In the morning?" Riley asked.

"Yes, I know it is a lot of ask of you, especially with our recent . . . argument. But I really need someone to watch Zoe that early. If it makes it any better, I would be willing to let you stay here."

"Like overnight?"

"Yes, it would be overnight. I have a guest room you can use, and it is right next to Zoe. You could wake up when she's up instead of driving in so early."

Riley felt a wave of relief wash over her. What were the odds Oliver would call and literally offer her to stay the night, and a distraction, when she had just been contemplating sleeping in her car, since she couldn't go back to her mom's, whether she was drunk or not? They were slim—that's for sure.

"Riley?" Oliver asked. "Are you still there?"

She blinked back into focus. "Yeah, I'm still here. Sorry I was just . . ." She couldn't think of a proper excuse. "Lost in thought."

"Is everything okay?" He sounded genuinely concerned. "You seem quiet."

Riley knew she could make an excuse about bad service or something to get him off of her back. It was easy to make excuses when not looking someone in the eyes.

"I've had a really bad night."

"Oh," Oliver said. "Have you been drinking?"

Riley felt embarrassed he was automatically assumed that, but the last time she had a bad night, she ended up doing just that; she couldn't blame him for asking, even though she really wanted to be annoyed.

"No. I went to a bar, but . . . I know I have work tomorrow," Riley said. "So, I was stalling in the parking lot. You called at a really good time, actually."

"Well, I hope everything is okay."

"It's not," Riley said. "It's really not."

"Is it the ex again?"

"The best friend." She leaned her forehead against the steering wheel. "My mom invited her over. They've been talking behind my back."

"What?" Oliver asked. He seemed offended on her behalf. "That's . . . so strange."

"It is. And basically, my mom kicked me out for the night. She told me if I drank anything then I wouldn't be allowed back, but even if I go back now, she'll never believe me. And Sarah might still be there."

"You're welcome here. Even if I didn't have the meeting tomorrow."

Riley let out a shaky breath of relief. "Thanks."

Oliver told her he would be up for a while and let her go. Once she was off the phone, she drove to his house, feeling emotionally exhausted, but also glad she had a place to sleep.

She was happy with her decision to not go inside the bar. Maybe she was doing something right for once, even if she ached for the taste of alcohol, ached for the release it provided her. Riley pulled into the driveway and turned off the car. She walked up to the door and knocked. Oliver answered in pajama bottoms and a T-shirt, which made Riley say, "Ah, getting casual I see."

He also looked really good in his outfit—like illegally good—but she made herself not stare for too long.

"It's casual Fridays after eight," Oliver said, and moved to the side so Riley could enter.

"I hope you don't have rules against wearing the same outfit two days in a row."

"I think I'll have to dock your pay," Oliver joked, and Riley felt relieved as the tension between them melted. A comfortable silence fell over the room. Eventually he added, "You look like hell."

"Wow, thanks." She crossed her arms. She wanted to be offended, but he was right. She could feel the bags under her eyes.

"I mean, you look like you've had a bad night. Like you're tired."

"Well, you wouldn't be wrong," Riley said. "I don't get why my mom is so hard on me. She never complains about Amanda like she does me."

Oliver looked uncomfortable for a moment.

"Sorry, I know you employ her. If it helps, everything I'm saying now is off the record," Riley said, and she looked away. "Besides, I know she has it together better than I do anyway. But instead of helping, my mom yells at me all the time."

Riley leaned against the wall, sighing.

"I think your mom is trying to help, but in a way, maybe she sees some of your dad in you that you don't. And that scares her."

"Doesn't give her the right to be a bitch, though."

"No, it doesn't. I think you're a normal person in her twenties and I think what I've heard about you is different than what I see."

"And what have you heard?"

"Do you really want to go down this path?"

"God, no," Riley said, shaking her head. Another silence lapsed over them. This time it was less comfortable.

"All right," Riley joked, "enough about me. Tell me one of your personal problems so I don't feel like the loser who has everything wrong with her life."

Oliver laughed, but then it faded. They stood in silence, and Riley noticed he seemed to be lost in thought.

"I guess we could talk about how Zoe needs a mom."

"Wait, I wasn't serious," Riley said, worried she pressured him into saying something. "But for what it's worth, I think you're doing fine on your own."

"Yeah, but how do I tell her that her real mother never wanted her and then drove off a cliff because she was too drunk to drive?"

"Oh," Riley said. "I didn't know that last part."

And suddenly, Oliver's reactions to Riley coming in hungover made sense. But what made less sense was why he even hired her in the first place.

Riley was going to have to tread carefully here. She did not want to lose this job, which meant she had to stop drinking.

"Zoe is asking questions I can't answer," Oliver said, bringing Riley out of her thoughts.

"Is that why you're moving so fast with Sophie?" Riley asked.

He paused, as if he wasn't sure if he wanted to answer the question. "Do you think it's fast?"

"A little." She shrugged. "David and I didn't move in until we dated for two years. Then again, maybe I don't give the best advice in that department," she admitted bitterly.

"She is the first person I've met in four years, and she likes Zoe. I mean, where can I find that?"

"I guess it's hard to," Riley said.

"People don't want to accept someone else's kids. If Sophie can, then she's a keeper."

"But don't just accept her because she likes your kid. What do *you* think about her?"

"I think she's beautiful, and nice."

Riley nodded. She didn't want to shit on her boss's relationship. She figured she had already pushed the line enough tonight.

"Just do this for the right reasons, not because you think you need a mom for Zoe," Riley said. "I think she's a happy enough kid right now."

"Well, that does make me feel slightly better. But I don't know, I grew up without a mom, and I don't want that for my daughter."

"What happened to your mom?"

"Cancer. When I was very little. I remember bits and pieces, but nothing else."

"I'm sorry."

"It's okay," Oliver said. "I didn't want to have kids until I could guarantee they would have a loving, two-parent household. We never meant to have her, because my ex didn't want children. She made that clear the day she found out she was pregnant, and I knew I had failed in finding someone who would give our child the perfect life I'd always wanted for them. But despite all that, I don't regret keeping her, though I do wish I could spend more time with her."

"You spend as much time as you can."

"I do what my dad did. I work all the time and have to depend on a nanny to take care of Zoe. I feel like I deserve the fact that she likes you more than me right now."

"That's not true. She talks about you all the time, and you're making sure she has a future."

"I guess, but it's lonely being a single dad."

"I wish I could relate," Riley said.

"Yeah, me too," Oliver said, and his phone rang. "I'm getting a call; I need to get back to work. Can you find the guest bedroom?"

"Yeah, of course."

Oliver smiled at her before he disappeared into his office. Riley walked upstairs and down the hallway, checking in on Zoe before opening doors to find the guest bedroom. Eventually, she found it and laid down to let sleep overtake her.

Chapter Eleven

Oliver

"I'm sorry, Oliver, but we don't have any other options," Jack said, sighing.

Oliver shook his head. "You know I have never been away from Zoe overnight."

"I know, but the company is in a position where we have to act if we want to close this acquisition. If anyone else had the clearance you do, I would send them."

Oliver knew this was true. His father would probably go himself if he wasn't going to be headlining something else that very week. Oliver was the only person who could logically get it done.

This was what his early morning meeting had been about. He was so grateful for Riley being there early that he told her to treat herself to coffee if she happened to take Zoe out for anything. Riley cracked a joke like she usually did but Oliver wasn't sure if she took him up on it.

Now, he had to ask another favor of her. His dad couldn't watch Zoe because he was as busy as he would be, so Riley was his last option as someone Zoe would be comfortable with. But he also knew he was going to have to be careful, since she had a second job.

Oliver: Can we meet for lunch somewhere?

It was a few minutes later before she responded.

Riley: Sure, everything okay? I'm not about to get fired, right?

Oliver: No, let's meet at Alexander's on 5th.

Riley: Expensive. You better be buying, buddy.

Oliver smiled at the text, and he was happy he was alone in his office when he read it because there would have been far too many questions if his dad had been around.

The time for lunch came much quicker than he expected. Soon, he was outside of the restaurant, watching as Riley pulled up and parked next to him. She greeted him with her normal half smile and opened the car door to pull out a sleeping Zoe. Zoe's head stayed against her shoulder as Riley picked her up.

"She must have fallen asleep on the way over here," Oliver said, his voice soft as he looked at his daughter.

"Yeah, she did. She's been going all morning. I think her waking up with me there made her day."

"Well, that's part of what I want to talk to you about. Do you want to head in?"

"Yeah, I do. I'm starving. I swear, running around with a kid is so tiring."

"It definitely is," Oliver agreed. Riley walked ahead of him, holding Zoe in her arms. Oliver found his eyes trailed down, before he could stop them.

Though she was in the same clothes from the day before, he couldn't help but now notice the way these jeans hugged her tighter than the other pairs. Oliver realized he was staring at her butt way longer than he should have, so he forced himself to stop looking and opened the door for her. Technically, he was exclusive with Sophie, so he didn't need to be looking at anyone, much less his nanny.

They walked inside, and somehow Zoe stayed asleep. They got a booth in the back, and Zoe seemed to be content to lay her head on Riley's lap while they ate. She must have been exhausted.

"So, what did you bring me out here for? Do you have bad news?"

"No, I need a favor," Oliver said. "I figured I could feed you and have a better chance of you saying yes."

"You might want to wait until I order an appetizer then," Riley said. "Wait, no, I'm curious. What favor do you want from me?"

"I have to go out of town for three days."

Riley said. "Oh. Really?"

"Yes, and I can't bring Zoe with me."

"So, you want me to watch her? Overnight?"

"Yes."

"Well, I can't exactly bring her to my mom's house. Things aren't great with her. If I ask for anything, she might flip out."

"No, no. I would never ask that," Oliver assured her. It felt wrong to him to have Zoe anywhere other than his own home or Jack's apartment. He liked knowing where Zoe was. "The favor is that I need you to watch her at my house for those three days."

"So, you're asking me to stay in your nice house for three days?" Riley reiterated, an eyebrow raised. "And you're going to pay me for it?"

"It sounds less like a favor when you put it that way," Oliver admitted, but he knew it still was. Riley would be solely responsible for his daughter, which was a daunting task. "But this would really be helping me out if you do."

"You're taking me out to lunch and asking me to be away from my mom for a few days? I am *definitely* okay with that."

"Really?" Oliver was relieved. "I didn't know how it would work with your other job."

"Even if I am scheduled, I haven't called out in like three years, so I think I'm fine," Riley said. "No worries. I love watching Zoe."

"This was easier than I thought it would be."

"I do like spending time with Zoe, okay? Don't feel like you have to convince me to come to work. I love it."

"I figured you would want your free time," he said.

"Oliver, the only thing I do in my free time is sleep, which I'm sure I will find time to do when Zoe goes down. It's really not a problem."

Huh. Didn't Amanda say she liked to party? Apparently that wasn't totally true.

Oliver, once again, was finding Riley wasn't as she seemed, which was becoming a pattern.

The next day, while Oliver packed, he received a text from Sophie asking to go on a date. He knew he was going to have to turn it down since he was about to be out of town.

Maybe he could still include her. He was going to have a few meetings, but he would have his nights free, and she was an independent woman. Maybe she could go with him.

He nonchalantly invited her on his trip and then began the arduous task of explaining to Zoe he was leaving for a while. At first, she was upset, but once he mentioned Riley was going to be staying, Zoe was excited about it. The fact she was okay with him being gone overnight was kind of painful. He knew six months ago, there was no way she would have been this calm about it.

The morning he flew out, he was saying his goodbyes to Zoe when Riley arrived with a small bag. Zoe immediately hugged her, and allowed Oliver to grab his suitcase.

"Got everything?" Riley asked.

"I do. I need to run by Sophie's apartment and then to the airport."

"Oh, you're stopping to say goodbye to Sophie?"

"No, I invited her to come along. I figured we could use some adult time to ourselves."

Riley's eyebrows raised. "Oh, well . . . you two have fun."

"We will. It'll be a good test to see if we like each other enough."

"Be careful or you will have way too many Zoe's running around. I cap off at three," Riley said. He could tell she was joking, but he was truly afraid of that happening again. He knew he and Sophie were probably going to be intimate, but he also knew he definitely didn't want to have another accidental child.

Even if he had Riley.

"Right, well, you would be getting a raise."

"I'm just kidding. Do what you will!" Riley said, laughing. "But seriously, be safe."

"I will," Oliver said, and he gave her a smile before heading out the door. Zoe called goodbye as he left, and he took a deep breath, knowing he was going to miss her more than anything.

Chapter Twelve

Riley

"Why is Daddy going with Sophie?" Zoe asked while sitting with Riley. Oliver had only been gone a few minutes, and while him leaving went well, Riley was worried about the next few days.

"He likes Sophie, so he wants to spend time with her," she explained. "Were you listening in when he said that?"

"Yes . . ." Zoe said. "But he likes me, so why wouldn't he take me?"

"Well, Sophie is grown, which means while he is in those boring meetings, she can take care of herself."

"I can take care of myself!"

"But can you cook your own food?"

"Can I go with him if I learn?"

Riley smiled at her. If only it were so simple.

"There are plenty of things you would have to learn, and you will over time. But sometimes, people have to go do other things, and that's okay. It doesn't mean he doesn't like you or love you, it just means he has other responsibilities."

"And he's coming back, right?"

"As soon as he can."

"Okay," Zoe said. "I'm glad you're here."

"Aw," Riley said, and she pulled Zoe into a tight hug. "I like being here too."

The rest of the day went well. Zoe followed all the rules and even volunteered for bath time. She went to bed after a short video call from Oliver and seemed to be in good spirits.

The next day was a little tougher. All Zoe wanted to do was watch TV and cuddle, and she seemed down. After half of the day went by with Zoe being lifeless, Riley shut off the TV and said, "Okay, let's go somewhere."

"But I don't want to."

"It'll be fun!" Riley said, trying to sound excited.

"Where are we going?"

"How about the park? You can even ride on my back!"

Zoe considered it. She loved riding on Riley's back to go places. Riley waited patiently, hoping it would work.

"Okay," Zoe said, and Riley got both of them dressed, and they headed to the neighborhood park. They walked around and climbed together. Zoe eventually found a tiny nook at the top of the playground where she tried to fit into and was delighted when she did. Riley laughed as Zoe made herself comfortable.

"This is my place, Riley!" she announced. "But you can't tell anyone so I can come and hide here."

Riley smiled. "It'll be our secret."

That night, Oliver called. Zoe happily talked to him up until he mentioned Sophie. Zoe then said she was tired and wanted to go to bed, and Riley and he stayed up late talking about how things were going. After hanging up the phone, Riley gave Zoe a goodnight kiss before heading to the guest room.

With her things strewn about, it was oddly beginning to feel like home. She knew it would never be, but it was nice to pretend. It was going to make going back to her mom's even harder.

Jane hadn't been too happy with Riley for a while. Ever since their fight, Jane had been ignoring her and doing other things. Thankfully, she hadn't invited Sarah back over, but it was rough either way. Their relationship had never been great but living together again seemed to only make it worse. Jane barely spoke to her, and Riley was honestly glad she worked as much as she did, so she didn't even have to be there.

The final day Oliver was gone proved to be rough for Zoe. She was missing her dad and asked Riley every five minutes when he was coming back. Riley messaged Oliver to see if they could meet at the airport to make it easier on Zoe, and she was grateful when he said yes.

Zoe waited anxiously to see him, and when she finally did, she ran to give him a huge hug. He seemed just as happy to see her and picked her up and swung her around. Riley walked up with a smile, happy to see Zoe was excited.

Sophie walked around the corner, hauling her suitcase. Her hair was perfect and she was wearing light makeup and exuding a confidence that matched Oliver's. She looked like the perfect girlfriend.

But Riley didn't care about Sophie. She cared about Zoe, and when she saw the normally happy little girl tense up and scoot toward Riley, it set off alarms—just like the night when Sophie tried to put her to bed.

Oliver didn't seem to notice it, though. Riley filed the information away, hoping it was her own imagination. She didn't want to fight with Oliver, but she wouldn't forget what she was noticing, just in case. She didn't exactly trust Sophie.

After leaving Oliver's place, Riley pulled up to the bar and sighed. For the last three days, Riley hadn't been able to drink, and she had been ignoring the headaches and grumpiness for Zoe's sake. But being at the bar made her too nervous to do anything else. The smell of alcohol and people drinking around her made her want to do it just like everyone else. She was afraid she would be too weak to stop herself if she went inside.

Riley found her priorities shifting to center around Zoe. It was a strange feeling, but the craving of alcohol was enough to make her worried her job at the bar was about to hurt the little girl she cared so much about.

She decided at that very moment she couldn't do it anymore. Her job as a nanny was more important. She walked in and told her boss she was quitting. He didn't say much but asked where she wanted her last check to be sent and told her to come back whenever she needed a job.

It was a split-second decision, but then again, choosing to work at a bar was too. She had only worked there because David said she would like it, but all of that changed now. She drove to her mother's house after finishing up at work. When she walked in, her mother looked at her, confused.

"Why are you here?" she asked.

"I quit the bar."

"What? Why?"

"It's not good for me to be working around booze all the time, especially when I have a day job."

Riley didn't know what she expected out of her mother at the news, but she remembered all the times Jane tried to get her to find a new job. Riley hoped there would be some sort of pride in her mother's eyes, but Jane sighed and shook her head.

Riley was offended. "What? I thought you would be happy for me."

"I thought you wanted to get your own place," Jane said.

"I mean, I do," Riley replied. "But what use is it if I'm unhappy?"

"It's going to set you back on your goals. And let's be honest, you can't keep this nanny front up forever."

"What does that mean?"

"Amanda told me you went to work hungover. This man is not going to give you a dozen free passes, Riley. You're dealing with *his daughter*. What happens when he fires you?"

"What do you mean *when* he fires me? I'm doing really well at this job, mom."

"Yes, for now. But you need to think about your future."

"Okay," Riley said. "Thanks for the advice."

She didn't stick around to hear any more. She headed to her room and laid on her bed, unsure of what to do.

Her mom told her to stop drinking, and she had. Her mom always said to find a better job, and she had. She was doing everything she thought was right, but nothing seemed to be good enough for her mother.

Chapter Thirteen

Oliver

"So, what do you think about marriage?" Sophie asked. "Ever considered getting married again after Zoe's mom?"

Oliver paused. He and Sophie were out for a walk in the park while Zoe hung out with Riley. They were holding hands and he felt at ease.

"Zoe's mom and I were never married, but yes I have. I think I would consider it if I met the right person."

Sophie's eyes twinkled. "Hopefully you do soon."

And that was where the conversation ended, but it was enough to get Oliver thinking. He knew he was moving fast, and that was okay with him. Sophie was great, and he really needed to find a mom for Zoe before she figured out what happened to her own mother.

Oliver had been looking at rings and he had been considering marriage, so much so, he decided he needed to bring it up with Riley. He was pretty sure Sophie wanted to be a stay-at-home mom. She always complained about her job and having to work to support herself. If she were to marry Oliver, she wouldn't have to do that.

A few days later, he decided to bring it up to Riley.

"Hey," Oliver said to Riley after coming home from work. "I have something I want to run by you."

"What's up?" Riley asked. Zoe was busy playing with her dolls while Riley had been cleaning up the house.

"I'm thinking of asking Sophie to marry me."

Riley looked stunned. "Oh . . . wow. That's a big step."

"I think she's great and Zoe would really learn to love her."

She glanced away, and then back to him, as if she were debating what to say. She then replied, "I don't think you should do this."

Oliver frowned. That was not the answer he was expecting. "Why not?"

"I don't think Zoe likes her," Riley said. "And besides, they haven't interacted enough to really get a good idea of whether or not they would like each other. Maybe this is too fast."

"You said it was fine."

"Well, I'm not trying to talk shit about your girlfriend, Oliver. But also, I want you to really think about this."

"Do you not like Sophie or something?"

Riley bit her lip, lost in thought. She sighed. "I don't."

"Why don't you?"

"You want my honest opinion?"

"You're going to give it either way." He grew frustrated. He didn't like people judging his choices, and he really didn't want Riley doing it either. He was the boss here. He was the one with a successful life and great kid. What did she know? Why did he even bother asking her?

"I think she's stuck up and after your money," Riley said, crossing her arms.

"Why?"

"It's the way she looks at you, and your house. Plus, Zoe acts really weird around her. I have a gut feeling something is wrong."

"So, you're telling me not to ask my girlfriend to marry me, and give Zoe a mom, based on a gut feeling?"

"I'm saying maybe you should wait."

"Yes, and I really should be taking advice from someone like you, right?" Oliver said. It was mean, but he never expected Riley to talk down about Sophie—to tear apart his choices like this.

Plus, she sounded jealous.

Several days prior, Sophie told him she was worried Riley was going to take advantage of him—that one day, she would snap about Sophie and tell him not to move forward with her.

Just like she was doing now.

"Excuse me?" Riley asked, offended.

"This isn't your decision. You don't get to come between Sophie's and my happiness."

"What? I'm only saying this stuff because it's true! I mean, how much do you really know about Sophie versus . . . well, me?"

"You?" Oliver asked. "I know far too much about you, but I also know plenty about her. I've just never told you."

That was kind of a lie, but also not the point. Sophie told him surface-level things about herself, and he had done the same. However, he was fine with that. He didn't need to know every detail about her life, and she didn't need to know every detail about his.

"Okay, then maybe have her and Zoe meet up a little more before you jump into this. I only have Zoe's best interests in mind here."

"Do you, or do you have your own?"

"Oh my God, are you really saying all of this stuff to me because I don't like your model girlfriend?"

"Model girlfriend?"

"Oh, let's not play around here. You like her because she's hot. That's it. You're like all guys, wanting women for what they look like and not who they are."

Oliver glared at her. "So, you're jealous because you don't look like her?" It was out of his mouth before he could stop it, but it made sense.

Riley raised her eyebrows. "What? Are you kidding me right now?"

"You're insecure."

"Fine, maybe I am. But I'm not wrong about the other things, okay?"

"You are wrong. Sophie and Zoe get along *fine*."

"You're delusional, Oliver. Sophie may play the part, but has Zoe ever asked about her? Has Sophie asked about Zoe, for that matter? At the airport, Zoe got quiet the minute she saw Sophie. I'm trying to warn you."

Maybe he would have remembered Zoe's shyness when Sophie arrived if he weren't so *mad* about Riley's opinions. He didn't want her picking apart his choices because of her own insecurities, and he didn't want her making him question his decision on giving Zoe the parental figure she needed.

"I'm asking Sophie to marry me."

"Then you're being a fucking idiot, Oliver."

And that was the final straw.

"Go home, Riley."

"Excuse me?"

"We're done here. That was unprofessional and if Zoe had heard it, she would have repeated it."

Riley's anger morphed quickly into hurt. "Zoe is in her room. I've never said anything bad in front of her."

"You came to work hungover. I should have seen it then."

"Are you firing me right now?" Riley asked, her voice high. It was obvious she was upset. Oliver almost felt bad, but he was too frustrated with her to allow it.

"I am. I can figure out childcare without you. Amanda and Sophie can watch Zoe."

"I just told you Zoe doesn't even like Sophie."

"You said they need more time together, so this is how I'm doing it. With how you're acting right now, how do I know you didn't tell Zoe awful things about Sophie anyway?" Oliver didn't know if this was true, and honestly, he couldn't see Riley doing that.

But she *did* benefit from keeping Zoe and Sophie apart. Sophie had mentioned that.

"You know I wouldn't do that," Riley said, her voice shaky and hurt. She stared, as if trying to decide if he was serious or not. "Fucking whatever. If you see me that way, then there's nothing I can do about it. I'm going to go say goodbye to Zoe."

"No, leave. I don't need you cussing in front of my four-year-old and ruining her vocabulary. You can go."

Riley's jaw dropped. "I can't even say goodbye to her?" Oliver shook his head.

"Fine. But for the record? This is how you screw up a kid. Forcing a stepparent into their life solely to replace their birth mother? This is wrong, and you know it. I hope Sophie is worth the risk, because it's Zoe who's going to suffer the consequences when this falls apart."

It hit harder than he wanted it to. He didn't want to think about whether she was right or not. "Leave, Riley."

Riley's eyes were wet. "Fuck you, Mr. Brian. I hope you have a terrible marriage."

And she was gone.

After she was, and the heat of the moment cooled, Oliver wondered if he made the right choice.

But Sophie would be good for them. She could be the partner he needed, and the parent Zoe didn't have. It didn't matter what Riley thought, because she didn't know him. She didn't know what he needed.

Oliver closed his eyes, trying and failing to convince himself he was right.

Then he remembered all the warnings about Riley, and he told himself it was for the best that this strange, unconventional woman was out of their lives. It gave him time to breathe, because when Riley was around, he didn't know how to. She was so unlike anyone he'd ever met, and he was sure it was better not to live with the uncomfortable, curious feeling he had around her.

If he felt this strongly about a woman who worked in a bar and drank her nights away, he knew Zoe would be feeling more. It was better to have Zoe get attached to someone he could keep around, not her nanny.

It didn't do anything to curb his guilt, but it at least helped him get to sleep that night.

Riley

Riley drank an entire bottle of whiskey after leaving Oliver's house. She didn't care if her mom found her. She was out of a job, she was pretty sure a little girl was going to be devastated, and there was nothing she could do about it.

She was as angry as the day she found out David was cheating on her. She was as hurt as the second she figured out it was Sarah. She felt like fate, or God, or whoever, had it out for her and was hell-bent on ruining her life.

Riley passed out at home, face down and snoring. No one bothered to talk to her. She almost wanted to call Sarah, because before all of this, she would have told her best friend everything. She would have confided every detail to her and felt comfortable doing it.

But Sarah fucked her boyfriend. Sarah was currently *engaged* to her boyfriend, so screw her. Riley had no one, and that was just how it was. She couldn't change it, only deal with it.

When she woke up hungover, she immediately thought about Zoe, who would wake up without seeing her. It would be Sophie, the blonde stuck-up bitch Zoe didn't even like. Or Amanda, who everyone thought was perfect but didn't love Zoe like Riley did.

That thought alone was enough to make Riley want to drink all over again.

Riley didn't care it was daytime. She needed more alcohol. She got up, prayed her mother wouldn't see her, and drove to the store. She knew she shouldn't spend money since she didn't have a job now, but she didn't care. She could easily go back to the bar and pretend none of this ever happened.

But as Riley drove, the headache hit her, and she wanted something to help ease it a bit. She didn't have any medicine, but she did know of a coffee shop a few miles away that made an amazing macchiato. She changed her course, now desperately craving coffee. She walked in and the smell overtook her.

Her need for a drink waned. All she wanted now was coffee. She walked to the counter and looked at the menu before she got to the front and instantly recognized the person taking her order.

"Oh my God," Riley said.

"Riley?" the woman asked.

"Camilla Reyes . . ." Riley said, remembering the girl she knew from high school. Camilla was wearing a brown apron with her dark hair in a ponytail. She looked the same as she did eight years ago, which was incredibly unfair.

Camilla and Riley were never close friends, more acquaintances than anything else. It had been years since they saw each other, but Riley saw her on Facebook every now and again, the rare times she was ever on it.

Camilla always had a coffee in her hand, even in high school. She was obsessed with it, so it made sense that she worked in a coffee shop now.

"Oh my God, how are you?" Camilla asked with a smile.

"I'm . . . here," Riley said awkwardly. She didn't exactly want to go into the details of her life, but she also didn't want to lie and say everything was fine. "How have you been?"

"I've been good! I own this place."

"That's amazing!" Riley replied, feeling genuine happiness for her. "I wish I was doing something half as cool as this."

"Well, I *am* hiring," Camilla joked, but in the moment, Riley was too tired to get it.

"I should apply. I need a job," she replied, and then realized Camilla probably didn't want her working there. Riley's muddled brain scrambled to take it back.

"Oh," Camilla said. Her eyes widened for a moment. She turned to the back and gestured for the guy making drinks to come up to the front. "You know what," she said, turning to Riley, "why don't I get you some coffee and we'll sit down? I think we need to catch up."

Riley blinked. She didn't think she and Camilla were good enough friends to catch up, but she still needed coffee, so she could deal with conversation while getting it.

A few minutes later, Camilla was sitting in a private part of her café. Her other barista, a guy named Dustin, was manning the counter on his own. Since it was a weekday, it wasn't too busy.

"So, you look like hell."

Riley's jaw dropped, but she knew Camilla was right. "I know. I wasn't exactly planning to be in public today. It's been a rough night. And day . . . and month."

"Ooh, yeah. I hate to ask, but isn't Sarah's new fiancé the guy you dated? I sort of saw some of the drama on Facebook."

"Yeah. He cheated on me. With her."

"What an asshole. I mean I never knew him, but you wouldn't think she would be the one to do that. And honestly, props to you for not blasting him on social media."

"Yeah, that and the fact I lost my job last night . . . it's rough."

"What were you doing there?"

"I was a nanny for the sweetest little girl, but the dad is getting married and when I warned him his daughter didn't like his girlfriend, he fired me."

"Jesus," Camilla said. "So, you don't work at the bar anymore?"

"How did you know I worked at a bar?"

"I got dragged to the honky-tonk bars when my wife moved here," Camilla explained, sighing. "It was pretty bad for me, but I saw you there. You were too busy for me to say hi, and honestly, I didn't think you would recognize me anyway."

"You're married?" Riley asked. "That's amazing! And I totally would have known it was you. You look the same as you did eight years ago."

"You're flattering me."

"No, I'm not. I am actually about to ask you what moisturizer you use because your skin looks great."

Camilla smiled. "Well, thanks. I know it's flattery, but I'll take it."

"It's really not," Riley said, shaking her head. "But about the bar, I quit not too long ago. I tried to stop drinking, and working at a bar was too much."

"So, what you're telling me is that you can mix drinks and you have the patience for a little kid?" Camilla asked.

"Those are all true things about me," Riley said.

"Can you learn about coffee?"

"I mean, sure. I would love to learn about the thing that keeps me running in the morning."

"Perfect! Then, you *could* work here."

Riley blinked in shock. "Um, I was joking earlier. I can't waltz in here and ask you for a job."

"Why not? I always want someone who works hard and is a quick learner."

"I don't have any experience."

"Well, lucky for you I need someone with a business degree, and I know for a fact you have one. It's on Facebook."

Riley felt her cheeks heat up. Were people from high school checking on her on Facebook? Did they see the dumpster fire that was her life? Maybe she needed to delete her profile.

"I do, but I haven't used it or anything."

"Well, you can now. I need someone to help with the numbers and be able to make coffee for people. I would like to hire you."

"Seriously?"

"Yes. I am being dead serious."

Riley paused. She would love to work at the shop with someone as kind as Camilla. It would be a day job, and nothing involving alcohol. Plus, she would *finally* be using her degree like her mom always wanted her to.

"Camilla, I would love to work here," Riley said. "But I feel the need to warn you I'm a mess and—"

Camilla cut her off. "Oh, *same*. We're all a mess here. My wife and I cannot keep an apartment to save our life. Dustin over there got dumped by his girlfriend and is heartbroken."

"Poor guy," Riley said, glancing over her shoulder at him.

"By the way, I totally shouldn't have told you that," Camilla said, looking slightly guilty. "I just really want you to work here."

"Why?" Riley asked, genuinely curious.

"Honestly? You were really cool in high school, and you aced math. I love my shop and everything, but I hate the math and taxes. I need someone who can work weird hours and do math really well, and you walked in here, like an angel sent to save me."

"You could hire an accountant," Riley suggested.

"I could, but they are ungodly expensive, and I also need help behind the counter. No accountant is going to do both," Camilla said. "And I want to help you out! I saw what your ex did, and I wanted to reach out, but we never knew each other all that well. This is the perfect way to do it now."

"Well, when you put it like that . . ." Riley said, laughing.

"Yes!" Camilla said, bouncing in her seat. "Okay, so I want you to go home, get your paperwork, and take a shower. You have a new job, and I really need help starting today."

It was only a few hours before she was back, and Riley had some hope for her future. The very minute Camilla had her name on the payroll, she showed Riley her finances, which Riley had to admit were a mess. But luckily, her hangover was gone, and she was feeling better so she could focus on it. In a few hours, she already had payroll and bank statements organized, and Camilla almost cried.

When Riley and Camilla discussed wages, Riley was relieved to find her new boss was able to offer her what Oliver paid her. It was only part-time, but it was enough to keep her on track for getting her own place. Plus, she would get paid when she took work home.

After the finances were organized, Riley worked on learning coffee and talking to people, which proved to be better than what she thought it was going to be. In the end, she hoped this would last, since she liked Camilla and liked what she was doing.

She could only hope she wouldn't screw it up like she had with Oliver.

Chapter Fourteen

Riley

It had been three weeks.

Riley still felt like she had lost a huge part of herself. It was ironic it was not her boyfriend of many years, or her best friend, but Zoe. She had been taken away from someone she truly cared about, and she didn't even get to say goodbye.

She hoped the little girl was okay. She hoped Zoe was fine with Sophie. The guilt of the abrupt end of their relationship was hard to live with, but she had to. She had no legal rights to Zoe, so she had to move on.

And she did. Camilla was quickly becoming a close friend, and Riley hadn't had anything to drink since the night Oliver fired her.

She was doing well at work too. She was happy to be using her degree and made a few business decisions that got people into the café. She crunched a lot of numbers and worked with Dustin and Camilla in helping customers, which kept her so busy it limited the time she could spend wallowing in her misery. Her life was going okay, minus missing Zoe.

"So, what are your plans tonight?" Camilla asked. It was just her and Riley as they closed up shop. The day had been wild, which was a good sign that it was so busy. They were both tired, but it was still daylight out.

"Probably nothing," Riley said. "Maybe I'll see a movie instead of going home. My mom is still gloating that Oliver fired me."

That was true.

Jane had been the first to say she knew Riley was not fit to be a nanny, and then told her working at a coffee shop was worse than the bar, even when Riley insisted she was using her degree.

Riley pushed that conversation out of her mind. It still made her sad to think about. Nothing she could do would ever please her mom.

"Well, I would invite you to my place, but my wife made me promise a date night since I've been working so much."

"Sorry, I knew the karaoke night would bring people in, but not this many people," Riley said.

"Um, because of you, my business is on fire. So don't apologize. Well, don't apologize to me. You might have to have words with my wife."

Riley nodded. "I'll be sure to tell her I'm sorry."

"I'm kidding, she's happy for me, but she will be even happier once we have some alone time," Camilla said. "Maybe tomorrow night you can come over. I know you don't want to be alone all the time."

"Yeah, maybe tomorrow."

Camilla said her goodbyes as they parted ways in the parking lot. Riley climbed into her car and looked back to where Zoe used to sit and sighed. Oliver hadn't taken the car seat when he fired her, and Riley hadn't taken it out of her car. It was almost like she was hoping she would get a call and get to see Zoe again.

Her phone rang. It was almost like fate, but it wasn't Oliver. It was Amanda.

"What's up?" Riley answered.

"Hey, look sorry to bother you and all, but I kind of need to ask you something." Amanda sounded worried, which was unusual. It filled Riley with dread.

"What's going on?"

"Would you happen to know where Zoe would go if she were upset or something?"

Riley froze. That dread morphed into straight fear.

"Why?" she asked.

"Zoe ran off today, and Oliver won't ask you, but no one knows where she is."

"She ran off?" Riley exclaimed; her mind raced.

"I just said that, and Oliver is freaking out," Amanda said. "And you don't need to yell."

"*I'm* freaking out," Riley said. "Why the hell would she have run off?"

"No one knows! Sophie was watching her and—"

"Fuck, I knew it was that bitch!"

"Jesus Christ, calm down."

"No, there is a four-year-old missing, Amanda," Riley said. "This is not the time to be calm."

"You're being dramatic!" Amanda snapped, but Riley could hear the tenseness in her tone. She was worried. "Do you know where she would be or not?"

Riley paused. Did she?

"Where was she when she ran off?"

"At home."

Riley thought about it until she remembered the park. Riley took her there almost every day. "I have an idea where she would go."

"Thank God," Amanda said, sounding relieved. "Just tell me and I can—"

"Oh no, if she's upset enough to run off, she's not going to come out for you or anyone. Just give me an hour."

"An hour? No, I need to tell Oliver—"

"Just trust me!"

"No!"

Riley needed to get to Green Hills, and fast, but if Amanda told Oliver she was coming, he could stop her from entering the neighborhood. And if Zoe was angry with Sophie, and Oliver kept bringing her around, it was likely Zoe didn't trust Oliver either.

"Amanda, I don't ask you for much." She tried to soften her voice. "But trust me this one time. I know where Zoe is, but I might be the only one she would listen to."

"Why?" Amanda asked. "Why would she listen to you?"

Riley sighed. Amanda wasn't going to believe Zoe truly liked her, but she did know what Amanda would believe instead. "Because I'm fun. I let her get away with whatever, so she would trust me more."

There was silence on the other end. Riley hoped it worked.

"Okay, fine. But I'm telling him in an hour."

"Thank you," Riley said, relieved.

Riley hung up the phone and threw her car in reverse and drove to Oliver's neighborhood. The security guard didn't stop her which told Riley that Oliver hadn't taken away her access to the neighborhood. She was grateful for his forgetfulness.

She got into the neighborhood and drove straight to the park. She looked around and saw it was deserted but knew better than to believe what met the eye. She climbed to the top of the play area and glanced at the tiny nook Zoe once found. She saw a shadow, and she wanted to run and grab Zoe to hug her. But that would do no good.

Riley took a gentler approach.

"Hey, kid," Riley said, sitting near her.

"Riley?" Zoe asked, her voice quiet.

"Yep, it's me."

Zoe immediately jumped out of her hiding spot and into Riley's lap. She hugged the woman tightly, and it took Riley a minute to realize she was crying.

"Where did you go? You left!"

"I'm sorry. Your dad and I had a disagreement, and he told me to leave."

"Daddy is the worst!" Zoe yelled with an aggressiveness that was unlike her.

Riley didn't disagree, but she had never heard anything like that out of Zoe.

"What happened?" Riley asked, feeling the anxiety drain out of her now that Zoe was near.

"He made you leave! And now Sophie is with me, and I hate Sophie!"

"Why do you hate Sophie?" Zoe asked.

"She's mean."

"Why do you say that?" And at Zoe's look, Riley felt a chill overtake her. She had a feeling she was about to get bad news.

"She told me not to tell anyone," Zoe whispered.

Riley paused. That didn't sound good.

"Well, you can tell me."

"Are you sure?"

"Yeah, in fact, I think you should. Maybe I can help."

"Okay . . ." Zoe said. "Sophie said I needed to be a better kid and stop ruining my dad's life."

"What?" Riley asked, her voice cold. She had been right. She definitely didn't like what she was hearing.

"And she said that when she married my Daddy, she would *make* me be a better kid."

"You *are* a good kid. She's wrong, Zoe."

"She's mean to me all the time." The little girl was quiet for a long moment, and then she added, "Once, I told her I didn't like her and she *pushed* me. I was so scared."

Riley froze. There were so many thoughts running through her head, she felt like she might explode. She took a long look at Zoe whose eyes were full of tears. She physically looked okay, but she knew people like Sophie would never leave a mark.

She remembered Oliver telling her to never use corporal punishment. Did he backtrack on that? Or did he even know?

God, if he was allowing this, then Riley didn't know what she would do.

"Does your dad know this?"

"She doesn't want me to tell him."

Riley took another deep breath, trying to keep her voice level, but her hands were shaking, and she had the urge to hit something . . . namely Sophie. "Okay, well, I am going to do something about this. I am going to talk to your dad to see if I can help."

Talk was not the word she would use, but Zoe didn't need to know that.

"Okay."

Oliver was lucky she still had the car seat. She strapped Zoe in and drove to his house, turning the lights off as she approached. She told Zoe to stay in the car and found a book for her to keep her distracted. She shut her door and finally let her anger show on her face.

Riley marched to the front door and pounded on it. Her fists were clenched, and when Oliver answered, looking disheveled and worried, she felt no sympathy.

"Riley?" he asked, obviously confused as to why she was there.

"Where is Sophie?"

"Excuse me? This is not the time—"

"Shut the fuck up, Oliver," Riley snapped with more venom than she probably should have. "I know Zoe is missing because Amanda called me to ask where she might be. Now where the fuck is Sophie?"

"What does she—"

"Oliver?" Sophie came into view. Unlike Oliver, she did not look concerned. When she saw Riley, her face turned into a frown. "What are *you* doing here?"

"I'm the one asking questions. Why did you threaten a four-year-old child?"

"What?" Oliver said.

"Excuse me?" Sophie asked.

"Oh, don't play dumb. I know what you did."

"Oliver, stop her from speaking to me like this!"

"Wait, how would you know?" Oliver asked. It seemed like he still had a shred of sense in him.

"Because Zoe told me," Riley said.

"Just now?" Oliver said. "You know where she is?"

"Yes. I do. And I am not letting you look at her until this bitch is out of this house."

"I did nothing wrong!" Sophie yelled.

"Oh, you did nothing wrong? Then why did Zoe run away, huh? Why is she keeping secrets from her father about what you say to her?"

Sophie was red in the face. Riley got immense pleasure from finally breaking Sophie's perfect exterior. "You don't know anything."

"I know you pushed her," Riley said.

The room went dead silent. Riley could feel Oliver's eyes were on her, but she couldn't care less. She was staring at Sophie, watching the woman's expression change from shock to anger.

"Did you push my daughter?" Oliver rounded on Sophie. He sounded angry, and thank God, or else he was going to get it from Riley next.

"Wait, you believe her?" Sophie acted appalled.

"Riley has never been a liar," Oliver said, his voice cold. "So, answer the question."

Sophie looked angry. "So what if I did?"

Hearing Sophie confirm it made Riley angrier than she had ever been.

"What if I pushed you?" Riley snapped. "There's a set of stairs right there."

"Are you threatening me?"

"You threatened a four-year-old!" Riley yelled so loudly her voice immediately went hoarse.

"She's a brat!" Sophie countered. "She had no set bedtime, no schedule, and she does what she wants! She needed to know I was the boss around here and not her! Oliver, you're with me on this, right?"

Riley didn't even want to look at him, because if he was on her side, and if he let Sophie stay, Riley didn't know if she could leave. She didn't know if she could let Zoe stay in this home.

"Get out of my house, Sophie," Oliver said in a low voice. Riley finally let herself look at him, letting out a breath of relief.

His fists were clenched and he looked ready to lose it at any moment. He also looked sad—a deep sadness Riley knew he wasn't going to get over anytime soon.

Riley almost felt bad for him, but this was his own damn fault.

"Excuse me?" Sophie said. She had the nerve to sound genuinely shocked Oliver wasn't on her side.

"Get out, before I call the cops," Oliver repeated.

"I can't believe this! You're making *me* leave?"

"Yes."

"You're choosing that brat over me?"

"Fuck you, Sophie," Riley interjected, though she probably shouldn't have, "that *brat* is his daughter, you inconsiderate bitch."

"I'm sorry. I don't speak to the *help*."

"Get. Out." Oliver's voice was so hard it made Riley tense, and be glad she wasn't on the receiving end of it.

"You'll regret this. Don't call me when she's a teenager ruining your life!"

Sophie stormed out of the house. Riley followed to make sure she wouldn't see Zoe in the back of the car and go after the little girl.

When Sophie peeled out of the driveway, Riley turned to Oliver.

"You," Riley said, pointing at him. "Don't think I've forgotten that bullshit you told me. I was right about her. I swear to God if I had any legal right to Zoe, she would not be coming back here right now."

Riley was prepared to deal with him diverting his anger to her. She was prepared to fight him too, but the minute Sophie was out of sight, all he said was, "Where's Zoe?"

She really didn't want to let him see her. She wanted Oliver to suffer more, but she knew that was selfish. She walked to her car and opened the door, where Zoe dropped her book and looked at Riley with wide eyes.

"Sophie's gone, honey," Riley said in a calm voice. "It's just your dad and me."

Zoe threw her arms up, obviously wanting to be picked up. Riley unbuckled her and complied, letting the little girl wrap her arms and legs around her torso. Zoe hid her face in Riley's hair.

"Are you okay?" Zoe only nodded and didn't move. Oliver reached for her, and she cried out and gripped Riley harder.

All of Riley's anger faded, and it was replaced with the pain of being away from Zoe for three weeks. And now that Riley knew Zoe had been suffering, it made it all worse.

"She's not really happy with you right now."

"Where did you find her?"

"The park."

"But we looked there," Oliver said.

"That's where she was," Riley said, not telling him about her hiding spot.

"Do you work at the bar tonight? Is there a way we can talk?"

"I quit the bar a month ago," Riley said. "And then you fired me."

Oliver looked guilty. "I didn't know."

"Would it have changed anything?"

He didn't answer, which told Riley everything she needed to know.

"Yeah, I can come in and talk," she said, but it was more for the girl in her arms than him. She didn't let go of Zoe as she followed Oliver back into the house. She looked around, noticing that not much had changed in that time, except all of Zoe's toys were missing from sight.

And that made sense. Sophie was in it for Oliver alone, and she wanted Zoe to be scrubbed out of existence. The house was devoid of any sign of a child. It made Riley feel even worse.

She sat on the couch, and Zoe adjusted herself, but did not let her go. Riley sighed and knew she was not going to be released anytime soon—unless Oliver made her, but Riley didn't think she could handle that.

"I messed up," Oliver said.

"Yes, you did," Riley replied. "What were you thinking?"

"I thought I could trust her. She never told me that there was a problem."

"But what about Zoe?"

"She was . . . quieter. Maybe that was my sign."

"No, your sign was the way Zoe acted every time you brought up Sophie. She never liked her."

"She's weird with strangers."

"Not that weird," Riley replied. "And besides, you didn't even let me say goodbye. Can you imagine how difficult that transition was for her?"

Zoe hugged her tighter. Oliver noticed it immediately.

"Sophie told me it went fine."

"Sophie is a liar, in case you didn't know."

"I know now," Oliver said. "I should have listened to you."

"You should have. You were cruel that night."

"I'm sorry." It sounded like a genuine apology.

"If you're sorry, then tell me why you did it."

"I thought you were jealous."

"That is the shakiest excuse. What were you really thinking?"

"I'm telling you—"

"I don't want to hear whatever excuse you told yourself to justify it. I want the truth—the one you don't want to admit to yourself."

Oliver looked pained, but Riley didn't back down. She may not have been able to hear the truth from David and Sarah, but this felt more important.

Mainly because of the little girl currently holding onto her like a lifeline.

"I'm tired, Riley." The words were quiet.

Pained.

Riley got the feeling he wasn't talking about the kind of tired you slept off.

"I've been doing this for four years," he continued. "Being a parent is *exhausting*. I pushed it because I thought I had done enough research on her and who she was so I could have some . . . help. Not just for childcare, even. I needed a partner."

Riley blinked. That wasn't the answer she was expecting.

"Did you even love her?"

There was no answer.

Then Riley understood. This was a transaction. This was Oliver trying to find the shards of a relationship. He found someone he was attracted to, and then made sure she would fit into his life like a missing puzzle piece.

"You knew this wouldn't work, right?"

"Of course," he said bitterly. "I knew you were right the moment you left when I fired you, but I couldn't . . . I couldn't admit that because it meant I was stuck like I was. I can't keep doing this alone. I *can't* go on like I have been."

Riley shut her eyes. The pain in his voice was so profound. He was actually being honest with her.

And she was about to do something stupid.

Dammit.

"Then don't," she said softly.

"Riley, I can't just stop being Zoe's parent. Even if she's mad at me, I—"

"I'm not saying you stop being a parent. I'm saying you stop doing it alone."

"As nice as that would be, I don't have childcare. That's what I was trying to do with Sophie, but we see how that turned out. It's not that simple."

No. It wasn't. But she was about to make it simple.

"I'll . . . I'll watch her."

Oliver looked at her, shocked. "What?"

"I'll watch her," she said slowly, as if testing it out for herself. "If you don't truly think I'm a bad influence, that is."

"Why would you offer to watch her? I fired you."

Zoe whined.

"Thanks for bringing that up," Riley said, her voice wry.

"No, that's not what I mean. You have no reason to want to come back."

"I have one reason," Riley replied, looking down at Zoe. Oliver's gaze followed hers, and he watched his daughter. "But I understand if you don't want me to come back. You did fire me, after all."

"I don't understand why you would offer to come back after how I talked to you."

"It's simple. I'm not doing it for you."

Once again, Riley looked down at Zoe, who was hugging her as tight as she could.

"I think it's obvious Zoe only wants you right now." Oliver sounded pained. "I know things aren't the same, but . . . if you're willing to come back, then I'd love to have you."

Zoe looked up at her hopefully.

"I have a new job that's during the day," Riley said. "So you're right. It can't be how it was, but I'll come back."

Oliver looked relieved. "Thank you, Riley."

She nodded, and Zoe laid her head down on her shoulder. She knew she was not going to be able to leave for a while, so she leaned back, and soon, Zoe was asleep.

"She doesn't even want me to hold her," Oliver said sadly.

"Give it time."

"I can pay you to stay overnight," Oliver said. "If she wakes up and you're gone . . ." He trailed off.

"I'll stay, but don't pay me. I'll feel weird accepting that," Riley said. "I'll have to leave at eight, though, to go to my other job."

"Of course," Oliver said with a soft smile. Riley gave him a half smile back, trying to decide if she hated him for what he said when he fired her, or really felt bad for him now that he knew he was wrong.

But all those emotions meant nothing in comparison to one thing. She had Zoe back, and it gave her a sense of peace so strong she couldn't find it in herself to regret the offer.

Riley had to sleep in Zoe's room since the girl wouldn't let her go. She had slept in Zoe's full-sized bed a few times, but never overnight. It was a tight squeeze, and her back bemoaned a full eight hours of it.

Zoe was up by six the next morning, and Riley got her dressed. Zoe didn't need to be carried anymore, which was relieving. Riley knew leaving to go to the coffee shop was going to be miserable.

Oliver was in the kitchen, cooking breakfast. He turned to see them, with dark circles under his eyes. He still looked awful, but Riley didn't say anything. He was probably already feeling bad enough.

"Hey, kiddo," Oliver said, and he knelt to be her height. "How did you sleep?"

"Will Riley be watching me today?" Zoe asked.

"Actually, I was going to stay home with you today. I already called work."

"But I want Riley to stay."

Oliver seemed lost for words, so Riley stepped in. "Hey, I have to go do something to make sure I can watch you later, so I have to leave for now. But Sophie won't be here."

"Do you promise?"

"I promise." Zoe held out her pinky, which Riley knitted through her own. If Oliver ever brought Sophie to the house again, she would kill him.

"Daddy, do you promise too?"

"I do," Oliver said, and he held out his pinky as well. Riley let out a sigh of relief when Zoe curled her pinky in his. Oliver looked like he felt a similar sense of relief.

"I don't like Sophie," Zoe said in a soft voice.

"It's okay, honey. I don't like her anymore either," Oliver replied.

"Good," Zoe added. Riley checked the time and saw it was already eight.

"I'm sorry," Riley said. "I have to go. I need to get to my other job. Zoe, will you be okay?"

"Will you be back?"

"Of course," Riley said.

Zoe gave Riley a tight hug with tears in her eyes. Riley felt bad about leaving, but knew she had to. Zoe didn't cry or scream as she walked out the door, which Riley could only guess was a good thing.

After driving to work, she tried to smooth down her hair and look somewhat presentable, but it was a futile effort. Eventually, she walked in and went behind the counter.

"Hey," Camilla said in passing, but stopped when she saw what Riley was wearing. "Aren't those the same clothes from yesterday?"

"Yeah, they are."

"Oh, did you finally get a rebound?"

"What? No, it was a bad night."

"Oh no. What happened?"

Riley checked to see if the shop was too busy before launching into the explanation of Zoe going missing and how she found her. Camilla listened with rapt attention, up until Riley mentioned Oliver offered her job back.

"Wait, are you going to take it?"

"That's what I was going to ask you," Riley said. "Oliver knows he has to make things work for me, but I was wondering if I could still do the books for you during the week, and then work mainly Friday to Sunday."

"Well, that's really what you were working anyway. Dustin and I have everything else. We can work something out, but . . . is this really what you want to do?"

"What do you mean?"

"I mean, this guy was an epic jerk to you. And he said some really nasty things. I know it was only one time but—"

"I'm not doing this for Oliver. I'm doing this for Zoe."

"You would work two jobs for a four-year-old who's not even yours?"

"Of course I would," Riley said.

"That is . . . really amazing." Camilla looked genuinely impressed. "There are some moms out there who wouldn't do half of that."

"I'm her nanny, not her mom," Riley reminded her.

"I know, but . . . you're there for her. I think that's great."

Riley smiled. "So, you're okay if I do go back?"

"I think you should do what makes you happy, but I want to meet this Zoe. She's gotta be cute, right?"

"Oh, she is. I'll bring her in soon."

Chapter Fifteen

Oliver

Oliver blocked Sophie from everything. He removed her from his life and didn't look back.

What was he thinking? He rushed into the whole situation. He didn't think twice about it, and he hurt his daughter, and Riley, for some woman he barely knew.

He took a few days off to try to get back in Zoe's good graces. She still eyed him warily sometimes, and she wasn't the same little girl she used to be, but she was gradually getting better.

Riley had come back into her life, and that seemed to brighten her day. Even when she didn't work, Riley was coming over to make sure Zoe was okay. Oliver and Riley had barely talked, and it seemed she wasn't too interested in being friends with him but was more interested in Zoe.

He didn't blame her.

Before he knew it, a week passed. He was back at work and Riley was watching Zoe. He was still reeling from everything that happened. He hadn't even told his father yet and was too ashamed of how he reacted in order to mention it. Thankfully, Riley didn't really talk to Amanda, so there was that. Oliver had, however, thanked Amanda for telling Riley that Zoe was missing, but no other details. He knew Amanda was curious, but they had agreed not to talk about Riley at work.

One night, Oliver returned home in time for dinner, which he was trying to do more often. He walked in and Zoe told him hello, and he set out food for them all. He walked into the kitchen to find Riley sitting at the counter, hunched over a stack of papers.

Trying to be polite, he said, "Hey. What are you doing?"

"My other job." Riley yawned. She leaned back to stretch. Oliver took note that, for the first time, her hair was down and it fell past her shoulders.

"What is your other job?" Oliver asked, confused.

"I work at a coffee shop near my mom's house."

"Wait, why are you working on accounting?" Oliver asked.

"Someone didn't balance right one night when the shop closed and . . . it's causing a lot of problems. Well, I say someone, but it was the shop owner. I love her, and I knew her in high school, but she's awful at math."

"They have you working on accounting there?"

"I have a business degree, Oliver," Riley said, so matter-of-fact it made him stare blankly at her for a prolonged moment.

"Really?"

"Yeah, I *did* finish college before David completely ruined my life."

He did not expect her to say that.

"Sorry," Riley said, looking embarrassed, "I might be so tired I'm not thinking before I say something."

"It's okay," Oliver replied. "I'm sorry for not knowing about your degree. You work for me, and I had no clue."

"I never mentioned it. Mostly because I never used it."

"Because of David."

"Yep. Because he convinced me my degree in business was boring," Riley said, her voice laced with annoyance. "And I was the idiot who believed him."

Riley really was tired enough not to have a filter, or even less of one than usual. Oliver sort of liked it. It had her talking to him again, at least.

"And I can definitely tell I never used it because this issue had to be obvious, and I can't figure it out."

Riley stretched again and Oliver could see how tired she was. Maybe working both of these jobs was too much. He wished there was someone else who could watch Zoe, but there was no one else the little girl would want to take care of her even if he could find someone trustworthy.

"Well, take a break," Oliver said. "You need some rest."

"I can't. The deposit is needed tomorrow." Riley sighed. "It doesn't help that I still need to go home and talk to my mom. I'm pretty sure she thinks I'm with half the city right now."

"You're not with half the city," Zoe said. "You're with me."

Riley nodded, still seeming zoned out.

"You could stay here," Oliver said to Riley, getting back on topic.

Riley sighed. "I could, but you don't know how judgmental my mom is."

"Please, Riley? Stay!" Zoe begged.

Riley looked at her before she sighed again and nodded. "Sure. I'll stay, but I have to work on some stuff. I can't be the primary person watching Zoe."

"That's fine," Oliver said. "Can you let Riley work, Zoe?"

"Yes, Daddy." Riley smiled at Zoe, her beautiful full smile, and went back to working. Oliver resumed taking care of Zoe as if Riley were not there. He took her to the dining room to eat, and they chatted about their day. Eventually, Riley joined them.

Oliver had to admit, it was nice having a second adult around the house. Even if Riley was still a bit distant from him after the Sophie incident, she was with him in solidarity as an adult.

Riley eventually retreated to the guest room to get more work done and Oliver got Zoe to bed as he usually did. Once she was asleep, he walked out into the living room and laid on the couch.

Her working another job sucked. For Zoe, of course. Riley was much busier, and since things had been rough at home with Zoe, he missed having her there more. But he knew she wanted two jobs so she could move out of her mom's house.

A plan was formulating in Oliver's mind, one that was probably a bad idea, but would work out, if Riley was up for it. Just as he thought of it, Riley came down the hall, looking frustrated. She had her things with her.

"Is everything okay?" Oliver asked

"Well, no. My mom is threatening to kick me out if I don't come home," Riley said, sighing. "So, I have to go and then come back in the morning."

"Are you still planning on moving out?"

"God, with what time?" Riley said. "And I don't know if I am ready to live an entire life in an apartment by myself. It seems sad."

"Then, why don't you live here?"

Riley laughed. "Right."

"I'm serious."

Riley blinked, as if she was finally taking him seriously. "Wait, what?"

"I was thinking . . . things are still rough here with Zoe and me . . ." He trailed off for a moment, unsure of how to word what he was trying to say. "But she's happiest when you're here. You could become a live-in nanny and be able to see her more and keep your other job."

"Wouldn't that be . . . weird, though?" Riley asked.

"Why would it be weird?"

"I . . . I mean, this is your house. I don't want to move in and mess things up."

"It would be a favor to me. And Zoe."

Riley paused for a long moment, and then she asked, "Can I think about it?"

"Of course, take all the time you need."

Riley nodded. "I do have to head out though. I'll see you in the morning?"

Oliver nodded and watched as she left. Hopefully, she would say yes. If not, then he was sure they could deal, but Zoe was still hesitant around him, and she was better with Riley around. It was all for Zoe.

Right?

Riley

Riley returned home feeling worn out. When she got in, her mother was sitting on the couch, looking frustrated. Amanda was there, with Luke and Landon running around the house. The last thing Riley wanted was to deal with her sister's kids. Zoe was more than enough.

"Shouldn't Luke and Landon be in bed?" Riley asked Amanda.

"You were supposed to have dinner with us," Jane said, frowning. Her mom completely ignored Riley's question.

"Oh." Riley dimly remembered something about dinner. "I'm sorry. I totally blanked on that."

"Where were you?" Jane asked.

"I was watching Zoe."

"Sophie is watching Zoe," Amanda said, crossing her arms.

"Oliver and Sophie broke up."

"He hasn't mentioned it at work."

Sometimes Riley hated that Oliver was so tight-lipped about his personal life.

"So, you're lying," Jane said. "You're never home, and I know you are working at a coffee shop, but it closes at four. So, what is going on?"

"I'm seriously watching Zoe."

"Are you dating someone?" Amanda asked.

"No, I'm not," Riley replied.

"It's someone I won't approve of, isn't it?" Jane said, sighing.

"I . . . No, I'm seriously not seeing anyone. You can ask Oliver, Amanda. He'll tell you the truth."

"I'm not asking my boss about this! We know you're lying. Tell us what is going on."

"I am!" Riley said. "I don't know what you want to hear from me."

"The truth," Jane said.

It was at that moment Luke ran past Riley laughing, and Landon suddenly screamed so loud she thought her ears were going to burst.

"Landon!" Amanda snapped, looking embarrassed. Jane pursed her lips.

"He took my toy!" Landon said, running over. "Give it back!"

"No!"

Amanda looked frustrated and Riley rolled her eyes. It was time she stepped in.

"Luke, I know you took it because I saw you and I know for a fact you have the exact same toy in your mom's car,"

Riley said, and she knelt down. "Can you please give it back?"

"But . . ."

"If you give it back, I'll go grab yours from your mom's car. If not, then it's a time-out."

"You can't give me time-outs."

"Sorry to break this to you, kid, but it's literally my job. I can sit you on one of the barstools and you'll be there for five minutes."

Luke stared at her before his eyes drifted to his brother. Riley already knew where this was going, so she turned to the other boy.

"Landon, if you make fun of him, you get a time-out too, and Luke gets your toy. We don't make fun of other people."

There was complete silence in the room. Riley had never stepped in with her sister's kids, but she'd been so deep in reading about childhood development because of Zoe that this was second nature to her.

"Can I have the toy, Luke?" Riley asked patiently.

Luke quietly handed over the toy, and Riley passed it on to Landon.

"Thank you. Do you want to come with me to get yours?"

"Yes," Luke said, and Riley hoisted him up on her hip much like she would Zoe. She turned to her family.

Jane and Amanda were looking at her like she had grown two heads, but Riley knew Luke wasn't a patient kid, so she said, "Amanda, can I borrow your keys?"

"Uh, yeah," Amanda said, handing them over. Riley went to Amanda's van and followed Luke's lead on where to find the toy. Once he had it, he seemed happy to play by himself.

Riley returned to the living room and sighed. "Those two are beyond tired," she told Amanda.

"What was that?" Amanda said. "You just . . . they actually listened to you."

"It was the shock value and nothing else," Riley said, rubbing her face. She'd never had to set her foot down so hard with Zoe, but she had looked into resources on it just in case. Those came in handy now. "Basic childhood psychology, but it's not going to work again. You need to get them home and in bed."

"I was waiting on you to get here."

"Yeah, and now you're dealing with two kids who are pissed off."

"Since when do you know childhood psychology?" Jane asked, her voice conveying her still-present shock.

"Since I started taking care of a four-year-old," Riley said. "There's a reason I got the job back."

Both Jane and Amanda stared at her, and she could feel herself getting more and more annoyed.

"Can I go to bed now? I've literally been working for fourteen hours straight," Riley said.

"I . . . I do need to get them to bed. It's past nine," Amanda said.

"Yes, you go, Amanda," Jane said. "And go to sleep, Riley. You're so crabby when you're tired."

"Thank you," Riley said, walking up the stairs quickly. She was asleep the very moment her head hit the pillow.

Riley had mostly forgotten about resolving the issue with Luke and Landon when she woke up. But when her mother told her to have a good day with Zoe, it occurred to her that her mother finally believed her.

Oliver

Riley, true to her word, came in before Zoe was awake.

Oliver didn't know if she realized how much she was doing for him and Zoe, because no normal nanny would be doing all that she was. But she never seemed to want to accept thanks, and he didn't want to push the issue and get her angry.

Oliver walked into work, knowing he had to leave early so Riley could get to her own job. These days, he was able to do certain things at home while Zoe played, which meant he could make Riley's schedule work as well. It was nice, but the times in his office were often very busy, with him trying to catch up with the things he couldn't do at home.

Amanda had been taking care of a lot of his meetings, but Oliver felt bad asking her to tote things back and forth from the office to his house. Amanda had a family of her own, and she was hired to be in the office only, so he resisted asking her. Of course, that meant they didn't really talk these days. Other than the few times Amanda watched Zoe while he was with Sophie, they hadn't communicated.

Oliver was fine with that. No one needed to know what a fool he had been to be with someone like Sophie. Oliver was waiting on Riley to tell everyone she knew, but that day hadn't come.

"Hi, Oliver," Amanda said from her desk as he walked in.

"Hi," he greeted back.

"Hey, do you have time for a quick question?" Amanda asked. "I know you're busy."

"Yeah, I do," Oliver said, even though he really didn't.

"Riley mentioned last night you hired her back. I didn't know if it was true or not."

Oliver froze. What was he going to say? He needed to be honest, but he didn't want Amanda, or anyone else, knowing what happened with Sophie. She was looking at him curiously, so he had to come up with *something*.

"Yes, I did rehire her."

"Does Sophie not want to watch Zoe or something?"

"No, Sophie and I broke up. She and Zoe didn't get along."

"Oh, I'm sorry, Oliver. I know how much you liked her."

Bitterness rose up into his throat. How could he have ever liked someone like Sophie? Someone who hated Zoe, someone who *pushed* her?

"It's not a big deal. Riley has been a big help."

"Like, romantically?" Amanda asked, shock apparent in her voice.

"No," Oliver said forcefully. "Never."

"Sorry," Amanda said, and judging by her face, she realized she had crossed a line. "My mom and I were thinking maybe she had a boyfriend or something, but now I know she is only working for you again. That was silly of me to think."

"It's fine," Oliver said. "But you don't have to worry about . . . that. Ever."

"Got it," Amanda said. "You two wouldn't exactly be compatible anyway."

Oliver opened his mouth to disagree, but *why?* Amanda was right, wasn't she?

With a tight smile, Oliver went into his office to try to get his long list of things to do done, but his mind wasn't on work, it was on what Amanda said.

Oliver and Riley weren't compatible.

Were they not? Sure, she pushed his buttons and was like no one else. She wore old flannels and jeans and always had her attitude in tow. He wore designer suits and tried to wall off everyone.

Everyone but her.

And that alone made him wonder if Amanda was right.

It was a dangerous thought to have since she worked for him.

He forced himself to work until he had to get back to his house so Riley could go to her other job. When she left, Oliver tried his best not to think about what Amanda said.

It didn't work.

Riley

"So, you'll never guess what happened last night," Riley said as the after-work rush calmed down. She barely had time to get in before they got buried under customers. The shop was staying open late for karaoke night and Riley knew how busy it was going to get.

"You finally rebounded," Camilla said.

Riley blinked. "What? No. Nothing like that."

Camilla sighed. "I keep hoping it's that. Whatever, what's up?"

"Oliver wants me to live with him."

"Wait, wait. Your other boss Oliver? I thought you weren't dating."

Riley's cheeks heated up. "What? Camilla, we're not dating. He wants me as a live-in nanny."

"And just that, right?"

"Yes!" Riley said. "And I'm considering it. Living with my mom is awful. It's a whole thing to get her to believe anything I'm saying."

"But what would living with him be like?" Camilla asked.

"I mean, probably the same as it is now."

"So, there's like no feelings there at all, right?"

"Feelings?" Riley asked. Her cheeks warmed again. At one point, maybe there could have been, but these days, she was only civil with Oliver. Riley was still getting over what he said to her.

"Like maybe you like him?"

Riley vehemently shook her head. "No! That is . . . not a thing that will *ever* happen."

"Are you sure nothing would happen if you guys did live together?"

"No, nothing would happen. I'm there for his daughter," Riley replied. And she would make sure it was true if she lived with him.

"Just think about it. Obviously, I'm a lesbian and I'm not going to say a guy and girl can't live together, but . . . you're straight, so living with someone of the gender you like could lead to issues. Just be sure you don't see him that way."

After everything that had happened, Riley knew Oliver's type. Blonde, beautiful, and perfect. She was not that. Once he found someone that wasn't awful, he would never think twice about Riley.

"If you saw the last girl he was with, you'd know he would never look at me that way. He has a type, and it's only women who are solid tens."

"And you're not a solid ten?"

Riley blushed. "Not like he wants."

Camilla sighed and her voice was soft when she spoke again. "I know what it's like to not think you're on someone else's level. I get it, I do, but types don't mean everything, and this whole thing could easily go somewhere."

Riley still didn't believe it, but she didn't argue.

"But I also know how hurt you were, so be careful, okay?"

"I haven't decided yet, but honestly, Camilla I don't think I can go on living with my mom. Getting an apartment by myself somehow seems worse. Plus, even if I work two jobs, I'll have to move farther out than I do now."

Camilla sighed and nodded. "That I get. It's hard to find a safe place to live that doesn't cost an arm and a leg."

"Right," Riley said. "And besides that, he lives in Green Hills in a gated community."

Camilla's eyebrows shot up. "Really?"

"Everything aside, it's safer than me living on my own."

"It sounds like you've decided then," Camilla said.

Riley shrugged. "Maybe. I still want to put more thought into this before I jump on it. I mean, at the end of the day, I would be living with my boss."

Camilla nodded, but then another wave of customers came in, which pulled them away from their conversation.

The words Oliver said to her that night when he fired her were still fresh in her mind, and it would be way worse if she lived there and had nowhere else to go. It was a tough decision to make, and she wasn't sure anything was going to be right.

Chapter Sixteen

Oliver

Oliver had been downplaying how much he wanted Riley to move in with them, not wanting to pressure her.

However, when Riley was around, things were easier. There was someone else to help answer Zoe's questions, someone else to help with her when she needed a bath, someone else to talk to.

Oliver lived alone for four years with no other adult to help him with his child, cleaning, or house maintenance. He felt like every second of his day was spent working on *something*. Riley took over some of the cleaning and most of the childcare while she was there, and it was amazing.

Plus, Zoe was better behaved when she was around.

Things still weren't normal between father and daughter. Zoe would be fine when Riley was there, but when Riley wasn't, it was a challenge to get the little girl to even talk to him.

That was the worst part of it all. But Oliver was respecting Riley's decision to think about it and he didn't want to guilt her into deciding before she was ready. An overeagerness might very well push her away from their little family.

But the carefully constructed peace he had made all came crashing down one day when Riley was leaving to head home. She had more paperwork to do and Zoe had so many questions that it was better if Riley were not around. Just as she was telling Oliver this, Zoe lost it.

Both Riley and Oliver turned to her, shocked. The usually happy little girl was screaming, her face red in anger. Oliver's immediate thought was she was hurt, as seemed to be Riley's. When they both knelt to comfort her, she said, "I don't want you to go!"

"Me?" Riley said. "Honey, you know I have to leave sometimes."

"No, you don't!" Zoe snapped.

"Remember what we talked about, sometimes I need to work?" Riley said patiently.

"But I don't want you to!"

"I have to."

"No!" Zoe said, and she ran and sat in front of the door.

Riley turned to look at Oliver with wide eyes. It was obvious she was not used to Zoe acting like this. He didn't blame her. He wasn't used to it either.

Oliver didn't know what to say. He wanted her to stay instead of dealing with the fallout of Riley inevitably leaving, but she was a free woman, so he really couldn't say anything.

"I'm sorry about this," Oliver eventually settled on. "I know you have a lot you need to do."

"I've never seen her throw a tantrum like that. Has she ever done this with you?"

Oliver knew he couldn't lie. "Sometimes she does this when you head out for the night, but usually she doesn't pick up on you leaving until you're gone."

"Oh," Riley said. "When were you going to tell me this?"

"I didn't want to influence you in your decision to move here," Oliver said. "I'm not trying to pressure you, because I want you to be able to be here because you want to be, not because you feel you have to."

Riley sighed. "I do appreciate that, but I didn't know she was suffering."

"This could be a phase. But it has been getting progressively worse."

"Great. Let's add this to the list of things to think about."

"This is why I didn't say anything."

"But I need to know these things," Riley said. "Be honest, would it really help if I was here all the time?"

"It would," Oliver said without hesitation. "Zoe is a different kid when you're around."

"A better kid?"

Oliver groaned. He hated to admit his daughter acted better for his nanny than her own father, but he nodded. "Yeah."

"All right. That changes things," Riley said. "But I don't want to trade one unstable living situation for another one. I don't think I could deal with us having a disagreement about something, and then I wind up jobless and homeless."

Oliver's first reaction was to say he would never do anything like that, but the night he fired her replayed in his mind, and he knew she had a point.

"How about we have someone draft up a contract that says I can't do that to you? It's only fair, plus you can bring your stuff with you, maybe from your old apartment or something? Just so the room feels as if it's yours."

"That's really tempting," Riley said, biting her lip. "I mean, I do really want to get out of my mom's house."

"And I'm serious about this. I think it will make things so much nicer around here."

"I'll need to talk to my mom about it. Which means I need to leave."

Oliver sighed. "I think it would go better if you stayed until she went to sleep."

"Yeah, I can do that," Riley said, and went to comfort Zoe, who was still upset. Oliver watched, almost feeling like a third wheel as they talked.

Once it was bedtime for Zoe, Riley put her to bed without asking. It took only a few minutes to get the little girl to sleep, and Oliver hovered for most of it, wishing it was him Zoe was reaching for.

After Zoe was asleep, Riley came out of her bedroom and began grabbing her things.

"Thank you for staying," Oliver said. "It would have been way worse if you hadn't."

"It's fine," Riley replied. "I'll also come back before she wakes up, so she won't even know I was gone."

"What would I do without you?"

"Well, you would be married to Sophie, for one." Oliver looked away. "I'm sorry. I didn't mean anything by that. It was an offhand comment."

"I know," Oliver said. "I try not to think about what I would have done if you hadn't been there that night."

"Don't torture yourself with that. In the end, when I brought the issue to your attention, you listened," Riley said earnestly. "I thought you weren't going to."

"I've never seen you that livid." Oliver shuddered as he remembered it. "I know you wouldn't have been like that for no reason."

"I know it sucks right now, and I'm sorry all of this happened. But I know you're putting it all on yourself," Riley said. "And that isn't fair. Sophie is the one who manipulated you and hurt Zoe."

Oliver watched her carefully. He expected Riley to hold a grudge against him forever. He figured she would hold onto what he said that night, and yet she was choosing to be forgiving and kind when she had no need to be.

"Thanks," Oliver said, his voice soft. "I might have needed to hear that."

"And Zoe's going to come around with time."

"You know, I've never had someone to be jealous of before," Oliver said.

"You're jealous of me?"

"I'm jealous she trusts you, even though it's my own fault she doesn't," he said. "That kid has been my life for four years and I messed it up."

"I hate to break this to you, but this isn't going to be the last thing you mess up, Oliver. Take it from me. I mess up daily," she said. "But it is what it is. We're human, and that's all we can be. All you can do now is learn from it and don't do it again."

"I don't think I ever want to date again," Oliver said.

"I feel you there," Riley said, a little bitterly.

Oliver sighed, and Riley seemed to be lost in her own thoughts. He glanced at the time and said, "Hey, I know you have to get going. I didn't mean to keep you late."

Riley smiled at him. "It's okay. You looked like you needed a talk," she said. "I'll see you in the morning?"

Oliver nodded with a smile and watched her go. Once she was gone, he felt the familiar loneliness set in. It was hard to bear, especially when he had that void ever since Zoe was born. He found himself wishing there was someone to talk to.

That had once been Sophie, but he now realized he couldn't talk to her like he could with Riley.

Riley

Riley sighed when she pulled up to her mom's house. She was exhausted, but it was still before her mom's routine bedtime. She knew she was going to run into Jane and she dreaded it.

She took a deep breath and climbed out of the car. She walked in to find her mom sitting on the couch.

"Hey," Riley said. She inwardly hoped her mother wouldn't say anything else.

"Where were you?" Jane asked.

"Oliver's," Riley said. "I was watching Zoe and trying to get some work done."

"From that coffee shop? They work you far too hard there. You need to find a better job."

"They pay me plenty of money to do what I do, and besides, I thought you would be happy I'm using my degree instead of working at a bar."

"You're working at a coffee shop. It is not different."

Riley sighed. She could not get Jane to understand that she did more than make coffee. She worked on the employee taxes, the bank statements, anything involving numbers. Camilla kept trusting her with more and more, since the two of them had been building trust as time went on. Plus, each added responsibility gave her a raise.

"Yeah, sure. Whatever you say." Riley shrugged. She knew there was no use in arguing.

"I'm looking out for what is best for you. You're twenty-six and working at a coffee shop, Riley. You could be doing so much more."

"I'm doing plenty," Riley said. "Mom, I'm really tired, and I have a ton to do. Can I go to bed? Can we skip the lecture for once?"

Her mother seemed offended. "Excuse me?"

"You know I am doing all of this so I can get my own place, right? I need a decent savings to be able to put a down payment on anything in town," Riley said, even though it was possible she wasn't going to have to pay a deposit at all.

"I do," Jane said. "What is the time line on that? Will you still be living here for the holidays?"

Riley shook her head. "I plan to be long gone before then." She didn't want to stay any longer than she absolutely had to.

"So, where will you be moving to?" Jane asked. "Another apartment? Please get somewhere nicer than that dump you and David had."

"You know Sarah lives there now, right?"

"I expected so much better from her."

Riley sighed. She knew she could bring up Jane still having Sarah as a friend on Facebook, but she knew better than to get into that argument.

"Actually, I do have a very nice place in mind . . . Oliver wants me to be a live-in nanny."

"Are you serious?" Jane said. "Or are you trying to lie to me again?"

"Zoe is a very demanding kid," Riley said. "And no, I'm not lying. I'm considering it. I mean, no rent, and I would live in a gated community. It seems like the perfect deal."

Jane frowned. "And what about you and this Oliver?"

"What about it?"

"It seems suspicious you would forgo finding a place of your own to live with another man."

"What? He's my boss," Riley said. She felt a blush make its way to her cheeks. Why did everyone ask about her and Oliver? He wouldn't look at her like that in a million years.

"You say you value your privacy," Jane said, crossing her arms, "so, this is very unlike you."

"I mean, it's not like I have a bunch of options, mom. Considering I would have to furnish an entire place by myself, it could really be a good thing to not have to do that. And, for once, it would be a nice house."

"And you're sure Oliver wouldn't take advantage of you?" Jane asked. "Think about it, Riley. You would be in his home, with his child, and he would always have something over you. What if he wants more?"

"We're having a contract drawn up, mom," Riley said. "I specifically asked for something like that so he wouldn't kick me out. But that other thing is kind of a good point too." Riley paused to consider it. "But he wouldn't do that."

Jane sighed. "I want you to have something for yourself for once. Nothing involving another man."

"Mom, I hate to break this to you, but men are 50% of the population. I'm not running from David to Oliver. We don't see each other that way."

"I disagree," Jane said.

"Well, it doesn't matter if you do. I'm still going to consider it."

"Why?" Jane asked. "What makes this something you are considering? Is it this man is rich or attractive? Are you planning to move on with him or—"

"Mom!" Riley snapped. "It's none of that!"

"Then, tell me why this is so important to you."

"I don't have to tell you anything."

"I'm your mother. I deserve to know."

"Okay, fine! It's Zoe, okay? Are you happy now?"

"The four-year-old?"

Whatever Jane was expecting to hear, it was obvious it wasn't that. She stared at Riley for a long time, and Riley was tempted to look away, or leave the room entirely.

"Yes," Riley said. "The four-year-old. It's not about Oliver at all."

Jane stared, trying to find any hint of a lie in Riley's response, but Riley knew she wouldn't find anything—there wasn't one. She was telling the complete and honest truth for once.

"You haven't brought anymore alcohol in this house," Jane said after a long silence. "And I expected you to fight me on that."

"I haven't been drinking," Riley said. "Not for a while."

"Why did you stop drinking?" Jane asked in a low voice. "I know it wasn't because of me. Nothing I ever say seems to get through to you."

Riley rolled her eyes, but knew she needed to answer. "Zoe's mom died because she was drinking and driving. That one time I went in hungover, Oliver was pissed. And honestly, I don't blame him. Plus, when it comes down to it, drinking hasn't done anything for me. Zoe, on the other hand . . ." Riley paused. "Somewhere along the line, she became more important."

Jane didn't say anything. Riley tried to gauge what reaction her response was going to get, but her mother's face was impossible to read. She wondered if she was about to get lectured on how inappropriate it was for her to care about Zoe, or how she was giving up her goal of getting her own apartment to live with a guy who was her boss.

But none of that happened. Jane didn't say anything.

"Mom, I'm really tired. Can I go to sleep now?" Jane nodded and Riley took no time getting up the stairs.

She felt uneasy, like she said something she shouldn't have. She knew she shouldn't be so attached to Zoe. She knew this was a job and nothing more. Saying it out loud, that she truly loved Zoe, felt like it was a bad thing, like she was taking her from Oliver.

Riley laid on her bed still feeling guilty. She knew for some time why she was edging toward moving in with Oliver

It was Zoe. At the end of the day, it wasn't about money, or how nice the house was. It was that she would get to spend extra time with Zoe.

And was that a bad thing? Shouldn't nannies want to be around their kids? Riley wasn't sure, but she knew she really wanted to move there anyway.

Oliver

The next morning, Oliver woke to find Riley already at the house. She was working on something, with her hair in a bun, and a flannel Oliver had seen a million times before. She was sitting at the counter in the kitchen, looking over an old laptop.

The moment she saw him, she said, "I think I'll do it."

"What?" Oliver asked, confused.

"I think I'll move in here," Riley said. "If you can get me a contract, I'll sign it."

"Okay." He tried not to let the relief show on his face.

Oliver excused himself to his office. It only took half an hour, and when he returned, Riley was reading to Zoe, who laid in her lap sleepily. Oliver offered it to Riley to read over before he headed to work. When he got home, it was signed.

Seeing Riley's signature cemented the fact that Riley was going to be living there. Oliver hoped this was a good thing for Zoe because that was what mattered.

He never considered a live-in nanny, even with his busy schedule. And it felt a little weird to lose his guest room to Riley. But he knew it was for the best and promised himself to make it work for everyone involved.

Riley

Riley moved in with Oliver the following Saturday. Zoe was excited and followed her around for days in anticipation. The day of, she ran outside to say hello to her the minute she pulled up, with Oliver in tow.

"Hi," Riley greeted, looking at Oliver. Packing up her clothes at her mom's felt strange, like she was staying at a hotel and not permanently moving in somewhere.

Jane hadn't actually said much since their conversation that night, but she looked at Riley differently. She couldn't tell if it was pride, or if it was a deeper disappointment than she had ever put her mother through.

Riley didn't think too hard about it.

"Can I help you grab anything?" Oliver offered, bringing Riley back to the present.

"I just have a few boxes, but sure," Riley said, and she opened her trunk for him to grab some stuff. It only took one trip, and when Riley got to what was now her room, she saw there was an empty wooden dresser and the bed was bare.

"I didn't know what all you would bring."

"It's fine," Riley said. "I need to go to the store anyway. Maybe now I can finally have my own bedspread."

"Can I go?" Zoe asked.

"Zoe, Riley needs some time to get settled in," Oliver replied.

"It's fine. I'll take her," Riley said. "Not a problem."

"Are you sure?" Oliver said. "It's technically your day off."

"I'm on salary now," Riley said. "And besides, maybe Zoe here can help me pick out a blanket."

Oliver seemed shocked, but he didn't say anything. He only nodded and left the room to give her privacy to get her things put away. As he moved into the hallway, he tried to coax Zoe out of the room by offering to watch a movie, but she wanted to help Riley put away her clothes. Riley had no problem letting her stay, even if the little girl talked for most of the time.

After that, Riley put her shampoo and conditioner in the ensuite bathroom. She made a mental note to get more towels to make the space truly feel like hers. It only took a few hours to get everything put up, and then Riley knew she had to go to get the rest of the things she needed.

Zoe still wanted to go with her, and she was happy to take her along. Oliver was apologetic for her clinginess, but Riley shrugged it off. She knew she moved in to get more time with Zoe which was exactly what she was getting.

It wound up being fun getting Zoe's opinions on bedspreads and towels. Of course, the little girl wanted the brightest of everything, but Riley wound up settling on a more neutral blue for towels and a gray comforter.

Riley roamed the aisles and grabbed a few other decorative items for herself, since Oliver gave her permission to make the room her own. It was the first time she bought anything since furnishing the apartment with David. But this time she was on her own, and she had more money saved up.

She wound up getting far too many things. Once she got an idea for a decoration, she got more items to go with it. Zoe rode in the cart and quickly picked up on what Riley liked and pointed out more things for her to buy. She got about half of them.

Later, with a cart full of things, Zoe begged for Riley to get her a toy, which led to a long cell phone conversation with Oliver, figuring out what Zoe already had or didn't have. At the end of the trip, Zoe picked a plush bear, and Riley spent way more than she meant to.

But it felt nice. She finally got to pick out towels she liked, rather than what David liked. She got to buy candles that she liked, when in the past, she could never have them since David complained about the smell. It was freeing.

Zoe fell asleep in the car, and Oliver was the one to get her into bed while Riley hauled all of her things to her new room. She laid it all out, proud of herself.

"You got so much stuff," Oliver commented.

Riley jumped, not expecting him to be around, but found him standing in the doorway.

"Slenderman returns."

"I was coming to see if I could help you with anything." Oliver laughed. "And now I see this is going to take you weeks to deal with."

"I know I went overboard, but this is the first time I have been able to get stuff I actually like without my ex's opinions. Also, Target had this whole modern farm thing going, and as a Nashville native, I had no choice but to buy it all."

"Well, you succeeded," Oliver said. "And it seems like Zoe had fun."

Riley pulled out her sheets and towels, setting them aside. "Oh yeah, she's responsible for half of this."

"Oh, are you now asking me to reimburse you because of my daughter?" Oliver joked.

"Nah, I'll take the hit on this one," Riley replied. "I honestly had a great time."

"I can tell by the look on your face," he said. "Also, I'm serious about helping you. I had a mostly kid-less day and I'm bursting with energy."

"And I am not," Riley said, laughing. "I would love some help, actually. Just don't judge what I got."

"No, I'm actually curious. I haven't been to Target in forever."

"You should go sometime. It was a blast."

Oliver helped her remove tags from her towels and sheets. Riley pulled out decorations and placed them on top of the dresser, nightstand, and throughout the room.

Occasionally, he would offer a spot, or compliment what she chose. He even smelled some of the candles and liked the scents.

Riley purchased a print that Oliver liked so much he asked if she would be willing to put it in the hallway.

After most of it was done, Riley was beyond exhausted, but felt a little more at home. Oliver offered to order dinner and they spent time chatting while they ate before Riley went to bed.

As she laid in her new bed, she realized she made the right choice. She and Oliver had a lot in common.

Riley had done this for Zoe, and was already reaping the reward for it, because maybe she would get a friend out of Oliver too.

Chapter Seventeen

Riley

Riley was at work calling out orders when she saw someone walk in who she could have gone years without seeing.

These days, Riley didn't think of Sarah very much. In fact, she was so busy with Zoe and Camilla, she rarely thought about Sarah or David. It sometimes crept up on her at night, and the hurt would fester until she fell asleep, but it wasn't as sharp as it had been when it was still a fresh wound.

However, seeing Sarah walk into the coffee shop brought it all back. Riley wished her old best friend was anywhere but here. She wished the other woman hadn't come to this exact place, because she knew the moment Sarah looked up, she would recognize Riley.

And it happened. Sarah looked at the counter and immediately saw her. Riley hoped she would leave, but deep down, Riley knew she wouldn't pass up a chance to try to talk. And she was right. Sarah strode right up to her with a smile on her face.

"Hey," Sarah said. "Do you work here?"

"Yep," Riley replied, trying not to sound curt. "I started working here a month ago."

"That's great! I'm so happy you found a good job."

"Yep, I work with Camilla from high school."

"Oh yeah, and do you still nanny? Your mom said you do."

Riley was annoyed her mom said anything about what she was up to these days. "I do."

"I never pictured you as a nanny, honestly. You're typically the fun aunt. Not very parental."

"Well, I guess I'm the fun nanny then," Riley said bitterly. "The little girl really likes me."

"Of course she would if you let her do whatever she wants."

Riley frowned. "I don't—"

Sarah interrupted. "Anyway, David and I are doing great."

Riley felt her mood souring even further. She didn't want to hear about David. She had been thriving while not even thinking about him.

"That's good for you guys," Riley said, though she didn't really feel it. She wanted to tell Sarah off, but she was in a customer service position. She couldn't be rude like she wanted to.

"Yeah. I mean we've been really worried—with your habits and everything."

Riley took a deep breath, knowing this was a jab at her previous drinking habits, but she didn't take the bait. Besides, David used to drink just as much as she did. If they were her problems, then they were his too.

"No need to be," Riley said. "Everything is all good here."

"Are you sure? I know it has to be hard."

"Can I take your order?" Riley changed the subject. She had had enough of Sarah asking questions about her life like they were friends, especially when she was the cause of most of her issues.

"Uh, sure," Sarah said, and she rattled off her order. Riley took it the best she could and tried to be professional. When Sarah received her coffee, she said, "I hope that despite everything we can still be friends."

"I'm not sure. Everything kind of happened only a few months ago . . ."

"Well, think about it. I want to move past it, and I'm thinking you do too."

Riley didn't say anything and Sarah gave her a small smile before walking out of the store. Riley watched her for a moment, feeling conflicted.

She really didn't want to talk to Sarah. She was in the process of getting over what happened. Could she ever trust Sarah again? What if she met Oliver and Zoe? Could she trust that Sarah wouldn't try to replace Riley, just as she had with David?

The thought made Riley sick. She didn't want Sarah near Zoe at all, ever.

Plus, Sarah had assumed friendship was better for Riley. What if it wasn't?

Riley was moving on. Despite everything, she was okay, and trying her hardest to move forward and leave the life she had with David behind.

She didn't need Sarah messing it up.

Chapter Eighteen

Oliver

"So, how are you doing without Sophie?" Jack asked Oliver as he walked into his son's office. Oliver had just finished with a meeting and was looking at his email when his father came in.

Oliver told him a few weeks ago he and Sophie broke up. He told him Zoe hadn't gotten along with her, but none of the details. The only person who knew the whole story was Riley and he was thankful she wasn't shouting it from the hills.

"I'm okay. I don't really miss her."

"Yeah?" Jack asked curiously. "Why's that?"

"Zoe is happier without her."

"But I know you liked her. I wanted to make sure you were okay. We talked about how you felt lonely without someone else around."

"I do," Oliver said. "But Zoe's happiness is more important to me than anything else. I'm an adult, and she's not. Plus, it helps that Riley moved in."

"Riley?" his father asked.

"The nanny. Zoe really likes her."

"Oh, I thought you never wanted to have a live-in nanny, for your privacy."

"Yeah, but Riley is good at what she does, so I don't mind. It's also much less lonely with another adult around. She's great."

"Right . . . well that's good to hear," Jack said. "I'm still working past where you asked her to move in. I tried to get you to do that forever ago and you never budged."

"I didn't feel comfortable with anyone else." It was the truth.

"Interesting. And you aren't concerned her living there could affect your dating life?"

"Honestly, I'm not worried about my dating life right now," Oliver said. "I'm taking this time to enjoy my kid while she's young."

"I think that's a great idea, but I thought Zoe was asking about her mom."

"She's actually stopped doing that since Riley started working with her."

"Really?" Jack asked, incredulous. "How old is Riley, if you don't mind me asking?"

"She's twenty-six."

"Oh, interesting," Jack said. "She's very young."

"Not really," Oliver said. "And besides, she handles Zoe just fine."

"How did you find her?" Jack asked.

"She's Amanda's sister."

"I didn't know Amanda had a sister."

"They don't get along, but I like Riley, and so does Zoe, so that's what matters."

"Out of curiosity, are there any feelings between you and Riley, or . . .?"

"No!" Oliver snapped, a little too loud and a little too quick. He took a deep breath to steady himself. "No, it's strictly professional."

Jack looked like he didn't believe him. But Oliver wasn't sure what else to say. He wouldn't lie and say he never looked at Riley, especially after what Amanda mentioned a few days ago.

She was beautiful—there was no denying it. Their personalities meshed well. She held him to a higher standard than any of his past girlfriends. He had seen her grow and change, and enjoyed watching her do it.

But she was his employee and he refused to take advantage of her. Plus, she was dealing with her ex-boyfriend and his infidelity. She probably didn't want him to look at her that way.

"Dad, please don't make this into anything it isn't. Riley is there for Zoe, and besides, she . . ." Oliver trailed off. "She doesn't exactly think of me as a friend."

That was *probably* true, and Oliver couldn't blame her. He had said some horrible things to her the night he fired her, things he didn't mean.

"Why not?"

"Riley knew Zoe and Sophie didn't get along, and instead of listening to her, I fired her. Since then, she is there for Zoe and nothing else. I don't think we get along in any capacity of friendship, much less romance."

That was . . . only mostly true. Riley warmed up to him quite a bit, but he could still feel she was keeping him at arm's length.

"Well, since it seems this Riley is not an option, keep your eyes open, son. Someone can be there at any moment, and if they are, feel free to let me watch Zoe. I'm sure she asks about me all the time."

"I wouldn't be so sure about that."

"Why not?" Jack said.

"Zoe is *obsessed* with Riley. She won't leave her side. Not even for me." Oliver couldn't help the bitterness that seeped into his tone, but it wasn't toward Riley. No, this mess was created entirely by him.

"Interesting," Jack said. "Is she working today?"

"Yeah, she is," Oliver asked. "Why?"

"Nothing, I find it quite strange Zoe has taken to someone who is not you. She must be a very special lady."

"She is. I've never met anyone like her."

Oliver hoped that was a normal thing to say about his nanny, but Jack seemed lost in thought. His father's phone rang and he excused himself to answer it. Oliver watched him go, curious as to what his dad was thinking, and if it had anything to do with Riley.

Riley

Riley had many regrets, and none of them involved David or Sarah, or even her mom. No, it had to do with Zoe and the movie Riley chose for her to watch, which involved dragons. Riley had assumed Zoe would enjoy the movie and move on. However, Zoe proved to be *obsessed* with it, and she was determined she could fly if she tried hard enough.

This led to Riley having to follow her around, trying to make sure Zoe didn't get hurt. Around lunchtime, Riley was getting tired and was looking for any reason to distract Zoe. However, the doorbell rang, and Riley wasn't expecting anyone, which led her to be slightly suspicious.

"Zoe, I need you to hang out here," Riley said, glancing out the window. She saw a BMW she didn't recognize. "I have to go handle something."

"Can I still try to fly?" Zoe asked.

"How about you wait for me to get back, and then I can help you?"

"Okay," Zoe agreed, and she mentioned something about pretending one of her dolls was a dragon. Riley knew the girl was sufficiently distracted, so she squared her shoulders and walked to the door.

Riley opened it wide to see an older man with salt and pepper hair and eyes plagued with crow's-feet. He was dressed in a suit and she hoped he wasn't a salesperson, because she knew her patience wouldn't be able to deal with that.

"Hi, are you Riley?" the man asked, smiling at her. "I'm Jack, Oliver's father."

"Oh, hi," Riley said, feeling relieved. Of course he wasn't a salesperson. They couldn't make it past the gate. She took another look at Jack and saw he shared many similarities to his son—the shape of his face, the color of his eyes, same height. "Can I help you with something?"

"I was stopping by to say hi to my favorite granddaughter. I've not seen her in ages."

"Oh, then come in." Riley stepped to the side. "Oliver didn't tell me you were coming."

"He doesn't know. I had a free minute between meetings and I figured I would use what time I had."

Riley led the way to the living room where Zoe was still playing. She turned when she heard Riley come back, and smiled big at Jack.

"Grandpa!" Zoe yelled, running to the man to give him a hug.

"There you are, my girl!" Jack said, kneeling down to give her a hug. "I've missed you."

"Daddy says you've been busy."

"He would be right," Jack said. "So, is this your nanny?"

"She's my Riley," Zoe corrected, and looked at Riley, who couldn't help but smile back.

"Well, I can let you two catch up," Riley offered. "And maybe go to the kitchen."

"No!" Zoe said.

"Okay," Riley said. So the clinginess had *not* stopped. "I can also hang out here."

"Hey, guess what?" Zoe said to Jack. He immediately gave her his attention. "I'm a dragon! I can fly!"

"Really?" Jack asked, sounding very interested. Riley could see where Oliver got his loving nature from.

"That movie was a mistake," Riley muttered. Zoe ran to the back of the couch and jumped off of it with no fear. Riley caught her.

"See?" Zoe said.

"I do," Jack replied. "Very nice. And it is also very nice that your Riley knows to catch you."

"Yeah, she's awesome," Zoe said, and she turned to Riley. "Can I go play with my dolls now?"

"I thought you were a dragon?"

"Now my dolls are," Zoe said.

"As long as your grandpa is okay with it," Riley said.

"It's fine." Jack smiled at her. Zoe ran off to play by herself.

"Sorry," Riley said. "She's a little all over the place right now."

"You seem to know her well," Jack commented.

"Yeah, I try to. I can't stop her from doing reckless things, but I've learned to anticipate them."

"I'm happy to see my granddaughter so comfortable with a caregiver," Jack said. "I never usually meet them because they move on so quickly."

"Yeah, I've heard," Riley said. "Honestly, I don't get it. Zoe's a great kid."

"A great kid for you only," Jack said. "And that's a good thing. I'm sure Oliver is relieved."

"I hope so," Riley said.

"He told me you two aren't exactly friends." Riley turned to him, shocked. "I do hope you two can become good friends someday."

"Oh," Riley said. This was news to her. "Yeah, maybe."

Were they not friends? Damn, had she read everything wrong?

"You seem upset about something," Jack said. "I hope I didn't cause that by coming."

"No!" Riley said. "Come by whenever you would like! I just didn't know Oliver didn't see me as a friend."

"Oh no. I am so sorry. I didn't mean to cause anymore disagreements."

Riley took a deep breath, trying to calm herself. "It's fine. I'm here for Zoe, so she's what matters, not what Oliver thinks."

Even if it did hurt.

"Still, I thought it was more of a mutual understanding. He said you had a disagreement about Sophie."

"Oh, that. Yeah, but that was weeks ago. On my end, things are fine."

"Hm, well it seems the problem lies with my son."

Riley suddenly realized she could easily be causing family drama, so she quickly said, "No, no. It's no problem, really. We're civil, and everything is fine."

"I see," Jack said, and his phone beeped. He excused himself to check it and sighed. "Ah, that is my cue to go. I'm sorry I can't stay longer."

"It's okay. Thanks for stopping by to see Zoe! I'm sure it made her day, even if she doesn't act like it."

"I hope so. I haven't been able to see her in a long time and with you being here, Oliver never asks me to watch her anymore."

"Um, I'm sorry?"

"It's fine! It means Zoe likes you," Jack said. "It was nice to meet you, Riley."

"You too," Riley said back. She called to Zoe that Jack was leaving, and Zoe came to tell him goodbye. After a heartfelt parting, he left with a wave.

Once he was gone, Riley pondered what she had found out. Oliver didn't see her as a friend. *Ouch.* Riley thought they were on good terms after everything that happened, and it seemed like he didn't have any problems with her when he was here.

She had to remind herself he *wasn't* her friend. He was her boss, and maybe he was keeping a fair distance between them for a reason. She told herself she wouldn't be upset about it and tried to move on with her day.

Oliver

Oliver arrived home from work at six. Other than seeing his dad, it was a normal, busy day. He had his usual meetings and emails but was tired after over eight hours of it. Oliver walked in to see Zoe being wild. When she saw him, she told him about a movie Riley had shown her about dragons, which seemed to have more than caught her interest.

Riley cleaned up while Oliver listened to Zoe try to convince him to watch the movie with her; by the time she did, Riley was done cleaning.

Oliver sat on the couch and tried to pay attention to the movie, but he couldn't exactly miss the fact Riley hadn't said a word to him the whole time he had been home.

To be fair, he had been listening to Zoe, but he figured once she was done cleaning, she would sit with them. Oliver turned to see her at the dining room table, working on something for the coffee shop.

Maybe she was busy.

Oliver eventually put it out of his mind and wound up enjoying the movie. Zoe fell asleep about three-quarters of the way through, so he moved her to her bedroom before quietly shutting the door. He came downstairs to find Riley still working. He grabbed a glass of water and sat across the table from her.

"So, how was today?" Oliver asked.

Riley slowly looked up. She smiled at him, but it looked a little different than normal, a little forced.

"It was fine," Riley said, and there was a pause. Oliver considered asking her if something was wrong. "Your dad came by today."

"He *what?*" Oliver asked, shocked. "Why?"

"He said he wanted to see Zoe," Riley explained. "It was a little weird, though."

"My dad normally doesn't show up to my house unexpectedly, so I'm sorry if it stressed you out."

"It's fine," Riley said, and she went back to her work. Normally, Oliver would leave it at that and go on with his night, but something was still off.

"Did he say something to upset you while he was here?"

Riley paused. Oliver grew worried. Jack was always a very kind and considerate person, so he couldn't imagine what he could have said to upset her.

"He just said you didn't really see me as a friend," Riley said. "Which I guess is fine."

"Oh no," Oliver muttered under his breath.

Riley looked up at him with raised eyebrows.

Oliver never imagined what he said would get back to Riley. After all, it was just to get Jack off of his back about Riley's age. But how did he explain that?

"It's not a huge deal," Riley said, oblivious to his turmoil. "I get that we don't have to be friends or anything. It caught me off guard."

"No, no. It's a misunderstanding. I did say something like that to my dad, but it was to get him off my back about you living here."

Riley leaned back in her chair, obviously confused by Oliver's explanation. "What do you mean?"

Oliver wasn't sure how to put it delicately, so he just said, "My dad thinks because of your age, and my relationship status, that there could be other . . . reasons why you live here. Or there could be in the future."

Riley's face turned red. "No, that's not . . . no!"

"I agree," Oliver said, feeling just as awkward. "But once he gets an idea in his head, it doesn't leave. I just said because of the whole Sophie thing we aren't really friends. And besides, after what I said a few weeks ago, I would completely get if you didn't want to be friends with me."

"Oh," Riley said. "I mean, I do think of you as a friend, and besides, it's not the worst thing that's ever been said to me." She shrugged and gave a half smile.

"That's not fair," Oliver said. "People shouldn't be saying anything close to what I said to you, and while we're on this topic, *I* shouldn't have said those things to you."

"You've already apologized," Riley reminded him.

"An apology doesn't make it right."

"Well, it's more than I get from most people, so I'll take it." She sighed.

"Who says bad things to you?" Oliver asked softly. He didn't mean to ask, but he desperately wanted to know.

"Everyone says things in anger they don't mean. Amanda's called me an alcoholic before. My mom has heavily hinted that I'm an idiot, and Sarah thinks that I have problems, which is ironic considering she's with David." Riley shook her head. "It is what it is, Oliver. I can't change that I made some mistakes and people don't trust me. So, when your dad said that earlier, I was a little hurt, but it's fine. You're not obligated to be friends with me, or even like me."

"We live in the same house."

Riley shrugged. "I'll be fine with whatever."

"No, Riley, I don't want you to be fine with whatever," Oliver insisted. "I like that you called me out that night. I like that you're honest instead of hiding your mistakes. That is one of my favorite things about you."

Riley didn't look like she believed him, "Okay. Whatever you say."

"Hey, I need you to take me seriously," he said firmly. She blushed a pretty shade of pink. "You saved me from a horrible marriage. You found my daughter when she ran away when you didn't have to. You could have walked off and never looked back, but you didn't. I owe you a lot."

"I owe you some too, for letting me come back and giving me a place to stay that isn't with my mom. So, we're even."

"Instead of being even, I'd like to be friends," Oliver said. "If that's okay."

"I think I can make it work." Riley gave him a smile.

But it wasn't her half smile. Both sides of her mouth curled up ever so slightly. He was only getting a fraction of the warmth Zoe got, but it made him not want to look away.

Riley wound up breaking eye contact first when she looked down at her work again. Oliver kept his eyes on her a little longer than was necessary before he busied himself with something else. Oliver's heart rate felt a little too fast.

Maybe what his dad said to him was getting into Oliver's head, because he was seeing Riley in a slightly different light.

Riley

The next day, Camilla begged Riley to come over to hang out. It was her first time doing anything like that in a while. She and Sarah only hung out to complain about other people, and David was her boyfriend—not her friend.

Camilla was fashionable, and Riley didn't feel like being teased for her endless collection of flannels. She picked up a few pieces of clothing from Target while she shopped with Zoe, so she wound up settling on a form-fitting floral shirt and jeans she thought made her look good. It wasn't too much, but she was happy with it.

Riley walked downstairs. Was Oliver going to say anything? Or would he even notice?

"You look pretty!" Zoe said, running up to her.

Riley smiled at her, even though the girl had basically given her away. It was nice to get a compliment, even if it was from a four-year-old.

"Thanks, kid."

"Are you leaving? Can I go?"

"I'm going out with a friend, but maybe next time," Riley said, feeling awkward.

"Oh, are you heading out?" Oliver came around the corner. He had been doing dishes and had a towel in his hand. He stopped in his tracks when he saw her.

Riley wasn't an idiot—she knew when a guy was checking her out. When she met David, he was very obvious about it. Oliver, however, was a bit more subtle. She noticed his eyes go up and down her figure, and then he looked away.

He must have not liked what he saw.

"You look nice," Oliver said politely. She tried to curb her disappointment. What was she expecting, for him to stride over and kiss her? That was ridiculous.

"Thanks," she replied. "I'm going to be out for a little bit."

"Have fun," Oliver said. "You deserve some time for yourself."

Riley nodded at him and gave Zoe a hug before she left. When she climbed into her car, she sighed and tried to pull herself together enough to go hang out with Camilla.

But the hurt was lingering.

Riley knew Oliver wasn't into her, and he never would be, but it still bothered her to get confirmation of it. She shook it off and drove to Camilla's apartment.

The night was far more casual than Riley expected. She was able to meet Camilla's wife, who she got along with great, and they wound up playing video games until late in the night. Luckily, neither of them offered her anything to drink, and thankfully, she didn't feel like she needed to. She was able to be herself without the alcohol.

Riley went home feeling lighter than she had in a long time.

"Hey," Oliver said from where he was sitting on the couch.

"Hey," Riley replied, as she sat next to him. "How has Zoe been?"

"Quiet. I'm hoping she's not regressing again."

"I'm sure she's not," Riley said.

"It also was weird for her that you weren't here," Oliver said. "But you need time for yourself, so don't feel guilty."

Riley already did.

"Besides," he added, "the more time she spends with me, the more we can move past what I did." There was a bitterness creeping into his voice that caught Riley's attention.

"Are you okay?" she asked suddenly. Oliver looked at her questioningly. "I know this whole attachment thing has been hard."

"I'm okay. Maybe a little jealous of you two, but that's my own fault."

"It's not going to be something that gets better overnight," Riley gently reminded.

"I wish I knew before all this happened," Oliver admitted. Riley resisted the urge to tell him she tried to warn him, even if it was late into the game. "But you did warn me. I wish I listened."

"Yeah, me too."

Oliver was quiet, and Riley wondered if that was the end of the conversation, but then he spoke again. "This might be my biggest regret."

"Really? Mine was getting those chunky blonde highlights when I was thirteen."

Oliver looked at her, bewildered.

"I'm kidding," she said, smiling. "The real biggest regret is David. Though, the highlights are a close second."

He laughed lightly, and she felt more than a little proud that she'd managed to cheer him up slightly.

"I know you regret what happened," she said, "and I know how much you wish Zoe had a mom."

"Yeah. I know one day Zoe is going to figure it out, and I am terrified of the day she does."

"It'll be a hard conversation."

"If it's anything like what I put my dad through, then it's going to be a little more than that."

"What do you mean?"

"I was angry because my mom wasn't there. I know that's silly because she was dead. She physically *couldn't* be there, but Dad never remarried, so I always felt like I was missing something. While every other teen was angry at their mom for basically everything, I was angry at my mom because she wasn't there."

Riley took a moment to process. That was more of a revelation than she was expecting.

"I felt the same with my dad," Riley replied softly. "Being a teenager is already such a weird time. It's like you're looking for someone to be angry at, and an empty space is an easy target."

"And I put Zoe into the same position."

"Oliver, even if she had a mother, she would find something to be angry about. If we don't mess up one way, there's another way to screw it up waiting."

He raised an eyebrow. "That's an interesting way to look at it."

"It's reality."

"You're right, and maybe if Zoe's mother stayed, there would have been something else to deal with. But Zoe's mom . . . the *way* she left . . ."

"Was it bad?"

"She didn't even look at her."

Riley didn't know how that was possible. Then again, some people were built differently.

"She wanted to give Zoe up for adoption," Oliver said. "That was *her* plan, but I wanted to keep her. I knew it was going to be hard, but I had a part in this somehow. So, I needed to be a part of my kid's life. Zoe's mom had one condition, and it was she wasn't a part of it. That's how I got here."

"You know you *can* play both parts," Riley said. "You can be both a mom and a dad."

"I thought I was doing a good job, but now she doesn't want me to," Oliver said. "Now it's you."

Riley held her breath. Her feelings about Zoe were a sensitive, unspoken topic.

"Is that okay?" Riley asked slowly.

"That's what I pay you for."

"Not really."

"Maybe not. But I'm grateful for it anyway. You're doing as much as you can. I feel like I'm doing nothing."

"You're not doing nothing."

"I work all the time and I let a woman into my house who ended up hurting her. I'm not doing great at this parenting thing."

"Sophie was good at pretending to be what you wanted," Riley reminded. "And you've been doing this alone for four years. It makes sense you would want to find someone to have a partnership with. But never say you aren't doing enough as a dad. You could have turned her away when she was a baby. You could be coming home and not listening about her day. You could be pretending to care instead of really caring. Don't let one mistake dictate how you see yourself."

"It's kind of hard not to when she only wants a person she met a few months ago," Oliver said. Some of the anger left his voice and was replaced by sadness.

Riley looked down at her feet, and then took a deep breath.

"You know," she said after a moment, "you're not the only one who's made monumental mistakes."

"Like ruining your relationship with your daughter?"

"Maybe not exactly that, but I've ruined my relationship with my mom, and then Amanda. Maybe even myself, if I think hard enough about it."

"What did you do?"

"I gave up," she said, shrugging. "You know, I used to be really good in school. I even graduated college a year early."

"Really?" Oliver asked.

"Yeah, I took classes in high school and nearly doubled the credit hours in my last two years. I loved learning. I never was the kind of student to get straight As like Amanda could, but I was efficient. I wanted to graduate and get this amazing job to prove to everyone I was mature and ahead of my time, but in doing that, I burnt out. I was tired of studying all the time, so I went to this party and that's where I met David."

She paused and looked at her feet. "We hooked up that night, but he didn't want to date until after I graduated. And by then, Amanda had done some amazing community service project that made my graduation an afterthought. I was angry, and he convinced me I didn't need my degree and I should work at a bar and not care about anything else." Riley sighed. "And my family kept telling me I was making a mistake, but I was so sure I was right that I didn't listen. I was an idiot."

"David sounds like the idiot."

She laughed. "He is. He did a good job of pretending to be someone he never could be. Just like Sophie did. We've all been lied to, Oliver. You're not alone, but you don't need to turn that anger you feel for her around on yourself. She's the one who deserves it."

"I don't even want to think about her," Oliver said. "God, I don't know what I was thinking even dating her."

"I mean, she was pretty perfect," Riley said, and it was true.

"No, it wasn't that," Oliver said. "I know you think it was about appearances, but it's not. She was there the night of the gala, and she sounded like she was interested in Zoe, but she wasn't. She kept changing the subject if I brought her up. I thought she was trying to get me to not be a dad for a while. I thought she saw that I was tired and needed a break, but she was in it for the status, nothing else."

"I'm sorry."

"I thought I had a partner, but I didn't."

"I felt the same way about David. I'm sorry, Oliver. I'm sorry you met Sophie, and I'm sorry you feel so alone. If there's anything I can do to help, just let me know."

Oliver sighed. "I don't know what you could do unless you married me."

Riley's eyes widened and she looked at him, feeling like a deer in headlights.

"I shouldn't have said that," Oliver said, turning to her. "I'm sorry."

Riley laughed, but it sounded awkward and loud to her own ears. She winced.

"Sorry," Oliver repeated, looking as awkward as she felt.

"It's okay," Riley said. "I think I'm tired. I'm working too much."

"Me too," Oliver agreed. She looked at him for a moment, wondering if there was anything she could do to help him feel better.

If it were Zoe, she'd offer a hug. Zoe seemed to love physical affection, but it felt different offering that to Oliver.

But why should it? They were friends and nothing more. There weren't feelings, but Oliver said he was lonely. She'd be a bad friend if she didn't at least offer it.

"Do you . . . need a hug?"

Oliver turned to her, his face slightly red. Riley bit her lip, realizing she had overstepped.

"Maybe I do, actually," he said.

She took a deep breath to steady herself. This was a hug between friends—nothing more. She wrapped her arms around his middle, pulling him close to her.

Oliver's body against hers was a new feeling. He was warm and tall. She felt completely surrounded by him, but in a good way—in a safe way.

He let out a slow sigh of relief and Riley could feel the tension melt off of him. She felt her own tension wash away too.

This was a good idea. This was a very good idea.

"You're not alone, you know," she said, her voice muffled by his shirt. "I'm here."

Oliver didn't say anything. His arms tightened around her, and it made Riley's heart stutter, but she ignored it. This was a hug between friends, and it was one of her first from an adult since she left David. It was totally normal to feel like this.

Right?

"Thank you." Oliver pulled away. "I really needed that."

"You're welcome," Riley said. She missed his warmth immediately and wished she was wearing one of her flannels to hide in. "Now, I would say let's get some wine, but we both know that's a horrible idea for me, so how about some hot chocolate?"

"Please and thank you," he said, and he followed her into the kitchen. "So, how are you doing?" he asked when he had his hot drink in hand. "I feel like I need to ask since you've listened to me this whole time."

Riley shrugged. "Nothing much has happened . . . Oh!" Riley said. "I just remembered—Sarah showed up at the coffee shop."

Oliver raised his eyebrows. "Really?"

"It was the other day. I think it stressed me out so much I forgot about it."

"Want to tell me about it?" Oliver asked.

Riley felt herself blush. She wasn't used to people being interested in her day, but she pushed it away. Oliver was being a good friend and nothing more.

"It was by chance because she didn't know I worked there. But the first thing she did was express concern over my drinking, as if I couldn't handle it on my own. Then she proceeded to tell me about how she and David are doing *so* well."

"Unprompted?" Oliver asked, shocked. "That's horrible."

"And then to top it all off, she says she thinks we could still be friends. I mean, I'm sure she does, but what about what I think? She's with my boyfriend. I can't get over that. Not yet."

"So, you don't want to be friends with her?"

"No, not really."

"Then, don't."

"And logically, that makes sense, but we've been friends most of our lives, so it's hard to let go of someone who was such a big part of everything I did."

"I think the question you need to ask yourself is are you a better person with or without her."

"I'm . . ." Riley took a second to think about it. "I'm a better person without both her and David."

Saying it out loud felt weird, like she was bragging about how far she had come. But deep down, she knew it was true.

"Then, you don't need them."

"Why do you make it sound so simple?" Riley asked.

"It's not, but it's what I had to do after Sophie. Staying around people that make you a worse person is not good for you, and you don't owe them an explanation for why you don't want to be around."

"Thank you, Oliver. For real, that really helps."

"I am a connoisseur of good advice."

She laughed and shook her head. "Sure you are." She wanted to say something else, but she was cut off by a yawn.

"Go to bed," Oliver said softly. "You need rest."

"I'll only go to bed if you go."

Oliver smiled and said, "Deal."

A few days later, Riley was busy at work when she saw Sarah again, but this time she was not alone.

David came with her.

It hurt seeing them holding hands.

Riley hadn't seen both of them together, not since the night of the bombshell. Sarah had specifically come in holding David's hand. It was almost like she was trying to show it off.

Riley had to remember she was at work and wasn't able to react like she wanted to. A part of her suspected Sarah was coming in while she was working so she wouldn't be able to avoid them.

"Hey," Sarah said, putting on a big smile. "It's good to see you!"

"Hi," Riley tried to sound as nice as possible.

"I figured I would bring David in, since it's been so long since you have seen each other. I hope you thought about what I said too. I think we could all be friends."

Oh, screw her job. This was not right.

"I don't think we can be friends. Sorry," Riley said bluntly.

Sarah's smile faded from her face. Riley tried not to feel proud of herself.

"Why not?" Sarah asked.

"What happened hurt. It's not going to go away overnight."

"Oh, come on, Riley," David said. "You knew it was never going to work out between us."

"No, I didn't know that," Riley said, glaring at him. "And it doesn't matter. You guys were together before you and I broke up. Sarah, you were supposed to be my friend."

"If you would let me explain—" Sarah began.

"I don't want to hear it," Riley said. "I don't really care how you got together, or how bad you felt about it. You two went behind my back and didn't tell me, so I am not interested in being friends."

There was a long silence.

"I see you're still as bitter as always," David said.

"Excuse me?" Riley asked, shocked.

"You always made me a worse person, Riley. We weren't good for each other."

"Finally, something we agree on," she said.

"But I'm changing and becoming a better man. You seem like you're still the same person as before, always blaming other people for your problems. Are you still drinking everything away?"

"We didn't come here to fight, David," Sarah said.

"Then why come here?" Riley asked. "Why bring David? You can't honestly think after only three months I want to be best friends again."

"I thought our friendship meant more than this, Riley," Sarah said softly.

"And I thought it did too," Riley said. "But what's done is done."

David shook his head. "I told you this would happen."

"Do you guys have a coffee order?" Riley asked. "Because you're holding up the line."

That was a lie. No one had come in.

"You know, I genuinely hope you find someone who makes you better, Riley," David said. "I hope you finally get over all your shit and move on because we are. Come on, Sarah, let's go."

He led her away from the counter and out of the store. Riley frowned and watched them go. She was trying not to let David's words get to her. What did he know? He hadn't been around these last three months.

But what if he was right? What if she was still the same person and she hadn't grown like she thought she had?

"Oh my God," Camilla said, walking up to the counter. "Was that Sarah and your ex?"

"Yep. That was them."

"Ugh, fuck those guys. That David dude is a piece of work, coming in and talking to you like that. I would have gone off if you hadn't done it for me. Good job, by the way. You handled that pretty well for someone who probably wanted to strangle them."

"Thanks," Riley said quietly. She was at least grateful Camilla wasn't mad about the loss of business.

"Hey, it's gonna be okay . . ." Camilla said in a softer voice. "You did the right thing."

"I know," Riley said, looking at the door. "But it still hurts."

Chapter Nineteen

Oliver

Oliver had a few problems, he was realizing.

It had been weeks since Riley moved in, and he underestimated how much time they would be spending together. It was a big house, so they could definitely be apart if they wanted, but they were always in the same rooms, hanging out with Zoe, or cooking together.

He had very few experiences living with someone else. For a short time, he lived with Zoe's mom. It was never official, but she stayed over more often than not. The same happened with Sophie. She was there quite often in the three weeks before they broke up. And yet living with Riley was different.

For one thing, there was evidence of her presence everywhere. There were new coffee cups in the cabinet that belonged to her. He found a few flannels that were hers when he did laundry. There was a new blanket on his couch he never bought.

Riley's stuff already spilled out of her room and into everywhere else, and Oliver hated to admit it, but it was his own fault. He liked her style.

But none of that was his main problem. In fact, it was Riley herself.

He knew to expect some disagreements between them. He knew it would be an adjustment having someone else live in his space, but nothing prepared him for reality.

He and Riley actually got along great.

Whoever woke up first made coffee. Whoever was up last made sure to tidy the house. Those rules were never made official—they just happened. And getting along great with Riley meant there were other issues.

The main one being Oliver was genuinely afraid he was falling for his nanny.

It started the night she went out with friends. She came out of her room looking like someone else entirely, with her patterned shirt and tight jeans, and yet she was still Riley. When he saw her, it was all he could do not to ask where she was going and who she was going to see while looking like that.

It didn't end there. Oliver caught himself staring at her nearly every time he was around her. He realized whenever she told him about something, and not even something that was about Zoe, he was listening with rapt attention. Oliver found himself trying to make her laugh whenever he got the chance.

None of these were good things for a boss to feel about his employee, and it was getting worse as time went on.

The weather cooled, though summer tried to hang around as long as it could. The trees turned from green to yellow and brought in a chilly breeze that forced everyone into sweaters.

Oliver discovered Riley hated the cold and had to have a heater in her room while she slept. There was a part of him that wished he could be the source of her warmth at night, but he put those kinds of thoughts out of his mind.

And the thing was, Riley more than likely wasn't going to be interested in him. She was still dealing with her ex-boyfriend who cheated on her, and she probably wouldn't want to date anyone anytime soon. Oliver knew he had to contain whatever it was he was feeling and keep some professionalism between the two.

But fate had other plans.

The holidays were coming up, and this was the first year that Zoe had an opinion on what they did. Usually, Oliver spent the day with his dad. However, Jack was going to be out of town and unable to attend anything on Thanksgiving, so they didn't have plans this year.

Zoe was not happy about it.

"Please, Daddy," she was saying. "We have to do something!"

"The two of us can do something," Oliver replied.

"That's boring! Riley won't even be here!"

"It might be our only option."

Riley walked into the room at that moment, dressed in a nightgown and robe. Her hair was down and messy from having just woken up. She looked amazing, but Oliver threw that thought out of his head the moment he had it. He really had to get his thoughts under control.

She muttered a quiet good morning before heading over to the coffee pot, but Oliver beat her to it, as the minute she was coming down the stairs, he had her mug out and was filling it up.

"Oh, thanks," Riley said, receiving the cup from him.

"Riley, what do you do for Thanksgiving?" Zoe asked, running up to her before she could even take her first sip.

"Uh, I usually eat dinner with my family, why?" she replied.

"Can we go?" Zoe asked. "We aren't doing anything this year and I want to have fun!"

"Zoe, we can't go along to Riley's family day. Besides, Riley definitely wouldn't want that."

"Yes, we can!" Zoe insisted. "Please?"

"I can ask," Riley said, and Oliver was surprised at her answer. "But only if your dad wants to go too."

He paused. Did he want to go? He obviously knew Amanda, but Riley's mom sounded like a force to be reckoned with. However, spending the day alone and eating his own cooking didn't exactly sound fun, either.

"It would be nice to do something," Oliver said truthfully. "But don't feel obligated to invite us."

"No, take us!" Zoe said.

"I'll call my mom on my way to work," Riley said. "Does that sound okay?"

"It's fine with me."

"Yes!" Zoe pumped her hands in the air. She raced out of the living room cheering and Oliver wondered how long she would be gone.

"You really don't have to invite us," he said.

"It's fine. I can't promise there won't be drama, but honestly there might be less of it if you're there."

"Okay."

"If you don't want to go then say the word," Riley said. "I won't be offended. You can also totally ask me to work too, but you'll have to deal with my mom's wrath."

"Yeah, no. I've heard enough about her to say it's not worth that."

"Darn," Riley said. "But for real, it's fine. Don't worry about it. Plus, my mom can cook, so if you do go, at least you'll know the food is good."

"Then, I look forward to it," Oliver said, smiling at her.

She smiled back and then she checked the time. "Hey, I have to get dressed, but I'll let you know what she says."

Oliver nodded and watched her go. As he thought about Thanksgiving, he realized he was excited to spend the day with Riley, even if it meant dealing with whatever drama could come his way.

Riley

It truly shocked Riley that Oliver was on board with spending Thanksgiving with her and her unhinged family. In fact, she assumed Oliver was looking forward to a day where she was out of the house. Was he not getting tired of her already?

But she would love the backup. She hoped her mom wouldn't bring out anything too awful in front of her and Amanda's boss. Well, if she even agreed. That was going to be another problem

Riley dialed her mom as she was driving to the coffee shop. They hadn't talked much since she moved out, other than the occasional conversation.

"Riley," Jane said, her voice level. "I hope you're not calling to ask to move back in."

She sighed, trying to avoid getting angry within the first two seconds of the conversation.

"Hi, mom, how are you?"

"I am fine, dear," Jane said. "But I would like to know the purpose of your call."

"What are the plans for Thanksgiving?" Riley asked.

"Why do you ask?"

"Because Zoe and Oliver would like to come."

There was silence on the other end for a moment. "Why?"

"Oliver's dad is out of town then and Zoe doesn't want to spend the day at home. She wants to go with me, and Oliver would like to spend the day with Zoe."

"I mean . . . I would have to prepare extra food, plus Amanda could be very uncomfortable with the idea as well."

"So, it's a no, then?" she asked. She figured this would happen. Maybe she could say she was working then to avoid leaving Oliver and Zoe alone.

"Well, I didn't say that," Jane said. "I would like to meet this child that has your attention."

"Then they can come?"

"That depends, do you want them to come? I am assuming you will be drinking on that day."

"No, I won't be," Riley said, keeping her voice steady despite the flash of irritation she felt. "I don't drink anymore."

Jane sighed. "Well, we will see about that. They are welcome to come, of course. Please let me know if they have any allergies. Goodbye, Riley."

And the line went dead. Riley rolled her eyes. Oliver had no idea what he was getting into by being willing to meet her mother.

And honestly—Riley herself had no clue what she was getting into, either.

Oliver

Thanksgiving came quickly. Zoe was a ball of excitement as the day crept closer, and when it did, she was bounding across the house, giving Riley a hard time as she tried to get her dressed.

Oliver offered to drive them there, and he was growing more and more nervous about meeting Riley's mom. From what he heard about her, she seemed like the type of woman who was going to judge anything he did or said. And coming from a father who was understanding, it was hard to figure out what to look like or how to act.

Oliver wound up dressing a little nicer than he usually would. He wore a button-down shirt and jeans, and tried to style his hair to be a little more well put together than his normal style. When he finished getting ready, he saw Zoe wearing a sweater and leggings, sitting on the couch.

When Riley jogged down the stairs, she was wearing an orange cardigan and jeans. She looked nicer than usual too, with her hair down and a touch of makeup on her face. Oliver realized he made the right choice in less-than-casual attire.

"Can we go now?" Zoe whined the moment she saw the two of them ready.

"Impatient, are we?" Riley asked as she grabbed her phone and keys.

"You guys take forever."

"I didn't take that long," Oliver commented as he picked up his little girl.

"Yes, you did. I'm going to be an old lady like Riley before we leave."

Oliver shook his head at Zoe. He didn't know why she teased Riley like she did, and he was worried one of these days Riley would have enough. But as always, she seemed unbothered. When she turned around, Riley even looked to be hiding a smile.

"Ouch, kid." Zoe stuck out her tongue. "All right, let's go."

They walked out of the house and Oliver strapped Zoe into her car seat. Once he was done, he climbed into the driver's seat and looked over at Riley.

"Got everything?"

"This is as good as it gets. I made sure to wear waterproof mascara for when I start crying today."

"Is it going to be that bad?"

"I've got no idea," Riley admitted. "But I am thinking since you're technically Amanda's boss she'll go easy on me."

"Aren't I your boss too?"

"Boss indicates that you have some level of control over me," Riley said. "And we both know you don't."

He sighed, knowing she was right. Riley treated him very differently than Amanda did. Whatever professional barriers he had with Amanda had long since fallen with Riley, if they even ever existed.

He pushed away his thoughts and backed out of the driveway. Riley played with the radio stations. They rode in an otherwise comfortable silence. Oliver could tell she was nervous about this dinner, but he wasn't sure what to say to make her feel better. He was anxious about it too.

The silence remained until they pulled up to Jane's house. It was a small, two-story townhome that looked well taken care of. Oliver recognized Amanda's van almost immediately, which was pulled up next to another small, red car.

"Okay, Zoe," Riley said, turning to the little girl. "Luke and Landon are going to be here, and they will probably want to play."

"I know. I want to play with them."

"Really?" Oliver glanced in the rearview mirror to check her expression, to see if she was being serious.

"They're not scary anymore, Daddy," Zoe said.

"We'll see how long this lasts," he muttered to Riley. It was weird Zoe was suddenly okay with Luke and Landon, after refusing to see them for so long, but he hoped it would stay that way.

Oliver got out and worked on unbuckling Zoe. Riley hung around the car, looking nervous.

"Are you going to be okay?" Oliver asked.

"I'm still not convinced that my mom isn't going to try to get you to fire me or something," Riley said. "Just don't listen to her if it does go south, okay?"

"I promise I won't," Oliver said. And how could he? Riley had been so patient with him and his daughter. She stopped drinking entirely on her own and saved him from being with someone who hated Zoe. He wasn't about to fall back down the path of listening to other people's opinions of her.

Riley let out a long breath as they walked inside. Oliver immediately noted that the house smelled like savory food and sweet cinnamon; he saw Luke and Landon were running around the house with a toy; and Amanda was sitting on a couch, watching TV.

When she turned, her eyes widened. "Oh God, Riley was serious."

"Why would I joke about this?" Riley asked, shaking her head.

Amanda didn't answer her. Instead, she greeted, "Hey, Oliver," and stood. She looked a little nervous. "I can't believe you're here!"

"Zoe wanted to come really badly," Oliver said, gesturing to the little girl who was watching Luke and Landon with a critical eye.

"Really? But the boys are here."

"She said she's fine with it," Oliver said, shrugging. Zoe eyes were roaming around the house. She didn't seem as concerned as Oliver expected, but she still kept a tight grip on his hand.

"So, you guys are staying the whole time?" Amanda asked.

"Until Zoe gets tired," Oliver said.

"Oh, okay, then." Amanda looked at the girl. "Hi, Zoe. How are you?"

"Fine," Zoe said. "Riley showed me you have a double chin."

"Really?" Amanda asked Riley, her voice tight. "You showed her that photo?"

"Hey, I had to get her to like me somehow." Riley shrugged.

"I'm surprised she remembers," Oliver said. "That was your first day."

"Oh, the guests of honor are here," another voice said. He turned to see Riley's mother entering the room.

Jane was Riley's height, with short, dyed blonde hair and a stern face. She reminded Oliver of some of the managers in the office who didn't take any flak or excuses.

He hoped that was enough experience to not making this dinner go totally haywire.

"Hello," he said, extending a hand out to the woman.

"Oliver," Jane said, giving him a firm handshake. "It's nice to finally meet you. I'm surprised you came."

"Well, Zoe really wanted to come."

"Oh, I have heard all about Zoe," Jane said, and she looked at the little girl, but the stern expression on her face eased slightly. "Hello, I'm Jane, but you can call me Gran."

Both Riley and Amanda had mirror image looks of shock on their faces. Riley turned a dark shade of pink, and she glanced at Oliver with wide, almost guilty eyes. Oliver shrugged in response. He didn't really care if Jane wanted to play grandmother to Zoe. It wasn't like she had another one. As long as Jane liked his child, he was fine with it.

"Okay," Zoe said, not even realizing that most of the adults in the room were shocked into silence. "It smells like cookies in here. Do you have cookies?"

"Those are for after dinner," Jane said. "But we will be eating soon, don't worry."

"Okay."

"Hey, Zoe!" Luke said, running over to the little girl. "Want to play with us?"

She seemed to consider it, and Oliver watched her, curious as to what she would do. "Okay, but I get to be a dragon!"

Zoe let go of Oliver's hand and chased Luke to where his brother was playing. Oliver hoped there wouldn't be any fights, and Riley looked to be in the same boat.

"Wow, she's never wanted to play with them," Amanda said. "She's really coming out of her shell, Oliver."

"As much as I'd like to take credit, it's not my doing."

Amanda looked to Riley but didn't say anything. Oliver couldn't read her face as well as he could read Riley's, so he had no idea what she was thinking.

"I have heard that Riley is apparently quite the nanny," Jane said. "Who knew?"

"Mom, do you have any wine?" Amanda asked. "I think it's time to break that out."

Riley rolled her eyes, and Oliver knew this was hard for her. With all of her trips to the store, and all of her nights out with Camilla, she still hadn't had anything to drink. Oliver himself hadn't really had anything either because he didn't want to negatively affect her progress in any way. Amanda obviously didn't care.

"Yes, I do. I've been able to stockpile since your sister moved out."

It was a subtle jab at Riley, who looked away and crossed her arms defensively. Oliver wanted to tell Amanda and Jane they were being rude, but he knew he really didn't have a place. Instead, he gently bumped Riley's shoulder with his and gave her a small smile. He hoped it was enough.

"Thank God," Amanda said. "I'm guessing you're having some too, Riley?"

Oliver wondered if she was actually going to accept, or if she was going to tell Amanda off, but instead she simply said, "Nope."

"Really, why not?"

"I don't owe you a reason," Riley said.

Amanda rolled her eyes and walked into the kitchen. Jane watched her go before she turned to Riley.

"You're still not drinking, then?"

"No, I'm not," Riley said tensely. "I've told you guys a hundred times. I'd appreciate it if you guys would stop pushing it."

"Well, I wasn't the one offering it to you. I never thought I would see the day when Amanda is having a glass of wine and you're not."

"I'm so glad you're proud of me, mom," Riley said sarcastically.

"I am," Jane said, and Riley obviously didn't expect that answer.

"Oh, well then . . . thank you," she said.

"Oh, I am so sorry about leaving you out of everything," Jane said to Oliver. "You really shouldn't have to be seeing all of this."

"It's okay," Oliver replied. "I was warned about some of it."

"He knew what he was getting into," Riley added.

"And, by the way, Jane," Oliver said in an attempt to get the conversation off of Riley, "this is a lovely house. I didn't even know this neighborhood existed back here."

"Yes, it's very quiet for being in Franklin. I raised both Amanda and Riley here."

"I can definitely see where Riley gets her taste for home decoration."

"Oh, you mean the home decoration you're stealing for yourself? I know you use that dishwasher sign even though you thought it was cheesy."

"You haven't seen anything," Oliver replied, shaking his head. He fought back a smile. He knew what he was doing, but refused to admit it to her face.

"Right," Riley said.

"Well, I get most of my things at a local furniture store," Jane said, looking between the two of them.

"Oh, mom, can you tell me the name of that place? They're the ones who had those blue dining room chairs, right?"

"Yes."

"Why are you asking about dining room chairs?" Oliver said.

"Zoe might have broken one yesterday."

This was the first Oliver was hearing about it. "Doing what?"

"Honestly, I have no clue," Riley said. "I think she was trying to get on the dining room table while I was in the bathroom, so when I came out, she was upset and thinking I was going to yell at her about it."

Oliver sighed, but Jane asked, "You didn't yell about it, right?"

"No, mom. We had a long talk about how certain things are more fragile than others and she has to treat them with respect. But it happened under my watch, so I'll replace them."

"You don't have to do that, Riley," Oliver told her.

"I mean, those chairs are ugly anyway, so it might make the house look better."

"Riley!" Jane chastised, but Oliver only shrugged.

"She's right, actually," Oliver admitted, "but they were a gift from my dad, which is why we still have them. But we can go furniture shopping when you're off from the coffee shop. I'll get the new chairs."

"Then, can I buy a new table? Because a glass table is not really a good idea with a four-year-old."

"It's been fine," Oliver said.

"I only have one thing to say: dragon Zoe."

Oliver sighed. "Yeah, I forgot about dragon Zoe."

"I regret showing her that movie."

"I'd rather it be that than *Frozen*," Oliver added. "But . . . you're right. Maybe I do need a new table."

He'd never say it, but he also would do anything to spend more time with Riley. Plus, it wasn't exactly aesthetically pleasing. He needed a new one.

Oliver glanced at Jane, remembering she was there. Guiltily, he realized he and Riley had totally forgotten about her. She was watching them with an unreadable expression, and he wondered what she was thinking.

But then Amanda came out of the kitchen with a wine glass in hand. Riley looked away from it and out a window. Oliver sighed, hoping this wouldn't push her too much into something she may regret.

Jane broke the silence. "I need to go check the food. Excuse me, you two." She walked back into the kitchen, leaving the three of them. Oliver tried to think of something to say to Amanda. After all, he did work with her every day, but luckily, his child came rushing into the room. Zoe seemed fine, but out of breath. She headed straight for Riley.

"Can we go outside, Riley?" she asked, her face red from running around.

"Shouldn't you ask your dad?" Amanda said, looking confused. Oliver sighed, knowing he never told Amanda everything that went down between him and Zoe, and how Zoe still preferred Riley.

"But I want to ask Riley," Zoe said.

"It's fine," Oliver said. "You can ask Riley too."

Zoe turned to look at Riley with pleading eyes.

"You have to wear your shoes, but sure," Riley said. "And don't expect to be out there very long. We're going to eat soon."

"Then I can have cookies?"

"After you eat."

Zoe nodded and turned to see Luke and Landon had asked their mom the same question. Amanda agreed, and they all ran outside without waiting for an adult.

"Should I go out there and watch them?" Riley asked after a moment.

"I could go," Oliver offered.

"Luke and Landon would eat you alive," she replied. "No offense."

"I can watch more than one kid, Riley," he assured her. "But I don't want to make Amanda uncomfortable with me watching her boys."

"Riley can go. Isn't it her job?" Amanda asked, taking a long sip of wine.

"Riley is off today," Oliver said, his voice flat. He really wasn't liking her tone. "But it's up to her."

"I'll go," Riley said. "Anything to get me out of here," she muttered so that Oliver could only hear her. Oliver had to admit, he was a little jealous she was getting to leave Amanda's cold gaze.

Riley went out the front door and caught up with the kids.

"It's weird seeing you in my mom's house," Amanda admitted, and Oliver turned to her.

"It's a little weird being here," Oliver said. "But Zoe is happy, and I don't have to cook today."

"What is up with Zoe?" Amanda asked. "I've never seen her run to anyone but you."

"She's a little attached to Riley," Oliver explained. "They get along great."

"And you're okay with that? I mean, she's your kid and Riley is just her nanny."

Riley was not *just* her nanny, and both of them knew it. It hadn't been brought up, but Riley filled the motherly gap in Zoe's life in a way Oliver never saw coming. But Amanda didn't know that, and he didn't exactly want anyone else to comment on it.

"It's been an adjustment," he said. "But I'm okay with it. It makes going to work easier, that's for sure."

"Hm. And Riley really hasn't been drinking at all while there?"

"Nope," Oliver replied, feeling himself get tense while talking about Riley.

"She's probably going out, but I guess it's good she's chilling out with it."

Oliver wanted to mention Amanda was having something to drink in that very moment, but he didn't. Thankfully, Jane came from the kitchen and told them the food was ready.

Oliver left the room to retrieve Riley and the three kids. She was standing in the sunshine, huddled in her cardigan when he found her.

"Your mom says dinner is ready," Oliver told her, and she called for Zoe, Luke, and Landon to come inside. The boys put up a bit of a fight, but once they saw Zoe was excited to eat, they seemed to be too.

Amanda was already getting food for her kids and Riley wound up holding Zoe to figure out what she wanted. There was a wide spread of food offered, and all of it looked good.

Riley helped to serve Zoe and then grabbed a plate for herself. Zoe sat in between them and ate slowly with a fork.

"I hope everything turned out okay," Jane said, sitting down. "I experimented with a few new things this year."

"Well, thank you for not taking the mac and cheese off the menu," Riley said, and she looked at the three kids' plates. That was the first thing all of them went for, though Luke was eating with his hands.

"I would never take that off the menu with this many children," Jane said. "Speaking of which, Oliver, Zoe is very good with a fork."

"Oh, thank you," Oliver said. "She woke up one day and suddenly could use one."

"I don't like messy hands, Daddy," Zoe said.

"Forks have graduated to pizza now," Riley said to Oliver.

"Really?" Oliver said.

"Yes, and that means I have to cut the pizza for her into little squares." Riley shook her head.

"Do you do a lot of delivery, Riley?" Jane asked. "I can imagine it would add up to quite a pretty penny over time."

"Not as much anymore." It was true. She did a lot of cooking these days, and judging by the food he was eating now, she inherited her mom's skills in the kitchen. "Oliver has a huge kitchen and it's pretty nice to cook in."

"Much better than that one in David's apartment, I'm sure," Jane said.

"Oh, loads," Riley replied. "Plus, there're actually kitchen appliances I didn't have to buy."

Riley hadn't really spoken much about David in regard to what living with him was like, but it made Oliver feel weird to hear her talk about her ex.

He had no stake in Riley's past or personal life. He didn't need to since it didn't affect her work performance. And yet, it felt like his girlfriend was talking about her ex right in front of him. The hurt felt like jealousy.

He knew he shouldn't feel this way. He didn't know the exact moment he didn't think of Riley as a nanny anymore, but regardless, nothing was going to happen. Oliver was not selfish enough to potentially ruin Zoe and Riley's relationship by putting himself in the middle of it. He was not prepared to have to find someone else to watch Zoe if things went south between them, so he was going to have to rein himself in. He was going to have to get past this without making any mistakes.

If only he could stop looking in her direction. His eyes were drawn to every upward curve of her lips.

Thankfully, they let the subject of David die down, and dinner passed without much more incident. The children all talked to their respective parents about what they had been up to, which dominated the conversation until they were done eating.

Once done, Jane retired to the kitchen to clean, and Amanda returned to the TV in the living room. In the choice between the two, Oliver went to help do the dishes and Riley stayed watching the kids.

"Thank you for having us," Oliver said as he walked in.

"It was no problem at all."

"Mind if I help with dishes?"

"You don't have to do that." Jane waved her hand. "I've got it under control."

"I don't mind," Oliver said.

"Need a break from my girls?" she asked knowingly.

"Uh, kind of," Oliver said, though Riley hadn't been the problem. But he didn't want to single out Amanda.

"Then I guess I will take the help," Jane said. "Would you mind drying?"

"Not at all," Oliver said, and he got to work.

Jack refused to hire a maid when Oliver was a kid. Back then, it drove him up the wall. He never wanted to do the chores of the house, but these days, he was grateful for it. The chores helped him learn he had to clean, and it was also the reason he hadn't hired any other help, excluding a nanny.

"You know, we were all surprised when Riley told us she was working for you."

It was posed innocently, but Oliver still considered his answer carefully.

"She did a really good job that first night, so I knew I could trust her," he replied.

"What constitutes that?"

"Zoe was happy, and actually went to bed without me for the first time. The house was a mess when I came home, but Riley stayed to clean it."

"I never saw Riley as being good with children," Jane said. "Don't get me wrong, she has always been smart, but after her relationship with David, I feared she would never change."

"Well, I am glad she did," Oliver replied.

"You know, I have been in contact with their father," Jane said. "It's only been a few weeks, but he found me on Facebook. He has a completely new life now, which isn't surprising, but he is still the same drunk he was all those years ago."

"Wow," Oliver said.

"He wanted to come to dinner tonight," Jane added, and Oliver set down the dish to look over at her in shock. "I almost accepted because I thought it would be a wake-up call for Riley."

"I'm very glad you didn't," Oliver said. "She is still very angry with her father and her sobriety is also very new."

"She told you about him?"

"Amanda did at first, but . . . she's told me more about him recently, and how she feels about him. But I don't think she needs the wake-up call you think she does."

"You weren't here when she lived here," Jane said. "She was angry and drunk any time she was home, and . . . I don't want her to be like her father, Oliver. David made it worse."

"Well, I live with her now, and I can assure you, she is nothing like that," he replied.

"I don't mean to offend you, but how much time could you possibly be spending together?" Jane asked.

"Every moment we're not working, we're together," Oliver said, and then he realized how that sounded. He didn't want to tip Jane off on his feelings toward her daughter. In fact, he knew she would probably do something about it, but before he could justify what he said, Jane was already asking a question.

"Why is that?"

Oliver paused. He could easily blame what he said on Zoe, or on Riley herself, but lying to a woman like Jane was pointless. She would never believe him.

"Riley is one of my closest friends. I enjoy spending time with her." Putting that out there was almost painful, but he did it anyway. It paid off because Jane looked like she believed him.

"I expected you to come here today and be shocked at what would transpire. I expected Riley to have a drink and be angry, falling back into the same patterns she always did. I assumed you wouldn't know any of them. But you do. You haven't been shocked by anything that has happened here, and that tells me you truly know Riley. I didn't expect that."

He took a deep breath. "Me either."

"Are you two going to stay friends, then?"

Oliver tensed. He was hoping he wouldn't have to answer this question.

"Yeah, we will," Oliver said. "That's not a road I am willing to go down."

Jane nodded. "I am guessing because you know of her past. Is it too much for you?"

"No, I don't care about that," Oliver said. "She works for me, and I don't want to mess with what she has with Zoe."

"I see," Jane said, nodding. "That does make sense."

Jane handed him the last dish. "Thank you for telling me these things. I see things much more clearly now."

Oliver nodded and dried it.

Riley

Riley knew it was probably a mistake going to sit next to Amanda who was still fuming, but the kids were fine without her, so it felt weird to sit and watch them. But the minute Riley sat next to her sister, Amanda turned to her.

"What were you thinking, inviting Oliver here?"

Riley sighed. "I didn't invite him—Zoe asked."

"That isn't any better," Amanda insisted. "What are you trying to prove?"

"Nothing," Riley said, feeling herself tense at the tone Amanda was taking with her. "Seriously, back off."

"No! He was my boss first, and now you're all buddy-buddy with him? How?"

"I don't know. He's a decent guy and we get along. Is that so bad?"

"Bad? It's unnatural. This is *not* how he is at the office. He keeps . . . *looking* at you."

Riley rubbed her face. Was he looking at her because she had food stuck to it or something? "At least he's not ruining dinner with by being jealous."

"Back off Oliver, okay?"

"What does that even mean?"

"It means I know you're trying to look all perfect for him so he doesn't know who you really are."

Riley didn't say anything. She was too shocked by the accusation to defend herself from it.

"You're trying to look better than me as revenge," Amanda said. "I know it. But it's not going to work, Riley, because who you really are is always going to show through whatever mask you put up. You're not fooling anyone."

Amanda took a long drink of her wine, and Riley almost wished she had some, but the moment she had that thought, she was up off the couch and walking to her old room. Riley shut the door and slid down to the floor, trying to rein in her emotions. She took deep breaths but could not get rid of the desire to get totally wasted after Amanda's comments.

Was that what she doing? Just trying to get on Oliver's good side to undermine Amanda?

Suddenly she was seeing everything differently. Maybe it *was* all a mask. Maybe she was lying and *acting* like a good person. Maybe she *did* want Oliver on her side. Maybe Amanda was right.

But one thing didn't fit.

Zoe.

Riley truly loved Zoe with everything she had. Hell, Riley would even watch her without being paid any day. That thought alone was enough to clear her mind to think straight, and to push away any cravings.

Besides, Riley never even thought of Amanda while she was at work. She never asked what her sister did at her job, nor did she really care. She hadn't been perfect around Oliver. In fact, she pissed him off as much as he pissed her off.

It wasn't true.

Amanda was wrong.

There was a knock at the door and Oliver poked his head in. He looked concerned. "Hey, Amanda told me you were up here. Is everything okay?"

"Mostly. Just a little drama. You know, the usual."

"I'm guessing Amanda said something to you."

"She did." Riley nodded. "So, I came up here instead."

"Good call," Oliver said. "She seemed like she was going to snap at any time."

"Yeah, she was not happy you came."

"I'm sorry. I didn't mean to cause any problems."

"You didn't. I told her you were coming, but I guess she didn't take me seriously."

Oliver sighed. "Well, Zoe's tiring out. I wanted to ask you if you were ready to leave."

"More than ready," Riley said, and she got up off the floor, excited to move on.

As they were saying goodbye, Riley's mom invited Oliver for Christmas Eve, which was surprising. Amanda went red in the face and Oliver said he should be able to swing it.

Still, even with her mom seeming to like Oliver, Riley was glad to be heading home. She wanted to be away from Amanda for a while.

Zoe fell asleep after about five minutes in the car.

"I don't have to come back for Christmas," Oliver told her softly as they neared his house. "I don't want to upset anything else."

"Honestly, that was the best holiday we have ever had, and I wasn't drunk for any of it. So, feel free to come. Zoe got along great with Luke and Landon."

"She did, didn't she?" Oliver said, smiling. "I never thought I'd see the day. I don't know what to do with all this time I have without Zoe always so attached to me."

"Well, I can always bother you. Don't forget I'm your friend. Plus maybe my mom, which is really weird."

"Do you think she will friend me on Facebook?"

Riley couldn't help but laugh. "Probably. And you'll have to accept her friend request. If you don't, she'll call me and grill me about why you didn't."

"Okay then, I will for sure add your mom on Facebook," Oliver said, shaking his head. "I haven't even added you yet."

"Well, I never use it, so you don't need to worry about that. Most everything on there is from a different part of my life."

Riley tried not to think too deeply about all the things on her Facebook profile. She probably didn't want to know, or else she would delete the whole thing.

"I know what all is on there. I looked you up a while ago."

"Really?"

"I was curious."

"And you still hired me?"

"Well, it was after I hired you, but yeah. It's not that bad. The only impression I got was David is a jerk and you didn't really use it much. Don't worry about it."

"Camilla found mine too. I guess it's pretty obvious what all happened," Riley said, sighing.

"That's all on David and not you."

Riley gave him a half smile. "Using my own advice against me, I see how you are."

"It's good advice." Oliver looked over at her.

When they got home, Riley said her goodnights to both Oliver and Zoe, and then happily retired to her room. Things at dinner hadn't been perfect by a long shot, but they were better than they had been in years.

And it was possible because Oliver was on her side.

Riley wondered what all she could do if they were truly together. Unlike with David, it would be an actually healthy relationship.

But it wasn't going to happen.

It didn't matter that, objectively, he was the hottest guy she had ever laid eyes on. It didn't matter he was kind and loving. Riley was never going to date him. He was her boss, and she knew she wasn't his type anyway.

Oliver: Can you bring my laptop to my office?

This was the simple text Riley got one morning while watching Zoe. When she received it, she only thought of how to get Zoe ready to go in time, and where parking was at Oliver's massively huge building. She didn't think about running into Amanda, who hadn't spoken a word to her since Thanksgiving.

Riley hated downtown, which was ironic since she used to work there. But the bar had a back parking lot, and after navigating to it once, she never worried about parking again. Oliver's office, however, was new and she was distracted by Zoe, who had been asking a dozen questions.

Eventually, she found a spot, but she was more than frazzled and wanted to go home. Oliver was in a meeting and she had to drop off his laptop at his personal office.

Riley tried not to think much about the building she was walking through, but it was hard. The company Oliver ran was large and had possibly three hundred employees crammed into cubicles. She had to get a receptionist to escort her to the wing where Oliver worked.

As she walked through the building, Zoe balanced on her hip, she felt so out of place. She was in her usual flannel and jeans. Everyone else was dressed for business, something she never had to do.

When she was a student, she figured a cubicle would be her future. She was good with math, and it was the only thing she could think to go to school for. But then she met David and she wanted to live her life while she was young, so all of that flew out of the window. Maybe in a different life, she would have been one of the many people in cubicles. Riley figured she probably would have hated it.

The receptionist walked away and left Riley in a row of offices. She sighed and turned to the one that had Oliver's name on it, only to be stopped.

"Riley?" Amanda asked. Riley turned to see her sitting at a desk outside of Oliver's office. "What are you doing here?"

"Daddy left his computer!" Zoe said. "We're on an adventure!"

Riley wordlessly handed the bag to Amanda, who took it with a frown. Riley knew things between them were still icy. Riley herself didn't exactly want to see Amanda anyway.

"And he asked you to bring it?" Amanda said. "I could have gotten it."

"He asked me to," Riley said. "So, can you give it to him?"

"Fine." Amanda rolled her eyes. "I don't get why he asked you to bring it."

"Maybe he wanted to save you the gas or something." Riley shrugged.

"And make you bring that ugly car you have? Please, that thing wastes way more gas than my van does."

Riley glared at Amanda for a second, trying to come up with something to say to her sister, but Zoe did it for her.

"You're being mean," Zoe said quietly, but there was no doubt it was said to Amanda.

Amanda's face morphed into a mixture of dismay and embarrassment, and she looked at Zoe with a slightly open mouth. Riley turned to look at Zoe.

"Hey, I've got this," Riley replied.

"But she's making you sad, and I don't like it when you're sad."

Riley stared at Zoe for a long moment. She felt a swell of emotion for the little girl.

"I'm okay, Zoe, I promise."

"You say you're okay, but you're not. Just like Daddy, and Miss Amanda is being mean to you."

"Amanda and I have our own thing going on, Zoe. We're sisters and sometimes sisters fight because we love each other."

"I love you," Zoe said. "And I don't want to fight with you."

Riley had forgotten Amanda was there. Zoe nestled her face into Riley's shoulder in some form of a hug while Riley was still holding her. She was filled with pride that Zoe cared about her so much to do it.

She leaned her head against Zoe's for a brief moment before she turned back to Amanda, who was staring at them. Riley didn't want to try to read her sister's face and see if there was any anger there. She was tired of fighting.

"I'm going to go," Riley said, her voice soft. "See you later, Amanda."

She walked off without waiting for a response. When she finally got to her car and buckled Zoe in, she leaned her head against her steering wheel and took a deep breath. Zoe waited patiently until Riley felt ready to drive again.

When Riley did turn the car on, the vehicle whined and sputtered, barely coming to life. When it did, it blew out cold air, even though the engine was warm. Riley groaned, annoyed at her luck.

"What's wrong?" Zoe asked from the back.

"My car sucks," Riley muttered. "But don't worry about it, Zoe. Let's go home."

Chapter Twenty

Oliver

The next few weeks were quiet. Oliver and Riley fell into a routine. He felt his loneliness ebb when he was around Riley, but it always came back when he laid alone in his room.

As Christmas drew closer, he found himself busy with work and home in a new way. Zoe was far more demanding they all do things together when they were free, and Oliver never had the heart to say no.

At first, it was going out to eat together. Then, Zoe would want to go to the park, even if it was freezing. Then, Zoe would see or hear an advertisement on the radio for Christmas events and beg to go see those.

It was keeping both him and Riley on their toes.

She insisted they check out the holiday lights at a nearby botanical garden, and she had begged for both Riley and Oliver to take her. It took a week for them to find a day off where they could go, and it wound up being a frigid December night when they were free.

"I hate this," Riley muttered. "I hate this so much."

They were walking into the garden. Zoe held Oliver's hand and she bounced around, excited to see the colorful displays. Riley was unhappily rubbing her hands together, complaining about the cold.

It didn't help that the heat in Riley's car had stopped working. Riley refused to take Zoe out unless she had a better vehicle, and Oliver loaned her his car a few times when she needed to get something and Zoe wanted to tag along.

"Are you going to survive over there?" Oliver asked, looking at her with a smile.

"No, I'm not. Could we have done the drive-through light show instead?"

"No!" Zoe said. His child was bundled up and seemed totally unbothered by the cold.

Riley groaned. "Kid, you're killing me."

She was wearing a long coat that looked plenty warm for the chill of the night. She also had on gloves and boots, but Oliver knew how easily she got cold, so none of it mattered.

"Lights!" Zoe exclaimed as they entered the gardens. She let go of Oliver's hand and ran over to look closer. Oliver jogged to keep up with her and Riley followed.

"Was that enough to warm you up?" Oliver asked after Zoe was in sight.

"Never," Riley muttered. "I can see my breath, Oliver. This is way too cold for human life."

"I'm sure Zoe will tire out soon." He playfully rolled his eyes.

"I mean, on the bright side, it *is* pretty." Riley looked around. "Even if I am going to freeze to death."

"You're gonna be fine," Oliver reassured her, and before thinking, he wound an arm around her shoulders and pulled her to his chest. It took him a second to realize what he had done, and he instantly let her go. "Sorry, um, I thought it would help."

"No, no. It does," Riley said, but her voice was quiet. Oliver took a risk and put his arm back, wondering if she would jump away from him or if she would stay.

She stayed.

They stood in silence. Zoe was busy looking at lights and calling out their colors, and he enjoyed feeling the pressure of

Riley's small body on his. He hoped she felt the same way about it.

"Oliver?" a voice said, and both of them jumped apart and looked behind them.

"Amanda?" Oliver asked, and he inwardly cursed. "What are you doing here?"

Amanda was dressed in a fancy coat and her curly hair was being blown in the wind. She looked embarrassed to see him, as if she had interrupted a nice moment.

Which she had.

"Are you on a date?" Amanda asked. "Where's Zoe?"

Before Oliver could answer, Zoe called out, "Riley, look at these green lights!"

Oliver turned to Riley who had been hiding behind him to avoid her sister. Her face was redder than he had ever seen it.

"That's really nice, Zoe!" Riley called back, but her voice was strangled. She looked at Oliver as if she wanted the earth to open up and swallow them both.

He agreed with her.

"Riley?" Amanda asked awkwardly. "You're on a date with Oliver?"

"No!" both of them said at the same time.

"I was cold!" Riley explained quickly.

"She was going to freeze to death," Oliver added unhelpfully.

Amanda looked between the two of them. When her eyes hit Riley, she opened her mouth to say something, but then they darted to Oliver, her mouth closed.

"You know what?" Riley clapped her hands together. "Why don't we do what we all do best and repress this and never speak of it again?"

Her voice was high, and Oliver could tell she was uncomfortable. What were the odds her sister would be at the same botanical garden they were at on the same night?

"Zoe!" Oliver heard a boy's voice call, and he realized Amanda must have brought her own kids to see the lights. He could hear Amanda's boys playing with Zoe, and he sighed

"You know what? That sounds great," Amanda said, looking uneasy. "I am so sorry if I interrupted anything."

"You didn't!" Riley said, laughing unnaturally. "I was about to die, as Oliver said."

Amanda nodded, but Oliver could tell she didn't believe them.

"Um, where's James?" Riley asked, obviously eager to change the subject. Oliver wasn't sure who that was.

"He's working," Amanda said. "Just like on Thanksgiving."

"Who's James?" Oliver asked, confused. He posed it to Riley without thinking, since she was the one who asked first.

"Her husband," Riley muttered. "Why wouldn't you know that?"

"It's okay. We don't talk about anything personal at work," Amanda said. "No worries."

"Awesome," Riley said, clenching her jaw. "This night is turning out great."

Amanda hummed in agreement, and then looked in the direction where the kids were playing. "I need to get Luke and Landon over to see Santa, so I could leave you guys . . ."

"No," Oliver said at the very same time Riley replied, "Please do!"

Amanda turned to look at the two of them, confused. "I'm . . . really not trying to interrupt anything. I only saw Oliver when I walked up, and I thought I'd say hi. You guys go do . . . whatever you were doing." She walked off.

Riley watched her go and turned to Oliver. "That was the worst thing that could have happened to me. I would rather walk in on David and Sarah having sex than my sister seeing what she saw."

"Really?" Oliver asked.

"My mom is going to kill me," Riley hissed. "Just when I thought I was doing well."

"It was innocent," Oliver said, a little hurt she was so upset.

"No, I know. But Amanda won't be able to keep it to herself," she explained. "And my mom asked me if we were going to be a thing when I moved in with you."

"She did?"

"Yes. Or well . . . she asked if you would expect sex out of me."

"What?" Oliver scoffed. "Why?"

"I don't know. I mean, thank God Amanda didn't walk in on *that*, but this isn't great, either."

Oliver's face was on fire. "Unless it was happening under the coats, we should be good."

She looked at him with wide eyes for a long moment, and then she burst into laughter.

He joined her only a second later.

"What is even happening right now?" Riley asked.

"I think Amanda caught us hugging and then I made a poorly timed sex joke."

Riley shook her head and wiped at her eyes, obviously still amused. "This has been a weird night."

"It really has," Oliver said, and he smiled at her, only to have it fade when she smiled back.

It wasn't a half smile like he usually got. She was directing a full smile at him, one he had only ever seen meant for Zoe.

His mouth went dry.

Oliver wanted to kiss her right then and there.

"You okay?" Riley asked, her smile fading.

"Yeah," he said, shaking it off. "Just like you said, a weird night."

It was then Zoe called them over, wanting to go somewhere else, and they were both distracted by the little girl. He still felt warm from the whole thing even when they were walking away, and it took him a minute to realize why.

He was in love with Riley Emerson.

Riley

Riley kept waiting for her mother or Amanda to call her after the night at the botanical garden. She expected Amanda to blab and her mom to corner her.

But it never happened.

And she didn't know why she was worried. It wasn't like she answered to anyone.

She was an adult.

An adult who kept wishing it would happen again.

Riley hadn't expected Oliver to hold her like he did in the park, but it set off something within her nonetheless.

But he was keeping his distance, and she didn't know if that was because they had been caught, or if it was because he realized it was a mistake. Riley wasn't confident enough in his feelings for her to do anything else, so she acted as normal as possible.

The worst part of it was going to be explaining to her mother that it was just a warming hug and nothing else. But after a few days of waiting, Riley didn't hear anything. Maybe Amanda hadn't told her after all.

The Christmas holiday arrived and Riley dreaded going to see her mom on Christmas Eve. She knew she was going, and Zoe had already been asking about it, so Oliver would be there too. This time, Amanda's husband James—who Oliver hadn't met yet—was going to be there. Riley barely talked to James since he worked all the time, and she didn't make it a habit of hanging out with Amanda and her family, so she didn't know what to expect if either her mom or her sister cornered her.

On Christmas Eve, Riley walked down the stairs in a red sweater and jeans, finding Oliver slightly dressed up like he had been on Thanksgiving. Her eyes lingered on him for a second, taking in how good he looked, before she found Zoe and helped her finish getting ready.

"Ready?" Oliver asked, smiling at them when they were both ready.

"Yes!" Zoe exclaimed, excited to head out. They piled into Oliver's car and began the drive down to Franklin.

"Hey," Oliver said when they pulled onto the interstate. "Are you going to be staying with your mom tonight?"

"Uh, no. Why?"

"I didn't know if you would spend Christmas Day there."

"Oh, no. My mom goes to Amanda's for Luke and Landon. They usually invite me but I'm not super into it. Are you guys going to be out all day?"

"No, my dad is coming over," Oliver said.

"I can leave if you don't want me intruding on family time," Riley offered. She had begun to think of herself as family, which was dumb, seeing as she was actually an employee. It would still hit a nerve if he wanted her to leave though.

"No, it's nothing like that," Oliver said. "I know Zoe wants you there. I want to be sure you're okay with my dad being there."

"Yeah, it's totally fine. Your dad is super nice. Plus, I have a gift for you and Zoe."

Oliver gave her a small smile. "You do?"

"Yeah, but now I need to figure out something for your dad."

"You really don't—"

"Nope, I'm going to," Riley said, and she pulled out her phone to see if Camilla would be willing to grab something from somewhere as a gift. "I already have plans."

The rest of the ride continued in silence, and Riley found herself staring out the window, wondering what was in store for them. She wouldn't lie and say she wasn't nervous about the night, but she hoped it would go just as well as, if not better than, Thanksgiving. They pulled up and Riley wordlessly climbed out of the car to grab Zoe while Oliver collected the gifts.

"We're here!" Riley called as she walked through the door.

"There you guys are!" Jane said, coming into the living room. "I thought you weren't coming at all."

"I'm not late, mom. Just because I don't come early like you want me to doesn't mean I've skipped."

"Oh, whatever Riley," Jane said, and she pulled her daughter into a hug. It had been a long time since Jane hugged her, but it was nice. "I'm glad you're both here."

"Hi, Gran!" Zoe said, wiggling out of Riley's grip and moving over to Jane. She hugged the older woman around the legs, and Riley had to wonder if she was in a parallel universe.

"Hi, Zoe," Jane said with a smile. "I'm especially glad you came!"

"What is happening?" Riley whispered to Oliver as Zoe launched into a long explanation about her day to Jane.

"I have no clue," he replied. Riley glanced back over to see Jane listening intently as Riley unbuttoned her coat. Oliver then helped her out of it, and his hands brushed her neck as he did so, which nearly made her shiver. Thank God she reined it in.

While he had been mostly normal but distant, there were times when he would take her coat or help her with dishes. Their hands would brush, or his would gently skim her skin, and she would have to force herself not to react. It could be read either way, but Riley didn't want to be the one to think it was anything but friendly.

Not when he was so out of her league.

"Thanks," she said to him, and Oliver nodded as if he did this with everyone.

Riley helped him put the gifts under the tree, and then she grabbed several small plates of snacks. She walked back into the living room and offered some of the food to Oliver, who took some and began grazing as well.

Amanda walked in the front door, with James, Luke, and Landon in tow. Amanda paused when she saw them. Riley felt Oliver stiffen. Obviously, he and Amanda hadn't talked about what she had seen either. "Hey," Amanda greeted. "I didn't know you were coming for sure."

"Once Zoe heard about it then it was a sure thing," he replied.

Amanda pursed her lips and Riley frowned. Were they really about to do this again? Riley was hoping Amanda was finally over her bad mood from Thanksgiving. Instead of worrying about it, Riley turned to James and smiled.

James was a stocky guy with a trimmed beard and blond hair. He looked like Luke, whereas Landon looked more like Amanda.

"Who are you?" James then asked Oliver in a blunt tone.

"Um, I'm Oliver, Riley and Amanda's boss," he replied. Riley could tell he was taken aback by the other man's greeting.

"I didn't know you would be here."

"My daughter really likes Riley's family," Oliver said slowly, as if trying to defuse the situation.

James gave him a critical look before he muttered something about going to the bathroom and left the room. Amanda followed.

"What was that?" Riley asked.

"I'm not sure," Jane said, frowning.

"Sorry that happened," Riley apologized.

Oliver was quiet for a second. His face was tense and he looked way more uncomfortable than he had been at Thanksgiving.

"It's fine," he eventually said. "Jane, do you need any help with cooking?"

"Oh, yes," Jane said. "Follow me."

Riley watched Jane leave the room with Oliver close behind her. She quickly checked on Zoe, who was happily playing with Luke and Landon, before she walked in the direction Amanda and James went.

Riley heard the hushed tones from the hallway.

"It's nothing, James!" Amanda said. "Riley invited him, just like at Thanksgiving."

"He was here for Thanksgiving too? I knew I should have come. That guy is making a move on you. I always knew he would."

"No! He's a normal guy. Besides, it's never been like that!"

Riley stepped back, feeling her cheeks heat up as she left the room. She darted to the kitchen where Jane was explaining something in great detail to Oliver, who seemed interested in what she was saying; but when he saw Riley, he looked up.

"Hey," Riley said before he could ask anything. "Could I, um, talk to you?"

All she wanted to do was tell him everything she had heard, but Jane frowned. "Now, why would you take away my helper right when I was explaining to him how I roast the turkey?"

"It's important, mom."

"Not as important as my turkey!"

Oliver looked at Jane and then back at Riley. "Can't you say it here?"

Riley groaned. "Fine."

"This is ridiculous," Jane said, sighing, but she put down her book and gave Riley her attention.

It looked like she was telling her mom too.

"James thinks you're making a move on Amanda," Riley said.

"What?" Oliver said loudly.

"Excuse me?" Jane added, obviously flustered. "You're not, right?"

"No!" Oliver said. "Why would he think that?"

Riley shook her head. "No idea, but they're fighting about it in the bathroom at this very moment."

"I shouldn't have come," Oliver said. "I knew it looked weird, but after Thanksgiving and Zoe . . ."

"Now hold on one moment," Jane said. "You are welcome here and I'm not having James ruin Christmas. He didn't even come to Thanksgiving."

"I'm not going to cause a fight at a family dinner," Oliver said. "Zoe can stay and I'll be at the house waiting for your call."

"This is ridiculous. You are here with Riley and for Zoe," Jane said. "James will have to deal. You must stay."

Oliver looked at Riley, as if begging for an out, but for once, she agreed with her mom.

"I think you should stay."

"Thank you!" Jane said. "He can stay in the kitchen with me, and he won't even be near Amanda."

"And maybe Riley can too," he suggested. "Since I have to stay."

"I can finally show you how to properly roast a turkey, Riley," Jane said.

Riley rolled her eyes.

"I know how to roast a turkey, mom."

"Not properly," Jane corrected, and she returned to her cookbook, an ancient tome weighing twenty pounds, and launched into an explanation on the details of the process. Riley was bored out of her mind, as she had heard her mom's recipe every year, but at least Oliver was interested.

Eventually, dinner was served.

When they were all around the table, Riley had almost forgotten about James and whatever was going on, but the man eyed Oliver as if he were sizing him up, even though Oliver had been nowhere near Amanda all night.

Thankfully, James was quiet during dinner, mostly because Jane kept the conversation focused on other things. In fact, Riley was beginning to get the idea this was going to pass without any drama. That is, until it was gift-giving time.

They were exchanging wrapped packages when James picked up a small box addressed from Oliver to Amanda. Riley knew it wasn't much, but with the current climate between James and Amanda, it didn't look good.

"Oh God," Riley said to herself.

"Why is your boss giving you gifts?" James asked, his voice tight.

"He's my boss," Amanda said. "Most good bosses give gifts."

"He's never done it before."

"He gave them to me at the office. Right, Oliver?"

He nodded, trying to appear innocent.

"Oh no," James said. "I know what is happening here. You're sleeping with your boss! That's why he's been here this whole time!"

The room was silent and then Jane quietly told the kids to go play with their new toys. Once they were gone, she looked at James and said, "You will not come into my house and speak to my daughter that way."

"I will when she's my wife."

"Oh my God," Riley muttered under her breath to Oliver.

"Next year, I'm not getting her a gift," he whispered back. Riley took a sip of her water and caught herself wishing it was something stronger.

"Don't worry, James," Amanda said, her tone solemn. Riley could detect a hint of panic in her voice. "Nothing is going on."

"And why would I believe you?" James asked accusingly.

"Because I saw Riley and Oliver kissing at the botanical gardens last week, okay?" Amanda snapped.

A few things happened in that moment. Riley, who had been taking another sip of water to avoid the drama, spit it out in shock. Oliver turned into a literal statue of himself. Jane looked at them both as if they had shit in her pecan pie.

"Is this true?" Jane asked.

Riley gripped her cup so hard she thought it would break. She considered hurling it at Amanda, but then she caught her sister's eyes.

They were pleading.

It then occurred to Riley that Amanda knew they weren't kissing that night. Maybe she only said what she did to get her asshole husband off her back.

Riley sighed. She could easily clarify it *wasn't* what it looked like. But judging by James's face, she knew he wouldn't let it go.

Riley leaned over to Oliver.

"Just go with it, okay?"

Oliver looked confused but nodded.

"Yes, it's true," Riley said to her mom.

Amanda let out a breath of relief, but Oliver did not. Riley silently begged for him to trust her and not make this worse than it already was.

"Really?" James said. "Her?"

"Hey," Riley snapped. "I'm a catch, you dick."

"Riley!" Jane hissed, and she looked around, making sure the kids weren't in earshot. Riley tried to rein in her anger. This whole dinner was a disaster, and it wasn't even her fault.

"She is," Oliver replied, his voice slow, as if he was struggling to figure out what to say. "And we're dating now, so there is absolutely nothing to worry about."

"Huh," James said. "I don't see it. You don't go together."

Riley glared at James, wondering if Amanda would be pissed if she threw her plate at him. It was one thing for James to come and be in a bad mood, but this was over the top.

"Anyway." Riley clenched her teeth. "We're not telling Zoe, so can everyone please keep your mouths shut?"

At everyone's nod, Riley blew out a relieved breath. She gave Amanda a look that said, "You owe me," and tried to go back to her meal, but Oliver grabbed her arm and motioned to the hallway. Riley knew she had to go.

"What was that?" Oliver asked the second they were tucked in the hallway. "I never agreed to being a fake boyfriend for your family."

"I didn't either, but something's up with James. He wasn't going to drop it."

"They think we're dating, Riley."

"You said that, not me," she reminded him. "And I can clear it all up once James isn't here, okay? I'm sorry you were brought into this, but I felt like a fistfight was about to break out."

Oliver groaned. "I did too."

"Listen, I know it's weird to have to pretend to date someone like me," Riley said. "But it's just for tonight."

Oliver frowned at her. "It's not . . . it's not you."

She didn't believe him.

Riley sighed, trying to get rid of some of her tenseness. It didn't work. She already felt terrible this happened, and now she felt worse dragging Oliver into it.

"I'm sorry," she said. "I could try to walk it back or something."

"No. We're in this now. We'll see it through," Oliver said, though it sounded like he didn't mean it.

She couldn't help but wonder if he was thinking about James's comments, about how they didn't match up—and they both knew it. Riley was bluffing when she said she was a catch, and maybe Oliver was realizing the same thing.

"Did Amanda really think we were kissing at the gardens?" Oliver asked, pulling Riley out of her thoughts.

Riley shrugged. "I don't know. I doubt it. Can we not worry about it for now? We'll figure it out later."

He was silent for a moment, his expression unreadable, but then he nodded.

She couldn't help but feel like she messed up everything as she walked to the living room. She would understand if Oliver was angry with her for what she said, but James was off Amanda's back for now, so it was worth it.

Oliver

As the night wound down, Oliver stepped away. He had been on autopilot after James's outburst and he didn't know if James believed him or not.

Because if he was Riley's actual boyfriend, there wouldn't be an inch between them.

Oliver couldn't stop wishing what Amanda said was true. He'd wanted to kiss Riley that night, but he didn't know if she wanted it too. But this pretend dating changed things. What if Riley was more okay with dating than he thought?

He wasn't sure what to do, but the quiet of Jane's kitchen helped him think it through.

"I'm happy for you and Riley, you know," a voice said, and Oliver whirled around so quickly he might have given himself whiplash.

It was Jane, who was looking at him with a soft smile on her face.

He wanted to come clean to her, but would she tell James if he did? He shouldn't risk it, not with what just happened.

"Thanks," he said. He expected her to see right through him. "It's good to hear that from you."

"How long?" Jane asked.

"Uh, it's new," Oliver said.

"And do you see yourself marrying her?" Jane asked.

He stared at her. *What?* How was this the life he was living? How did he get himself into this ridiculous situation?

And then the question replayed in his mind. Did he want to marry Riley—if she ever showed interest in him?

The thought made Oliver weak in the knees. Of course he would want to marry her. If only they met at different points in their lives, maybe they would be married now. Riley could easily be the one for him.

If she even liked him back.

"I think I know how to take your silence," Jane said, and Oliver snapped back into focus, because what did that mean?

"I think Zoe is tired." Riley walked into the room holding the little girl. "Are you ready to go?"

"Yeah," Oliver said, nodding, "I am."

He looked across the room and caught Jane's eyes and she smiled at him.

The drive home was silent. He couldn't get the words out of his mouth to say what happened and Riley seemed lost in her own thoughts. Zoe fell asleep during the ride, and it was easy to get her into bed once they were at the house.

Riley sat on the couch, leaning back, and covering her face. "I can't take any more wild shit today."

"How about we watch a movie or something?" Oliver offered. He would do anything to get rid of the awkwardness of the night. "Just to relax?"

"Sounds perfect."

They sat next to each other and watched a Christmas movie to honor the season. About a third of the way through the movie, Oliver was dozing off and having a hard time focusing. Then, he felt weight on his right shoulder and looked over to see Riley was asleep.

He stared at her for a long time, taking in her features and her subtle floral scent. She looked calm in her sleep, as if she didn't have a worry in the world. He gave her a moment, making sure she was fully asleep before he spoke.

"I think I love you," he whispered. Riley didn't wake, and he knew she didn't hear it. "Actually, I know I do. If you weren't my nanny, or if I knew you would be able to say it back, I'd tell you any day. But I don't know, and I can't justify ruining what we have for love."

He wondered if she would stir, or somehow be awake enough to hear what he was saying.

But Riley slept on, and Oliver wished he'd had the guts to say it to her face.

Riley

Riley awoke to the sun in her face, which was strange. The sun never hit her room at the back of the house in the morning.

Shifting slightly, she realized her pillow was a little too warm, and her surroundings were too much like the living room to be her bedroom. Quickly realizing she slept on the couch, it hit her that she was not alone. Oliver was underneath her, fast asleep against the armrest. Her head was on his chest, and Oliver's arms were wrapped around her back.

Riley cheeks felt so hot they could start a fire. How did this happen? Was she that tired last night she didn't notice falling asleep on top of her boss?

Her body protested as she moved off Oliver. She stood up, heart racing, wondering if she should say something to him, or if she could pretend this never happened.

But then Zoe came running down the hallway, announcing it was Christmas and it was time to open presents. Oliver jolted awake but was too busy stopping his daughter from ripping open the gifts to even notice Riley. She was grateful for that.

After Zoe grumpily sat on the couch waiting for Jack to arrive, Oliver made coffee. Riley remained beside Zoe, still wearing yesterday's clothes, and made sure she wouldn't head for the presents with no adult watching her.

Oliver and Riley never talked about sleeping on the couch.

Jack arrived around eight. She tried to ignore her nervous emotions and focused on making sure Jack felt welcome.

"Hello, Riley," he greeted when he arrived. "It's nice to see you again."

"You too," Riley said, and Jack smiled as he moved over to the giant tree Riley and Oliver had decorated.

She busied herself by taking photos of everything to ensure it was all remembered. Zoe opened her presents first, and then Riley got a text from Camilla that she dropped Jack's gift off outside the door. Jack seemed shocked to have been remembered, and he took the present with a warm grin on his face.

"How did you even manage that?" Oliver asked her while he was opening it. "We've been busy this whole time."

"Magic," Riley replied, and Jack thanked her profusely for her gift. Camilla got him a notebook she had seen a lot of the regulars use at the shop. Riley made a note to buy her friend dinner as a thank you, especially considering Camilla had to argue with the security guard for thirty minutes before getting into the neighborhood.

After that was a flurry of gift opening. Their presents to each other were nothing too fancy. Zoe was the one who had all the fun ones.

Oliver cooked them a late breakfast, and they ate at the new dining room table they had picked out.

"This is a lovely table, Oliver," Jack commented. "Where did you get it?"

"Uh, I don't know. Where did we go, Riley?" Oliver asked.

She blushed. The way Oliver worded that made it sound like she was far more involved in things than she really had been.

But she pushed it off, trying not to think too hard about it.

"It was Farmhouse Thrift out in Franklin," Riley replied. "My mom recommended it."

"Oh, grandpa. I have a Gran now!" Zoe said, and thankfully took Jack's attention off of them. Zoe apparently loved Riley's mom and told Jack all the details of their holiday dinners. Unfortunately, that made Jack glance between them a few times, and Riley knew how this all sounded.

After sunset, Oliver put Zoe to bed while Riley cleaned up the house. Jack offered to help, which she graciously accepted, seeing as it was a total mess.

"It's good to see you and Oliver are now friends," Jack said. There was a questioning edge to his voice, and for a moment, Riley wasn't sure what to say.

"Um, yeah. We're definitely friends."

Jack didn't push it, but his eyes roamed to the dining room table, and Riley could tell what he was thinking.

"He's a great boss," Riley said. "I love working for him."

"Oh yes. Sometimes I forget he's your boss," Jack said. "With the way he talks to you, it's like you're his wife."

There it was.

Riley laughed awkwardly. "Definitely not. I mean why would I sleep in the guest room when I could have the master bedroom?"

"Why, indeed," Jack echoed, and Riley wondered if she made the situation worse. Luckily, he didn't say anything else.

After cleaning up, Jack left Oliver's, but not before giving them both a hug.

"Be kind to each other," he had said as he walked out the front door. Next to her, Oliver frowned.

"What a weird thing to say."

"Might be the Christmas exhaustion talking," she said. Maybe it wasn't best to mention her conversation with Jack after their debacle the day before. "I think I need to relax after all that. Zoe was wild today."

There were plenty of chores left to do, but she couldn't find any energy left to do them.

"Well, we never did get to finish our Christmas movies." Oliver gently guided her to the couch. He looked a little uncertain about the offer, as if Riley would ever say no.

"Oh yeah," Riley said. "We should definitely watch them before they're out of season for the next year."

Oliver smiled at her and they sat on the living room couch. They wound up watching something light and funny. It was easygoing between the two of them, and Riley finally felt herself relaxing after such an intense day.

"You know," Riley said, as the credits rolled, "it's been years since I sat down to a good Christmas movie."

"Why's that?"

"Well, Amanda has her kids. My mom isn't really into movies and David . . . he never watched Christmas movies with me."

"Really?" Oliver asked.

"Nope. He hated the entire holiday," Riley said. "We never even had a tree."

Riley's eyes glanced over at the giant artificial tree she and Oliver put up only a few weeks earlier. She had never decorated such a huge tree before, and she would always remember Zoe's laughter as she handed Riley and Oliver different ornaments.

"What?" Oliver said. "That's . . . really sad, actually."

"At the time, it was one less present to buy," Riley said, waving him off. She hadn't minded it at the time, but now, looking back on it, she really hadn't been happy.

"The next guy I date," Riley started, an impulsive thought springing out of her mouth, "has to at least like Christmas."

"The next guy you date . . ." Oliver said, his voice quiet.

"Yep. That's where the bar is. It's practically on the floor."

"What would you be looking for?" Oliver asked, looking over at her.

"In what?"

"Dating," he clarified, as if it were an obvious answer.

Riley felt herself blush, and she fought against the instinctual need to lie to him or avoid the topic entirely.

"Um, to tell you the truth, I haven't put much thought into it. The idea of dating and getting back out there . . . I don't know. I don't even look at people in that way anymore."

Other than Oliver. But Riley sure as hell wasn't going to say that.

"No one? Not even . . . some guy in the coffee shop?"

"No, not really." She shrugged. "I've got the long-term relationship mindset of I'm taken . . . without the relationship, I guess."

"Are you ever going to date again?" he asked. He sounded breathless, almost as if he was more invested in her response than he should be. Riley didn't know what that meant.

"I'm sure eventually," Riley said, shrugging again.

If it were anyone else asking her this, Riley would be honest and say she wouldn't be able to date anyone else until Oliver either found someone, or she moved on from the nanny job. Whether she liked it or not, she did have a man in her life, a man who was her boss and also her closest friend. It seemed like a betrayal to look at anyone else.

"Why do you ask?" Riley was eager to find out why he was even interested. Did bosses always care about their nanny's love life? Or was she simply reading into it a little too far?

"No reason," Oliver said, shaking his head. "I was . . . curious."

"I mean, I sort of feel like I'm doomed to date losers, you know?" Riley said, feeling the odd need to explain herself further. "It's like when I'm at my level of attractiveness, the guys in my league suck."

"What?" Oliver said.

"Men suck?"

"No, no. What you said about guys in your league. What does that mean?"

"It means . . ." Riley began. "You've heard of the number system, right?"

"For what?"

"For rating people's attractiveness."

"I don't think that exists."

"Okay, for some it doesn't but for a lot of people, there's this scale of one to ten of like . . . a hotness level."

Oliver looked at her like she was speaking another language. "What?"

"I consider myself an eight when I dress up," Riley continued, feeling mortified she brought it up. "Most guys who are also an eight are either way too full of themselves or assholes."

Oliver paused. "So, you use this rating system?"

"I don't really mean to, but, yes, I do."

"What am I?"

"Uh . . ." She trailed off. How in the world did she answer something like that? To her boss no less?

"Do you . . . not want to answer? How ugly am I?"

"You're not—no! This feels weird to tell you."

"But you brought it up," Oliver said.

Riley groaned. "I regret it. I regret it so much."

He laughed. "Okay, so you're an eight. What am I, like, six?"

"You consider yourself a six?" Riley asked in complete disbelief.

"I'm a dad who gets no sleep and works all the time. I don't know what you're into."

"You're telling me you don't think you're one of the hottest guys on the planet?"

"No, I don't. But do you think that?"

Riley suddenly realized what she said and wanted to melt into the floor. Oliver looked at her with wide eyes.

"I shouldn't have said that." Riley's cheeks were on fire. "I am so sorry."

"You really think that?"

"Can I plead the Fifth here?"

"No."

Riley sighed and hid her face in her hands. "I really don't want to say any more."

"No, you have to say it now," he urged. His tone was somewhat joking, but she could tell he wanted an answer.

"Fine. You're really hot, okay?" Riley said, blushing furiously. "With your stupid hair and beard and . . . general tallness, but—"

"General tallness?"

"Yes! You look very . . . proportionate." Riley tried to talk back what she said. "Any woman would be really lucky to have you, but a girl in your league, of course. I am not, and I know it, but if I was then I'd totally try to date—"

Riley didn't get to finish her sentence because Oliver leaned across the couch, capturing her lips with his.

Her heart hammered and the room seemed to heat up ten degrees. Was this really happening?

Oliver was kissing her. She could feel the heat of his body near hers and his lips moving against hers.

He pulled away and looked at her like he was afraid she would be angry because he'd kissed her. It occurred to her she hadn't moved to kiss him back.

Her breath came out haggard and she felt like she was going to wake up at any moment. There was no way this was real, right?

"I . . . maybe shouldn't have done that," Oliver said as horror and worry etched its way onto his face.

Before she could stop herself or question it any further, she grabbed the back of his neck and pulled his lips back to hers.

He smelled like cedar and oak. His lips were soft and warm. His hand was gently cupping her cheek. It was both the best and worst kiss of her life. This was Oliver, and he was such a good kisser it was almost unfair. She worried she couldn't keep up, that she wasn't good enough.

But he continued kissing her, coaxing her back until she was lying on the couch and he was on top of her. Their bodies pressed together, much like it had been before when they hugged, but it was very different now.

Riley arched up, trying to feel more of him through their clothes. She wanted to be closer to him—to take advantage of his interest as long as she could. She didn't know how long it would last.

But it did last.

Riley lost herself in the feeling of someone else for the first time. She felt herself come undone, then weave back together only to fall apart again. Oliver seemed to enjoy it as much as she did, and they both lost track of time while they explored each other's bodies.

When they were finally done, he pulled her to him, his naked body pressed flush against hers, and he asked her to stay, and she couldn't say no.

Riley had never been in Oliver's room before. So, when she woke up, naked and in a room she didn't recognize, she wondered what had happened the night before. Then, she remembered she actually had sex with Oliver, and not only that, but it was mind-blowing, amazing sex.

She wondered if it was all some fever dream. Maybe her mind imagined him undressing hurriedly as he tried to kiss her. But there was no way it was a dream. There was an ache between her legs she hadn't felt in a long time, and there would be no other explanation for the fact that she wasn't wearing clothes.

Riley rolled over and looked around. Oliver was nowhere to be found, so she got up to find her clothes and explore. She used his bathroom, which was far nicer than the one she regularly used, and splashed some water on her face to try to wake up. Then, she got dressed in last night's clothes and went to her own room to change into something better suited for the day. When she was done, she headed downstairs, wondering if Oliver was going to mention what happened.

He was talking to Zoe and gave Riley a generic smile when he saw her. He did hand her a cup of coffee, but he always did that.

Riley felt disappointed. Things so far seemed to be normal between them. Was she a one-night stand? Did he feel lonely for Christmas and want someone there? Did he get caught up in the fact she called him hot?

Riley felt awful. Why did she have to go and sleep with her boss? She was filled with regret and the day hadn't even started yet.

"Well, I'm off to work," Riley announced as she finished her coffee.

"Aw," Zoe pouted.

"I'll be back tonight," Riley replied, trying to appear normal for Zoe.

"Okay, love you!" Zoe said.

Riley smiled and said, "Love you too," and left the house.

She arrived just in time to clock in. It was a busy morning, which further made her unable to think about the night before. Then, when it slowed, she went into the back corner of the seating area to work on the bank statements for the shop.

With her mind so jumbled, she didn't get far. In fact, she wound up putting her head on the table instead of working for about ten minutes until Camilla walked up and asked, "What has you all out of it this morning?"

"I slept with Oliver last night," Riley said, sitting up enough to put her head in her hands.

Camilla nearly dropped the cup she was holding. *"What?"*

"Yeah."

"Like you guys slept in the same bed or like you two had sex?"

"Both," Riley said.

"How did that happen?" Camilla sat across from her at the table. Riley glanced up and she looked shocked, more so than Riley had ever seen her.

She explained every detail she could remember about the night before. Camilla listened intently as she rambled for what felt like forever.

"And that's it," Riley said. "This morning, he looked at me like it never happened."

"So, you think he was lonely last night and that's why it happened?"

"That, or it was what we were talking about when he kissed me, but it doesn't change the fact I was there and available to him."

"Well, maybe you should ask him tonight," Camilla suggested.

"And then what—I totally get rejected?"

"If that's what is happening, then yes. But he could easily be willing to start a relationship with you."

"But what do I do if he does reject me? What do I do if this guy I really like, who is also my boss, tells me he's not into me?"

"Then, you let yourself be sad for a bit and you eventually move on."

Riley sighed. She understood what Camilla was saying, but something was stopping her. She knew it was the fear of being turned down, and she also knew it was because her feelings for Oliver went a little deeper than she wanted to admit.

"I don't think I'm ready to deal with the fallout from it," she admitted.

"Well, then this is where you're at right now. He's treating you normally and you're not going to know why for sure."

"Oh God, what have I done?" Riley asked. "Why did I sleep with him?"

"Because you've had feelings for this guy for a while," Camilla said. "And that's okay, but with you denying them like you have been, something was bound to happen."

Riley leaned her head against the table again, and Camilla rubbed her back comfortingly. She was right, and Riley knew it. Maybe one day she would be ready to face the music and ask exactly what had happened between her and Oliver.

That day wasn't today.

Riley felt like she was about to walk into a war zone. When she pulled up to the house, a part of her wanted to drive far, far away.

However, she couldn't.

"Hey," Oliver said in an even tone. He and Zoe were sitting on the couch.

"Uh, hey," Riley replied. "Have you eaten?"

"Nope, we were waiting for you," he said.

Dinner went on as if nothing happened. It was so normal, Riley was sure she imagined sleeping with Oliver. Maybe it had been a vivid dream.

She put it out of her mind and got Zoe to bed after dinner. When Zoe was asleep, Riley stepped out of the bedroom and walked into the kitchen, where Oliver was drinking a soda.

She was determined to act as she usually would and not let on that she had nearly had a breakdown at work. She tried to think of something to say that would ease the tension she had been feeling, but nothing came to mind.

"So, how was your day?" She inwardly cringed. Was that the best she could do?

Oliver laughed and set down his drink. He walked over to her and wrapped his arms around her back and pulled her body against his. "It was great, but what I really missed was this . . . and you."

She felt her brain short-circuit. Why was Oliver acting all sweet and attentive? What had changed since when she got home to now? The only thing that had happened was that she put Zoe to bed.

Oh.

Zoe.

"Just out of curiosity, are you trying to play it cool in front of Zoe?" she asked.

"Yes. I thought about what you mentioned at your mom's house. It's probably better to leave her out of it for now."

Riley nodded, feeling relieved. "That makes a lot of sense actually."

He kissed her then, sending away any of Riley's thoughts.

Maybe she wouldn't have to tell him about her feelings after all. Maybe her feelings were loud and clear without words.

"Do you know how hard it was to get out of bed this morning when Zoe woke up?" he asked pulling away once more. "I could have stayed there all day."

"I almost did," Riley admitted. "I was cutting it pretty close today."

"And yet you still made time for coffee," he said, smiling at her.

"I will always make time for coffee."

He moved to kiss her neck, and she tilted her head, giving him more room.

Her anxieties faded as his lips brushed against the skin of her neck. Her body came alive, feeling like the night before.

"Will you come back to my room?" he asked. The words pressed against her neck made her almost moan.

"Yeah," she said, her voice husky. "Of course."

Chapter Twenty-One

Oliver

Oliver was on cloud nine.

He woke up with Riley next to him, all loneliness gone.

She was on her side, facing him. Her hair was everywhere and her mouth was open as she slept. And somehow it was one of best things he had ever seen.

He didn't know where they stood. He didn't know what the future held, or where they would go, but he was still getting more than he hoped for. He moved to be closer to her and gently placed his hand on her back to pull her over.

Riley made a noise and nuzzled her face into his neck, making him smile. She continued moving, gently waking up.

"Good morning," he whispered, and all he got in response was a yawn. Riley had never been articulate first thing in the morning. "I have to head in to work today."

"I know. I'm watching Zoe today."

Oliver kissed her once more, hovering over her with his hand on her hip. He would have loved to stay there and turn his kiss into something more, but he knew he didn't have the time. Reluctantly, he got up to get dressed. He could feel Riley's eyes on him as he moved.

"I'm going to make coffee," Riley said, and Oliver turned to see her slightly flushed, but getting dressed as well.

"Before you go . . ." He kissed her once more. It was a long, lingering kiss, just enough to tide him over until tonight.

"This is nice, but I will kill you if I can't at least brush my teeth before Zoe's awake," she said, pulling away. He laughed and kissed her one last time before she left the room.

Zoe was not awake as Oliver was leaving, so he stole one more kiss before he was out the door.

He drove into work, feeling on top of the world. Maybe soon he could risk asking Riley out on a proper date. Maybe she would say yes.

He got into office and began his daily tasks. His days were still very busy, since he was trying to get everything done in order to get home at a decent time.

But at lunch, his father knocked on his door. Oliver sighed, closed his email, and called for him to come in. When Jack walked into the office, he was followed by a young woman who was Oliver's age. She was a tall woman with bright blue eyes. Her brunette hair was the same shade as Riley's.

"Oliver," Jack said. "I am so glad I caught you. I want you to meet Alina. She's someone who works for me, and I thought you two would like to get to know each other."

"Oh," Oliver said, confused. "Hi, Alina."

"Hello," she said, smiling at him. Oliver wondered if she was supposed to be helping him out with something for work, or if she was here as a new member of his team.

"I thought you two could go to dinner next week," Jack said, and Oliver realized his bringing Alina to his office had nothing to do with work. It was strictly personal.

His dad was trying to set him up. He wanted to be angry, but he knew Jack didn't know about him and Riley.

Still, Oliver's first instinct was to say no. He didn't really want to go on dates with anyone else while he was figuring out things with Riley.

But, if he did say no, Jack would ask endless questions, which could easily get back to Riley. And then she could get nervous he was thinking they were exclusive before she was ready to be, or he was hiding things from her.

Oliver didn't know where he and Riley stood. Nothing was written in stone, so technically he was single.

He said sure and took Alina's phone number. He knew when he got home, he would mention it to Riley and see her reaction. If she was upset, he would cancel. If not, then he could put two and two together and know she wasn't truly ready.

Oliver thought about it all day, and when he got home, he found Riley and Zoe on the couch. Zoe told him about her day and everything that went on, but soon, she went back to her movie and Oliver pulled Riley aside.

"Hey, we need to talk about something," he said.

"Okay," Riley said, her voice hushed.

"So, I have a date with someone from work," he said.

Riley's mouth opened in shock, and Oliver carefully watched her expression. He didn't know what he expected. Maybe it was for her to be angry, or maybe she would ask him to cancel, but it was neither of those.

She quickly collected herself, and there was nothing written on her face.

"Good for you," Riley said.

Oliver stared, as if willing her to say more.

She didn't.

"I'll add it to the calendar."

"Yeah, sounds great."

Riley

Riley felt like an idiot.

Why in the world had she slept with Oliver? Why had she crossed lines she knew she shouldn't have? Things were fine before, and she should have left things as they were.

She focused all of her energy on Zoe that night. She pointedly didn't look at Oliver because she didn't want him to see she was upset.

Of course this was a hookup for him. Why would he want a relationship with *her* of all people?

After Zoe went down for bed, Riley sat in her room and tried to figure out what to feel. If she let herself be as hurt as she truly was, then it would be all-consuming. She wouldn't be able to even look at Oliver for months, and that wasn't going to work since she lived with him.

She couldn't wait until she went to work and could talk to Camilla. The worst-case scenario happened, and Oliver wasn't interested in her beyond sex. Now how did she deal with it?

Riley laid back on her bed, trying to figure out what to do. She was going to have to be okay that Oliver was dating people, and she wouldn't be having sex with him again.

Or was she?

A horrible thought entered Riley's mind. What if Oliver kept her around to sleep with her while he found his perfect girlfriend? The thought made Riley sick to her stomach and she knew she had to say something before it went any further.

Riley found him in the dining room. He was working on his laptop, but he looked up when she appeared. For a second, he looked surprised to see her, but she put it out of her mind.

"I need to talk to you," Riley said.

"Oh, okay." He closed the computer. Riley thought she saw him take a deep breath, as if preparing himself for something big, but she couldn't be sure.

"So, about this date," she began. "If you're going on it, then I want to clear something up."

Oliver blinked for a moment, but then leaned forward, as if he was hoping to hear a certain thing from her. Did he want to hear that she'd be okay to sleep with him while he dated around? Riley had to suppress a shudder at the thought.

"I don't want us to continue . . . um . . ." Riley paused, unsure of how to word what she was trying to say. ". . . sleeping together if you've agreed to go on a date."

"Oh," Oliver said. "And if I canceled?"

"You already agreed," she said. "So go."

He opened his mouth to say something, but Riley wasn't sure she wanted to hear it.

"Besides," she said. "Things are too complicated for me right now to move forward with anything."

His mouth shut and she wondered if she saw disappointment in his face. She looked away.

And yeah, it wasn't the total truth. Maybe she could have gotten over her fear of being cheated on. Maybe she could have worked through her insecurities if he had asked.

But she would always be Riley. And he would always be out of her league.

"Totally fair. I can do that."

"Thanks," she said. She took a shaky breath and walked away—her heart a rock in her chest.

She went to sleep feeling like nothing was truly resolved.

The next morning, things were awkward. She wasn't sure if he was giving her space or ignoring her.

Oliver didn't make her coffee, nor did he even really stick around to say hello. He muttered something about needing to work and retired to his room. Riley felt the urge to follow him to try to work this all out, but it fizzled the second Zoe asked her for something.

It wore on her, and when she headed to work at the coffee shop, she was lugging it around like a heavy suitcase in an airport. Camilla instantly took notice, but didn't say anything until a few hours later during a lull in customers.

"Are you going to mope all day, or come clean about why you look like a kicked puppy?"

"Oliver told me yesterday he has a date."

"Seriously?" Camilla asked. "And not with you?"

Riley shook her head. "Not with me."

"What the hell? He agreed to it before asking if you guys were anything serious?"

"I don't know," she said, cleaning one of the coffee machines. "But we're not anything serious. I got cheated on only a few months ago, and I . . . I don't think I can do this. If I did continue, eventually Oliver would find someone else—someone better—and then I'd lose Zoe. So, it's best we stay professional."

"I don't think he's going to find anyone better than you, Riley."

"But *I* do," she insisted. She took a deep breath. "And I'm more committed to Zoe than to Oliver."

"I get it," she replied. "I can tell you've thought about this, and I won't be able to change your mind. But these feelings aren't forever. You'll get over this. I mean, as long as you guys aren't going to continue sleeping together."

"We aren't. I told him last night," she said. "Now he's avoiding me, so I guess I lost a friend too."

"Maybe not forever. Maybe this was a wake-up call. He could have feelings for you and just now realized it."

Riley shook her head again. "I doubt it."

"It's a possibility," Camilla said.

"I really don't even want to think about it right now." She groaned. "Because if I give myself hope and nothing happens, then I don't know how I can see him every day."

"Fair," Camilla said. "Have you thought about hooking up with someone else? Maybe it would get your mind off it."

"I doubt it's going to be anything like the two times with Oliver," she muttered under her breath.

"You never told me about it. Was it any good?"

"I can honestly say that is was the best sex of my life," Riley replied. "So good that if I hadn't been cheated on by David then I would consider letting him date around while we were sleeping together."

"Damn," Camilla replied. "That makes this so much worse."

"I know," Riley said, sighing. She studied the wood patterns on the counter. "And it doesn't help I am totally and completely in love with him."

Camilla didn't say anything for a moment, and Riley glanced up to see her friend looking at her with nothing but sympathy.

"I thought you might be," Camilla said softly. "I'm sorry."

"It's okay," Riley said. "Like you said, it'll get better."

"That's the spirit."

Chapter Twenty-Two

Oliver

Oliver met Alina at an art gallery. His heart still ached remembering Riley and he took a step back, but he wanted to see where this date would go. He didn't have high hopes for it, but at the same time, he trusted his father's judgment.

Alina was standing at the entrance of the gallery. She was wearing a simple outfit and she looked nice.

"Hi," Oliver greeted.

"Hello," Alina said. After a long, almost painful silence, she added, "Sorry if this is awkward. First dates are always weird."

He nodded, grateful she seemed down-to-earth. "Yeah, they are."

"I haven't dated anyone in a while, so I'm on autopilot. But it was really nice of your dad to set us up."

"It was."

Even though it totally ruined what he had with Riley.

"So," Alina started. It was almost like she was following cue cards for how to have a first date. "I work for your dad, and I have a five-year-old."

"Oh, you're a mom?" Oliver asked, interest piqued. He didn't expect that—but he now understood why his father chose her.

After being with someone who didn't care about Zoe, Jack made sure to find someone who had a child, who would understand what Oliver was going through.

"I am. To a little boy."

"I have a little girl," he said. "She's four."

"Oh, that was a great age. They are so excited to explore the world."

"They are! She loves seeing new things."

And the rest of the date went very well. They discussed all of their memories of their kids and shared pictures. It was great—much better than Sophie had been—but it felt like he was catching up with an old friend and not on a romantic date. Any time he thought about kissing Alina, or doing anything with her, his heart stopped him.

Six months ago, Alina was someone Oliver would have loved to be with. She was kind, had a child of her own, and seemed to have a few things in common with him. This woman was what he had been looking for. She was someone he could get along with, and yet, now, he felt nothing for her.

When the date ended, without a kiss but with a shy, knowing smile, Oliver knew he couldn't do this. He couldn't date or even be looking for anyone else.

Oliver drove straight to his father's apartment. He needed to set some of the story straight.

Jack lived in a high-rise apartment in the same building he and Oliver worked in. Oliver opted for something with a yard for Zoe, but sometimes he envied his father's commute.

Jack opened the door after only a few knocks. He looked ready for bed and surprised to see Oliver.

"Well, I guess if you are here and not with Alina then it didn't go well," Jack mused.

"She was great, but I didn't feel anything for her."

"Really?" Jack asked. "I thought she would be perfect."

"Dad, we need to talk about something."

"Okay, then sit down and we can talk," Jack said, and Oliver sat on his couch with a heavy sigh.

"I don't want to be set up on any more dates."

"Really? Why not? I thought you wanted a mom for Zoe."

"I'm in love with Riley."

"Oh."

"Yeah," Oliver said. "I don't want to date right now."

"Well, honestly son, I can't say I'm surprised."

Oliver frowned. His dad wasn't surprised?

"Why not?"

"I saw the way you looked at her at Christmas. It was fairly obvious, but she told me you guys were only friends, so I thought it was time to see if you would be willing to date again."

Oliver leaned forward and sighed. "Of course we're friends, but there could have been something more."

"Really?"

"Yeah," Oliver said. "I didn't want you to know because I didn't want you to push her into something with me she isn't ready for. Her last relationship didn't end well."

"Oh, I see. Why didn't you tell me that?"

"I don't know, Dad. I can't keep my head straight around her. I never can, which has led me to look like an ass."

He remembered the night he fired her because he couldn't take her criticism and shuddered.

"Did you love her when you were with Sophie?" Jack asked. "Because I thought you liked Sophie a lot."

Oliver shook his head. "I didn't like Sophie, not really. I rushed it because I thought I needed a mom for Zoe. Meanwhile, Riley took on that role without me even having to ask. She's . . . amazing, and I wish I had a chance with her."

"Why don't you?"

"She's not ready for a relationship right now," he explained. "So, we can't be anything."

Oliver was surprised by a laugh from his dad. "Well, why not? Just because she isn't ready for a relationship *now* doesn't mean she will never be."

"But what if she isn't?"

"Oliver, you don't have to rush into everything. Just give her time and wait. If she wants to be with you, she will tell you."

"I don't think that's possible," Oliver said. His father looked at him questioningly, and he told Jack everything.

He told him about what happened with Sophie, and what he said to Riley that night. He told him about Christmas and then the night after. He ended his long tale with his date with Alina.

Jack listened quietly and didn't make any comments. Oliver wasn't sure what his dad was going to say, but it felt freeing to get it off his chest.

"That is . . . a lot of information," Jack replied. "But what I get from this is your feelings for her are different than anything you've felt before."

"Yeah," Oliver confirmed.

"And you have already made some mistakes from before you realized you had feelings, and because of that, you're afraid she is never going to want to be with you."

Oliver leaned back. His dad was right, like always, even if he hadn't put the pieces together himself. His job depended on him keeping it together and not being an ass at work. All of his relationships had been him trying to do the same thing.

He never pushed or got mad at Zoe's mom. He never snapped at Sophie—not like he had at Riley—even when he told her to get out of his house. And with Riley, he showed her a part of himself he hated, the part of himself that was rude and jumped to conclusions.

"Oliver, I think you need to give her time to deal with everything that has happened over the last few weeks, and then you need to tell her how you feel."

"But I have told her, not with words. But I know I showed her."

Jack shook his head. "That's not enough. She could be seeing everything completely differently. She could easily think you aren't interested in her because of your status and hers, or because you said yes to that date. She could think you are having a great time right now and she is simply not good enough."

"But that's not true. None of that is what happened."

"Not on your end, but she doesn't know that. I think you both need time to think and recover, and then you need to make sure she knows what happened. You both need to start talking to each other, for real this time."

Riley

Riley was tired. She was tired from her conversation with Camilla, tired from the hurt she was feeling, and tired from Zoe running around the house. All she wanted to do was sleep, and instead, she was watching Zoe while Oliver was on a date with someone else.

She tried to keep a positive outlook on everything, but it was hard. She could tell Zoe was noticing, and the little girl was nice enough to have them simply watch movies near the end of the night instead of doing anything too wild.

They watched *Brave*, and at the end of it, Zoe asked, "Can I call you Mommy?"

Riley felt like she had been hit by a train. "You want to call me Mommy?"

"Yes."

On one hand, she was honored the little girl thought of her in such a way, but deep down, she knew she was not Zoe's mom. She never had been, and, on paper, she wasn't even a staple in Zoe's life past being her nanny. It didn't matter that she *felt* like she was more.

"Zoe, I'm sorry, you can't," she said, even though it was the last thing she wanted to say.

"Why not?" Zoe frowned.

"Because I'm not your mom. And I may not be here forever."

"But you promised."

"I know I did, but honey, one day I might not be your nanny, and that's what I am. I'm your nanny. One day, you might have a new stepmom or someone else. I'm not your mom."

"No!" Zoe yelled and jumped away from Riley. "You said you would never leave again!"

Riley now realized what a mistake that was. "Zoe, honey—"

"No!" Zoe repeated and ran upstairs to her room and slammed the door. Riley chased after her. "You can't leave! I don't want you to!"

"I'm not leaving now," she said through the door. "But you have to know that maybe one day I will."

"I don't want a stepmom! I don't want anyone else."

That broke Riley's heart, more than anything Oliver could ever do. She leaned her head against the door tiredly.

"Zoe . . ." she said softly. Then, she knew she had to make a call. She knew Zoe was going to be a mess when Oliver got home because she wasn't going to understand the delicate situation Riley was in. But there was something she could do. "Kid, you have a mom, but it's not me."

Zoe opened the door. "Then where is she?"

"She's gone now but was here at one point. And I can't replace her."

Riley's full attention was on Zoe, so she didn't notice when Oliver came home, or that he had heard what she was saying to Zoe. It was an unspoken rule to never mention Zoe's mother, and Riley broke it. So, when Zoe's eyes drifted behind her, Riley felt her blood turn cold as she spun and saw Oliver standing in the hallway. He looked pissed.

"Oh no," Riley said, mostly to herself.

He only shook his head at her. "Seriously? You're telling her the one thing I asked you not to?"

"Oliver—"

"I don't want to hear it, Riley," he snapped, but whatever he was going to say next was interrupted by Zoe.

"Don't be mean!"

"Zoe," Oliver said in a tight voice, but he was interrupted.

"No!" Zoe yelled, and when Oliver tried to grab her, she screamed so loudly Riley winced. Zoe ran to hide behind Riley, which made the whole situation worse.

"Zoe, come here," Oliver instructed.

"No!" Zoe repeated. "No, no, no, no, no!"

"Then Riley can leave!" he barked.

Everything was silent for a moment, until Riley asked, "Really?"

"Yeah, I need you gone for a bit," he said. "Obviously I need to explain things to Zoe that I really don't want to."

"No . . ." Zoe muttered again, but Riley knew Oliver was serious. She hoped he was going to honor their contract and not kick her out, but she wasn't so sure.

Riley turned to Zoe. "Okay. You heard your dad. I need to go."

"Daddy is being mean!" Zoe yelled, holding onto Riley's shirt.

"Zoe, you and your dad need some alone time. I'll be back in a few hours, okay?" Riley said, and she gently took Zoe's hands off her. It almost killed her to do it. But she stood up and left, even though her heart was crying much like she knew Zoe was.

Her car struggled to turn on, which sent a jolt of anxiety through her, but she knew she had to go. She ignored it and drove away. She didn't know where she was going, and a part of her wanted to head to the nearest liquor store and buy all that she could, but she merged onto the interstate instead and headed north.

Or she would have—if her car hadn't completely died on the highway.

Riley cursed and managed to safely pull to the side of the road. Everything including the radio and the interior lights were not working. She stared at the wheel, completely shocked her car finally died, and it was when Oliver told her to leave, and she had nowhere to go.

That was when she lost it and finally cried.

Tears streamed down her face and she let it all out. She sobbed, and then screamed, and then cursed. Eventually, her raw emotions subsided a bit and she figured out she had to do something. Her phone only had 4% of its battery left, so she called the one person who probably wouldn't ignore her call.

Camilla answered on the second ring. Riley told her that her phone was about to die, her car was broken down, and where she was, and Camilla promised she would be there in a few minutes. After the call, her phone shut off, and she resumed crying, staring at the dead screen while she waited for her friend.

Oliver

Things got worse when Riley left. The minute she was gone, Oliver realized it may not have been a good idea to tell her to leave when Zoe was saying how much she wanted Riley to stay. Zoe was crying, screaming, and hitting him.

"Hey, Zoe," Oliver said. "What's going on?"

"I want Mommy!"

Oliver sighed. Damn Riley for even mentioning it. "Honey, your mom . . ."

"I want Mommy!"

"Your mom isn't here. She's . . . gone."

"No, no! You told her to go away!"

"What? When?"

"Just now!"

Oliver was confused. "What? Zoe, only Riley was here."

Zoe sobbed. "That's my Mommy."

And then it hit Oliver like a ton of bricks. That's why Riley was talking to her about her birth mom. That was why Zoe was mad—because Riley was trying to explain why she couldn't think of her that way, and he went and assumed the worst. Again.

Oliver had been so tense after his failed date and then the conversation with his father. With Zoe crying, it took him back to the days before Riley, when he came home to that more often than not. Then, he overheard Riley and Zoe's conversation, and it was too much.

"Honey, you know Riley isn't your real mom, right?"

"I know," Zoe said quietly. "But she loves me and takes care of me, so she is my Mommy."

It was such a simple statement, yet it meant so much.

"I'm not sure it works that way."

"That's why I asked her, but you were mean and sent her away."

Oliver glanced at his feet. That was exactly what he did, and he was for sure going to be paying the price for it now.

"Well, when she gets back, we can talk to her about what to call her, okay?"

Zoe only nodded, and Oliver got his phone to send a simple text.

Oliver: Please come back. I'm sorry.

Now, all he had to do was wait for her to return.

Riley

"You look awful," Camilla said when she pulled up.

"I've been crying for like twenty minutes."

"Jesus . . . are you attached to this car or something?"

"No, but it's been a bad night. Zoe wants to call me Mommy."

"Oh. Did you tell her no?"

"I had to," Riley said. "And then Oliver came home, and he thought I was trying to tell her about her mother behind his back and told me to leave."

"Like he fired you?"

"No, he needed to explain to Zoe without me there. At least I think so. We have a contract, so technically I could take him to court."

"Would you?"

"No." Riley sighed. She took out her phone, remembering the battery died. "Do you have an iPhone charger at all?"

"Nope, Team Android all the way."

"Great. I guess I don't need to charge it anyway. I'm sure things are fine."

"So, what are you going to do about a car?"

"Get a new one? It was my ex's so I'm not all that attached."

There was a long silence. Riley stared out the window, eyes unfocused as they passed by interstate signs and trees.

"So, how do you feel about Zoe calling you mom?" Camilla asked.

"What do you mean?"

"Like . . . are you weirded out by it?"

"No, I mean in a perfect world . . . I don't know. Maybe if I wasn't her nanny, I would be okay with it, but since I am, it complicates things. I mean, her dad could fire me at any time and it would be nothing. I can't say I'm going to be this permanent thing in her life when legally I'm not."

"So, the only thing that has you upset is that you're her nanny and not something more?"

"Right," Riley said.

Camilla let out a disbelieving laugh. "I always fail to get why you think you're such a bad person. The fact you're willing to be her mom is more than most would do. I mean, there are a ton of stepparents who hate their kids."

Riley laughed humorlessly. "You wouldn't feel that way if you knew the whole story."

"What do you mean?"

"I'm . . . I'm not perfect."

"I never said you were."

Riley sighed and leaned back on the headrest. "I really want a drink right now, like really bad."

"Oh, well I have some wine at the apartment."

And that was enough to cause Riley to cry again because she almost said yes. Camilla immediately apologized.

"I can't drink."

"Why not?"

"Because when I do, I lose control and use it to avoid my problems. That would be exactly what I would be doing now."

"Oh, I know you said you tried to stop drinking, but I didn't know it was serious. I shouldn't have even mentioned it. I'm sorry."

"It's okay."

"You can have water though. If you want something stronger, I have soda."

"Thanks," Riley said, giving Camilla a half smile.

"And you can crash on my couch."

"That would be nice."

"And also, it's going to be okay," Camilla said. "I promise."

Riley really hoped it would. She really did.

Oliver

What if she drinks?

The thought was unwelcome, but it made Oliver's blood run cold.

He knew Riley had been sober for the last few months. She had been doing great, but she had been drinking for years before she stopped. He knew she struggled with it when upset, and he went and upset her. He had a bad feeling something was happening, mostly because she hadn't responded, hadn't even read the text, and she hadn't come home yet. He stayed awake, even after Zoe fell asleep, and didn't hear from her. He could only hope she was safe and all right.

Eventually, he fell asleep too, and when he woke up to sunlight streaming through the windows, he immediately went to Riley's room but found it empty. Her old SUV wasn't in the driveway. His heart raced and he pulled out his phone to call her again.

Then he heard the door open. Her car wasn't there, meaning she may have been at a bar. But that wasn't his worry. He was more concerned that she was safe and home.

"Hey," Riley greeted, but Oliver strode to her and hugged her tightly. "Whoa," she said. He inhaled her scent as he did so, and she smelled like somewhere unfamiliar. It could have meant anything.

"I was worried," he said, in explanation for his hug.

"Oh, well the SUV crapped out on the interstate."

"What?" he asked. "Are you okay?"

"Yeah, I'm fine. I would have texted later, but my phone died after I called Camilla, who I figured would answer. I spent the night at her house to give you two some space."

"We were fine in minutes. I texted you." He was reluctant to let her go.

"Oh, sorry. I haven't charged my phone yet," she replied. She rubbed her eyes. He decided not to bring up anything difficult.

"It doesn't matter, I'm glad you're okay."

"Yeah, I'm fine. Is everything good here?" she asked.

"Yeah, but you and Zoe do need to talk about what she asked you."

"I know," she said, looking at him nervously. "The plan was to bring it up to you, but she was being insistent and I—"

"I know, and I shouldn't have assumed you would tell her about her real mom behind my back," he said. "I'm sorry, Riley."

"It's okay. It was a bad situation. This whole thing is . . . unexpected. I didn't think she would ever ask me that."

"Me either," he said. "So, what will we do about it?"

"It's more about what's appropriate rather than what I *want* to do."

"What do you *want* to do?"

"It doesn't matter. I love Zoe. You know I do, but . . ." She trailed off. He expected her to say this was too much responsibility—that she wanted space.

After all, this was more than most people could take.

"I'm her nanny, and as much I wish I was more, I'm simply not."

Oliver stared at her. "You mean you would be willing to be her mother?"

"If I had a choice? Any day." There was no hesitation in her voice or expression. "But I'm not. You pay me to watch her. That could end at any time, and it isn't fair to her."

He sighed. She was right, of course. While they did have a contract, it wasn't for forever. One day, Zoe wouldn't need a nanny and then that would end their working relationship.

If he and Riley worked out, then it would change things. She could be around for a very long time, nanny role or not. It was something he needed to talk to her about, but the morning after a possible relapse and a fight between them was not the right time for it.

"Then, we tell her no."

Riley looked at her feet. When she finally looked back up, her eyes were wet. "Yeah, that's probably for the best."

"You're upset."

"Of course I am," she said, her voice thick. "I'm very aware I have no legal rights to her. If something happened to you, I have no recourse. She's not mine, no matter how much I want her to be. Ugh." She rubbed her face, looking frustrated with her own emotions. "If there was *any* way I could change this, I would."

There was a way. It was totally unorthodox, but there was a way. Oliver never thought anyone would have wanted his daughter so badly, especially if they didn't have access to his bank account. He figured a mother for Zoe would come with marriage.

Not a nanny.

"There is a way."

"How? I get named a guardian when she's got a perfectly good father? I don't think any court is going to go for that."

"Zoe's birth mother signed away her parental rights not long after she was born. It made it easy for me when I finally found someone who would actually *be* her mother in the future. Anyone looking to adopt her only needs my permission."

Riley stared at him, and then laughed incredulously. "No, no way. You can't be offering this."

"You don't want to do it?" he asked. He couldn't curb the disappointment he felt at her refusal.

"I want to do it, but why the hell would you offer this to *me?*"

"Because you're the only person in the world that could be here for her if I was gone. Her current next of kin is my dad, and I love him, but he's busy. He can't be there for her like *you* could."

Riley blinked at him, disbelief written all over her face. "You're really offering this."

"Yes. I am," he replied, and the weight of the offer hung between them for a long moment. She stared at him and he couldn't tell what she was thinking. "There's absolutely no pressure for you to, but . . . the door is open?"

In that moment, he wished—more than anything—he could read her mind.

"I think I have to quit."

"What?" he asked. "Hang on, you can't—"

"I don't want to be paid for watching a child I'm adopting."

Oliver froze.

She wasn't quitting to get away from him. She was quitting to *adopt* Zoe.

"Then . . . I guess I accept your resignation," he said.

There was a moment where nothing happened. The room stayed still, but he could feel something shift. He never thought he could love her any more than he already did, but somehow, she found a way to prove him wrong.

She jumped on him, eyes wet, pulling him into one of the tightest hugs he had ever been a part of.

Her body pressed close to his, right where he liked it.

He couldn't help himself. He hugged her back just as tightly and lifted her off the ground to swing her around. She laughed in his ear and was smiling when he set her down.

"I can't believe you're even willing to do this," he said.

"Oliver, I love her. I genuinely want to do this, even if I lose the income doing it."

"I want to cover the legal fees."

"But—"

"No, it's the least I can do."

"I can cover them," Riley said. "I've been saving a ton of money living here."

"And you'll need to buy a new car. A family car," Oliver reminded her. "Save it for that."

"We'll think about it."

He shook his head. He was *so* finding a way to cover the legal fees.

"Thank you," Riley said, pulling away.

"Why are you thanking me?"

"Because you're willing to let me adopt Zoe. I never thought you would be okay with that."

"It's you, so . . . of course I'm okay with it."

Riley smiled one last time before she turned to Zoe's room.

"I guess I need to tell her, huh?" she asked.

Oliver nodded, and Riley walked away, toward Zoe, who would be her daughter. He stared after her, wondering what he had done to deserve such a woman in his life.

Riley

Riley gently knocked on Zoe's door. The girl was still asleep, so Riley tiptoed to the bed and laid down next to her. As she stirred, Riley combed her hands through the little girl's hair.

"Mommy?" Zoe whispered.

"Hey, kid," Riley said softly.

"Are you back?"

"Yes, I am."

"Can I call you Mommy now?"

She smiled. "Yes, you can. And I have something else I want to talk to you about."

"What?"

"Your dad and I talked, and instead of being your nanny, I'm adopting you."

"What does that mean?"

"It a more official way of me becoming your mom. It's as close to forever as we can get."

"So you're never leaving?"

Riley shook her head. As long as she could help it, she would always be by this little girl's side.

"Yay!" Zoe said, hugging Riley tightly. She laughed and curled up with the girl, feeling like she was making the right choice. It was a wild one. She knew most nannies didn't adopt the kids they watched, but it was right for them.

Zoe was happy, and she wouldn't have it any other way.

Zoe slept in the next day, and Riley woke up earlier than her soon-to-be daughter. Oliver was up and getting ready for work when Riley walked into the kitchen.

Looking at him brought back a lot of feelings she would rather avoid. Zoe's meltdown distracted her from everything that had been going on between them, but now, in the quiet of the morning, the feelings bubbled to the surface. She pushed them away, determined to act normal around him, but the memory of his hands on her body flashed through her mind, and it was hard to ignore.

"Morning," Oliver said, his voice soft. "Want some coffee?"

"Yeah," she replied, and as he prepared it, she wondered if there was any work she could do to avoid thinking about what had transpired between them.

"Are you having second thoughts?" he asked.

Riley blinked, confused. "What?"

"About Zoe and adopting her."

She glanced at him and he didn't look accusatory. If anything, he looked worried. "Why do you ask?"

"You seem lost in your thoughts this morning."

"Oh." Her cheeks heated up. It wasn't that she was having second thoughts about Zoe, because the moment she made that decision, it settled in her heart as if it had been there a long time. It had been something she wanted, but never allowed herself to have. "No, I'm not."

"You would tell me if you did though, right? This is a huge decision, and I don't want you to feel forced into it if you don't really want to do it."

"I want to do it," she said, feeling a little insulted Oliver would think she would go back on it, as if it were a rash decision. "I'm serious. I'm not going back on it."

"Okay."

"Did you think I would?"

Oliver was quiet for a second.

"I thought," he started, "I thought you would think about it overnight and realize you don't want this, or think it's too much."

"Well, I didn't," Riley replied. "I don't think you understand how much I love Zoe."

"I guess I don't," he said quietly. "I never expected that, you know."

"Neither did I." She took a sip of her coffee.

"Well, if you are still serious about this, I will get a lawyer involved to figure out what all we need to do. It should be easy since I'm on board."

"How expensive do you think it will be?" she asked, numbers running through her head. "I have savings, but I need to know what I need to have for this since I now also have to buy a car."

"I said I would pay for it," he reminded, shooting a half smile in her direction.

Riley straightened. "No, I can do it," she said, a bit defensively.

"We talked about this . . ."

"I know, but I *can* do it."

"Right, but you also have to buy a car," Oliver said. "You really don't like accepting help, do you?"

It was said in a friendly manner, but it had Riley pursing her lips because he was right. She hated accepting help. "No, I don't."

"If you think about it, though, don't most employers offer adoption assistance?" he asked. "And besides, I haven't been able to give you health insurance, so maybe this will make up for it."

Riley stared at him. Her savings had become a comfort, something to rely on if everything fell apart again. Now that her car was broken down, it was either she used her savings to fix it, or she used it to put a down payment on a new one. If adopting Zoe was expensive, as she was sure it would be, then it could wipe out everything she saved. That was a scary thought for her.

"Fine," Riley said begrudgingly. "That would be great."

"You sound very happy about it," he replied sarcastically. "But I know how hard this is for you, so thank you for accepting it for once."

"I probably wouldn't if I didn't have my car to think about. I have to get it towed and figure out what's wrong with it." She put her head down on the counter and groaned. "I have so much to do."

Riley didn't realize he had walked over to her, but he gently patted her back, which made her feel slightly better about the situation. He promised to give her the lawyer's information before he left for work.

She felt the thoughts begin to sink in again, about Oliver and his date, the fact he never told her how his date went, and the fact she was in love with him. To avoid these intrusions, she straightened up and took out her phone, calling her mother.

"Riley," Jane said, answering the phone. "Why are you calling me this time? Is it for Oliver and Zoe? Or is it bad news?"

"Do you have any tow truck companies you like?" she asked. She knew if there was anyone to ask for recommendations, it was her mother. Jane vetted everyone who provided her a service.

"Yes, I know of one. Why do you ask?"

"Well, you'll be happy to know my car broke down last night."

"And why would I be happy about that?"

"Because you hate that car."

"Yes, you're right about that," she said with a sigh. "I didn't like David giving you his trash."

In a different time, Riley would have been offended. She would have defended David until her mother dropped it. But Jane was right. David gave her that car a year ago when it was on its last leg anyway, and now it was finally done.

"Does this mean you are going to get another?" Jane asked.

Riley paused. Is that what it meant? She could probably fix up the old car. It was in decent shape, and was an SUV, which made carting Zoe around easier. But the radio barely worked, the seats were uncomfortable, the heat didn't run hot, and it was a sore reminder of a life she no longer lived.

"Yeah," she responded, "I probably will."

"Oh, good," Jane said. "I have been meaning to give you the information of the man who sold me my own car. He gave me a fantastic deal. I am sure if you bring Oliver and Zoe, you can charm him into an even better one."

The idea of taking Oliver anywhere with the current state of their relationship was laughable.

"Yeah, I'll probably go by myself," Riley said.

"Why would Oliver not go?"

"He's busy, mom."

"Well, I hope he isn't too busy for you, dear," Jane said. "He is your boyfriend after all."

Riley felt her eyes widen at the term, but then she remembered Christmas Eve dinner. The lie they told.

It felt like ages ago, but in reality, it was only a few days.

"Mom, um, I hate to tell you this, but Oliver and I aren't dating."

"What? You two broke up?" Jane asked. "Whose fault was it? Yours or his?"

"Neither," Riley said, feeling embarrassed. "We were never together in the first place. We said that because of James."

There was silence on the other end, and then Jane said, "Are you serious?"

"I am," Riley replied. "It's not a huge deal, but—"

"And there are no feelings between you?" she interrupted. "None at all?"

Riley was silent. Did she want to tell her mom everything that had happened? Would it even help if she did?

"Well, I guess I have my answer," Jane said.

"He doesn't see me that way, mom," Riley said, rubbing her face tiredly. "We already had a discussion about it."

"He doesn't see *you* that way? That is not the impression I got at Christmas or Thanksgiving."

Riley paused. Her mom thought Oliver liked her? There was no way that was true, but even so, she couldn't bear to think about it. If she did, then she would go down a rabbit hole she may never recover from.

"I-I don't know, mom," Riley said. "But we're not together."

"But you have feelings. So, are you going to keep working for him? Living with him?"

Riley paused. Things had changed on that front. Technically, she didn't work for him anymore. Technically, she was Zoe's mom, or at least would be once the adoption went through.

"I need to talk to you about that. My job, I mean."

"Are you going to quit?" Jane asked.

"I already did," she replied. "But not because of my feelings or anything. Mom, I'm adopting Zoe."

The noise Riley heard her mother make was one of absolute shock. Jane was a lady who kept herself together at all times, but what Riley said knocked her out of her poised figure.

"Wha—You're . . . Are you serious, Riley?"

"Yes. And before you say anything about it, she asked me to be her mom, and Oliver and I agreed I could be, but I want some backup on a legal standpoint."

"My God, Riley. This is a huge decision!"

"I know," Riley said. "But it feels like it's been a long time coming."

Jane was silent again. Riley pictured her mother going back to the poised woman she always was, and she was right to do so, for when Jane spoke, she sounded like her normal self. "I suppose it is."

"Anyway, I told Oliver I'm not going to work for him if I'm adopting Zoe. So, as of now, I work at the coffee shop."

"And you two are roommates?"

She hadn't exactly thought of what they were now that she was no longer his employee. In fact, she didn't want to. Saying Riley and Oliver were roommates felt wrong, like it was a misrepresentation of their relationship. She would say friends, but not all friends lived together.

"I think the word co-parents sums it up better than roommates," Riley eventually settled on.

"Well, this is certainly not what I expected from this conversation," Jane said.

"I thought you would like to know." Riley suddenly felt embarrassed about it. Was her mom going to judge her? Or tell her she was wrong for doing this?

"Be sure that the coffee shop pays you enough to support Zoe on your own," Jane said. "They may ask that when you apply for the adoption."

"Yeah," she said. "I'll talk to the owner about it."

"Good. Then you shouldn't have any problems. Also, I went by there the other day. The woman, Camilla, I think, was there."

Riley's thoughts were torn away from the adoption and put on that statement. "You met Camilla?"

Camilla and Riley's mom meeting felt like a merging of two worlds she wasn't ready for.

"She was a sweet woman," Jane said. "I didn't tell her I know you, of course. I didn't want her to give me a free drink or anything."

"She *would* do that," Riley agreed. "She does it to her baristas' families all the time."

"You should become friends with her," Jane mused. "I think she would be good for you."

"I am friends with her," she said. "And she is."

They ended the call there, and Riley put down her phone, wondering when the other shoe would drop about her decision to adopt Zoe. What was Amanda going to say when she found out Riley had been lying about her relationship with Oliver, and about adopting Zoe? Was she going to judge her too?

Looking at her life from Amanda's perspective, Riley's was even more of a mess now. She, Riley Emerson, was adopting a kid and lying about a relationship with Amanda's boss. She slumped and put her head back on the cool granite, half expecting her phone to explode at any moment. She was so used to everything she did being regarded with scrutiny that she didn't know what to do when she finally did something right.

Oliver

Oliver walked into work, wondering why Riley was quiet. He wanted to ask her, but he didn't want to pressure her into answering, especially with the current state of their relationship.

He hoped it wasn't that she was having second thoughts, and if she was, that she would tell him before they got too deep into this. Hopefully him getting her in contact with a family lawyer was enough to have her tell someone if she truly was rethinking the decision.

Off the top of his head, Oliver didn't know of any lawyers, but his company had an entire list that employees often used in their adoption processes. His father would know, since he curated most of the list.

He found Jack in his office in a rare, free moment. Jack was looking at his computer, glasses perched on his nose, but he took them off when he saw Oliver.

"To what do I owe this visit?" Jack greeted pleasantly.

"Do you know of any adoption lawyers that owe you a favor?"

"Of course," Jack said. "But I have to ask why. You aren't thinking of adopting a child, are you?"

"No, not me. Riley."

"Riley is adopting a child?" Jack looked confused.

"Yeah, she's adopting Zoe."

Jack's eyes widened almost comically. There were a few times Oliver's father was shocked, and this was definitely one of them. "I'm . . . I'm sorry? She's adopting Zoe?"

"Yes," Oliver said. "Zoe asked if she could call Riley her mom, and Riley didn't feel comfortable being her nanny anymore."

"So, she's *adopting* her?"

"Yep."

"So, let me get this straight. Riley, who you are not in any romantic relationship with, is okay with being your child's mother and is also wanting to adopt her?"

"Yes, she is," Oliver said, and he knew the weight of her decision. It weighed on him too. He didn't understand why Riley was willing to do this, but it made him love her even more that she was.

"Is she sure?"

Oliver paused. Riley had been quiet this morning, seeming lost in her thoughts, and she had denied it when he asked if it was about Zoe.

"I think so. I at least want to give her a lawyer's information. She says she's serious, and I am willing to do this if she is."

"I suppose you got what you wanted then: a mom for Zoe," Jack said with a small smile to him. "And if she goes through with this, she will have earned more than my respect."

"Mine too," Oliver said quietly.

And that was the truth. While it definitely wasn't out of character for her to do something like this, Riley Emerson had surpassed every expectation he had for her when he opened the door that fateful afternoon.

He never imagined someone would come into his life and take care of his daughter the way she had. She had done her job responsibilities and more, ever since that first day, but it was never her job to love Zoe. It was never her job to care for her at night, or to move in at a moment's notice, and yet she did, never with complaint.

Riley

Within twenty-four hours, Riley had a meeting with the lawyer Oliver referred her to. He was a nice guy on the phone, and Riley couldn't wait to get the process started. It was all Zoe could talk about.

Oliver kept looking at her like she was going to change her mind, which was annoying, but she could understand why he was concerned about it.

Riley had a hard time talking to him these days. While she loved Zoe and was okay with living with Oliver to be close to her, the fact that she still didn't know what happened on the date with the other woman hung over her any time she would talk to him.

Luckily, they had a new contract put together for their living situation where Riley was shown to be a full-time resident there, but Oliver insisted she didn't pay anything.

Once that was settled, she put her focus on finding a new car. The lawyer mentioned she needed a stable car to prove she was capable enough to be the sole caretaker of Zoe. She worked with her mom to find something that suited her. What they eventually settled on was another used SUV, but a smaller one that was blue and only a few years old.

Jane had worked with the salesman before, and he gave it to Riley for a fair price. Her savings weren't wiped out, and her new monthly car payment wasn't going to eat through what she made in the coffee shop.

There was also the matter of Amanda. They hadn't talked since Christmas, and she wasn't sure what to even say to her sister now that so much had changed.

Amanda had always been so strange about Riley's relationship with Oliver. This was going to take that and blow it out of the water.

It all came to a head right after New Year's Day when Jane called Riley to come over to celebrate the fresh year. Riley wasn't sure what to expect, but Amanda sitting on the couch was not one of them.

"You two need to talk," Jane said. "Both of you have had a lot of life changes in the last few months, and this feud between you has to end somewhere."

Riley was taken aback but sat down anyway. She wasn't so full of pride she couldn't admit she *was* jealous of Amanda. She opened her mouth to say just that, but Amanda spoke up first.

"I think James and I are going to get a divorce."

"Oh, shit," Riley said.

"That's not a very eloquent response," Amanda said. "But it's not wrong."

"What happened?"

"He's . . . he's been like this for a while. He thinks everyone is making a move on me. Not because I'm perfect or anything, but because he's *never* home. I barely see him."

"Yeah, it's kind of weird he's out so much. He works in construction, right?"

"He does," Amanda said. "But I don't think he's only working when he says he is."

"You think he's seeing someone else?"

"I don't think so, but I do think he's lying. Whether he's out with a friend or . . . someone else, it's still not being honest with me."

"I'm sorry," Riley said.

"So there you have it," Amanda said bitterly. "I'm not perfect anymore."

Riley fought against a wave of resentment. The only person striving for perfection was Amanda herself.

"I-I'm sorry if I ever made you feel like you had to be perfect," Riley settled on.

"One of us had to be."

Riley glared. "I know I've been a mess, but you have to stop being so mean about it. I've always *tried*, and comments like that make it harder to."

Amanda's face went red and she looked to Jane to back her up. Riley tensed, waiting for her mother to jump to Amanda's defense, but nothing came.

Jane wasn't even in the room anymore. She must have left when they'd began talking.

Amanda sighed. "Fine. Maybe I . . . maybe I used being perfect against you, but for the record, you went off and dated a loser for five years."

"That doesn't mean I'm less of a person, Amanda."

She blinked. "No. I guess it doesn't."

"Did you or mom ever stop to think maybe I needed compassion instead of shame? That maybe some fucking kindness would have helped me more than constantly lecturing me?"

"I . . ." Amanda blinked, her eyes growing wet. "No, I never did. God, I'm so sorry. I never . . . I never meant to hurt you."

"You did. Both you and mom did."

"And you still saved my ass at Christmas? If it were me, I wouldn't have said anything with James acting like he was."

"I did it because you're still my sister," Riley said. "And I'll always be here for you, but I'd like for you to start treating me better."

"I'll . . . I'll definitely try. God, *thank you* for saying what you did at Christmas. I know you aren't actually dating him and thank you for probably making Oliver mad by going along with it."

"Why would Oliver be mad?" Riley asked. "And if you say he'd be mad because I'm ugly then I will throw something at you."

"No, it's not that," Amanda said. "Oliver doesn't ever talk about his personal life with his employees. I can't imagine what he thought about me saying you were kissing. I bet he went off."

"Oh, right." Riley asked.

Yeah, that was a rule that didn't apply to her, and not because she was no longer his employee.

Amanda nodded. "He's a brick wall about it. He told me off for saying anything about you from the beginning."

"He did?"

Amanda nodded. "Yeah. I'm sure he gave you the same lecture about not talking about me. He wasn't rude about it or anything, but he can be firm when he needs to be."

"I agree he can be firm but . . . never mind."

Amanda frowned. "No, what?"

"Trust me, you don't want to know. It's only gonna piss you off."

"Why would it piss me off?"

"You're very . . . protective over Oliver. Any time I talk about him or anything I do with him, you get mad."

"I don't . . ." She trailed off, face red as she realized Riley was right. "Okay, maybe I do. But it's not you, it's just—he was *my* boss."

"And he still is only *your* boss. I don't work for him anymore."

Amanda's eyes widened. "Why?"

"I quit, because I decided to adopt Zoe instead."

Amanda's jaw dropped and stayed open for what felt like minutes. "Adopt? You? Zoe?"

"Yeah," Riley said, face aflame at Amanda's shock. "Zoe asked me to be her mom, and I want it on paper. Oliver said there's no one else he'd want Zoe with if something happened."

"Oh my God! Oliver agreed? He is *so* protective over her. He let you adopt her?"

"Don't say it like I'm some garbage troll under a bridge," Riley said. "I love Zoe."

"B-but the drinking—"

"I stopped drinking months ago."

"What? You did?"

"Yeah, I haven't touched it in a long time. I keep telling you and mom that and you both refuse to believe me."

"Holy shit," Amanda said. "That is . . . this is so incredible. I never expected you to stop drinking, of all things."

"Zoe became a lot more important to me."

"Oh, you even sound like a mom," Amanda said, shaking her head. "I never thought I'd see the day."

Riley nodded, cringing at the fact that this was *not* everything to the story.

"What?" Amanda said. "You have more, don't you?"

"Oh, you're gonna like this even less."

"Now you have to tell me."

Riley sighed. "So, you know how Oliver is very professional at work with you?"

"Yes."

"He was never like that with me. I don't know if it's because he trusted me because I was good with Zoe, or if I somehow made cheesy jokes so bad they got past his defenses, but . . . we were friends."

"*Were* friends?"

"I mean, we still are, but . . . at Christmas, we slept together."

"What?" Amanda said. She looked somewhere between pissed and shocked. "How?"

"He kissed me, and things went from there."

"While you were employed?"

Riley nodded.

"How?" Amanda almost yelled. "He didn't even tell me Zoe's name until I worked for him for two months!"

"I don't know! It's not because I'm special or anything. I know I'm not. I genuinely think it was because I got through to Zoe and we became friends because of that."

"I'm-I'm torn between being insulted he never attempted to befriend me and jealous of whatever skill you have to make him open up."

"Don't be jealous. It wasn't a skill. I think I just got lucky. Plus, I'm obviously going to know a lot about him considering how much I see his daughter and stay in his house."

"Yeah, maybe," Amanda said. "Was it good?"

"Was what good?"

"The sex."

Riley felt her cheeks heat. "I mean, yeah it was good. Look at him."

"I would ask for more information, but I don't want to be fired. At least he lives up to his looks."

"And then some," Riley said, trying not to think of their two nights together, and failing.

"So, what, you're co-parents with benefits now?"

"No, just co-parents. He wanted to date other women, and I couldn't be a sidepiece during that."

Amanda groaned. "Ugh, why do attractive men have to ruin their good looks like that? He really wanted to date other people?"

"Yep, I had to watch Zoe while he went on one."

"Gross," Amanda said, rolling her eyes. "Good on you for not letting him get away with that. I don't think I even want to know what standards he has for an actual girlfriend."

"You saw Sophie."

"Ugh, yes. I always got a weird feeling about her."

"You should have. She pushed Zoe and made her run away that night."

"What?"

"Yeah, and when I found out, I threatened to push her down a set of stairs. It wouldn't have been enough."

"Holy *shit*. That's badass."

"She deserved it."

"Uh, yeah. If there's one thing everyone knows not to mess with, it's Zoe."

Riley nodded in agreement. "Same goes for me."

"I can't believe I'm getting a niece," Amanda said. "I never thought you'd have kids."

"I always wanted them, remember? David didn't."

"Ugh, David." Amanda rolled her eyes again. "I don't know what it is about you, but you attract shitty men."

"Both of us do."

"Fair enough," Amanda muttered. "Maybe we should go for the men we're not attracted to and get the opposite result."

"You do that," Riley said. "I'll . . . I'll need some time before I date."

"Did David mess you up that bad?"

"Yes, but not just him. It's a little hard to date with Oliver right there."

"Do you have feelings for him?"

"Yeah," Riley admitted sadly. "Ones he will never return."

"He did say that once," Amanda said. "I accidentally misread what he was saying, and I thought he was into you or something. He was very sure he wasn't."

"Ouch," Riley said miserably.

"There are other guys out there," Amanda tried to say comfortingly.

"Yeah, but they'll have to wait. I think if things work out with this woman he went on a date with, I'll be able to move on."

"Maybe," Amanda said. "But I wouldn't worry too much about him. You have a lot of other good things going for you."

Riley smiled. "I really needed to hear that."

Amanda smiled back. "Any time."

Once the two sisters had talked for a solid hour, Riley had to get home. She tightly hugged Amanda, happy that things were feeling good between them for once. Amanda seemed to feel the same.

On the drive home, Riley's mind couldn't help but double back to Oliver. They now stood as co-parents and nothing else. Plus, he apparently had no feelings for her whatsoever. She also wasn't sure if he was still seeing that woman, or a new one, but ever since that first date, he had stayed away from her. So, she stayed away from him in that way too.

They were friends and co-parents. Maybe one day she would learn to be okay with that.

Chapter Twenty-Three

Riley

It was a chilly day. The sun was bright in the sky but doing nothing to warm the city. In the cold, the coffee shop was extremely busy. People lined up to get fresh coffee and Riley felt the heat of the business.

The lawyer had emphasized her need to be able to support herself and Zoe, so Riley was willing to put in more hours and work harder. Camilla appreciated it, but it meant she had less time to spend with her future daughter, which made childcare difficult.

She rarely saw Oliver too.

But it was worth it. The adoption was going smoothly, and the lawyer didn't anticipate any problems. While she felt bad for being so busy, she knew it was what she had to do.

Plus, the days went by incredibly fast. Camilla gave her a raise and let her close the shop with the newer employees. In the afternoons, she was there by herself to be able to balance the books and clean the storefront.

Things were calm for once.

Riley should have known something would ruin it.

As she was walking to her car, she stopped when she saw someone parked next to her. She gripped her keys tightly and wondered if she would be strong enough to knock someone out that wasn't drunk.

But then she recognized the car.

David.

But what in the world was he doing here? He was standing outside in the cold when Riley got to her own car and looking right at her. All he said was, "Sarah and I are done."

If it had been months ago, maybe Riley would have felt something hearing those words. Maybe she would have been happy or sad, anything. Instead, there was nothing.

"I'm sorry," was all she said.

"It was never going to work out anyway," David said. "She wasn't right for me."

"Why are you telling me this?" Riley asked.

"I still love you," he said, stepping closer. "I made a mistake; I should have never left you."

Riley wasn't sure what to do. "Uh, look David—"

He was right in front of her. There was a time when she would be excited to see him, where she wouldn't hesitate to kiss him and go back to their place. But that was a long time ago. She didn't feel that way anymore.

"We were right for each other," he said, taking her hands. Riley took a deep breath.

"Are you drunk right now?"

"We should get back together." David ignored her question.

"No," she said with a shake of her head. "You said it yourself, we're not good for each other."

"I was a fool."

"I can't believe I'm saying this, but you weren't."

"Riley—"

"No, David, I don't want to—" David cut her off by suddenly planting his lips on hers. She pushed him away with a force she didn't even know she had and yelled, "No! I don't love you anymore!"

"What?" he asked, but Riley was done listening to him. She wiped her mouth and jumped into her car, making sure to lock her doors.

Riley could taste he had been drinking whiskey. It burned on her mouth and threw her back to a time she desperately wished she could forget. Instead of thinking about it, she turned on the car and sped out of the parking lot.

She managed to keep her cool as she drove home. Her knuckles were white from gripping the steering wheel and she focused on nothing else. She arrived safely. The moment she pulled into the driveway, all thoughts flew out the window on what was going on with Oliver.

She didn't care if things were still awkward because of the woman he took on the date, or if he didn't like her. He knew her at her worst, and she needed him.

"Hey," Oliver said, meeting her in the foyer. "I think we should—"

He didn't get any further than that. Riley lost it and grabbed him, pulling him into a tight hug. His familiar scent calmed her and she sobbed into his shirt. His hands immediately went to her lower back and he began rubbing comforting circles against her skin.

"What is going on?" he asked softly. "Are you okay?"

She shook her head but did not let him go. Her hands bunched into his shirt.

"All right, it's gonna be okay." His voice was as warm and gentle as his hug. "Up you go."

He carried her to the couch and set her down. When he moved beside her, she scooted next to him and practically sat in his lap. She tearfully recounted what had happened while he listened intently. His face was kept in a tight, straight line, up until the part where David kissed her. At that, he took a deep breath, looking pissed.

"I can't even believe I used to be with him," Riley added. "I could taste he had been drinking. It was disgusting."

"He's disgusting. Going from you to Sarah and back to you is . . ." He trailed off. "I should start taking you to work."

"No, you're too busy for that. I'll get pepper spray."

"Riley, he kissed you without your consent."

"I'm aware." She opened her mouth to continue, but stopped when she saw his murderous expression. "I'll start scheduling more closers. I won't be alone at work anymore."

Oliver looked somewhat pleased with that answer.

"Good. But let me know if he does something like this again."

She nodded, but then remembered the one person she hadn't seen in the house.

"Oh God, where's Zoe?" she asked. "I really hope she doesn't see me upset."

"Zoe's at my dad's."

"Why?" She couldn't remember a time when Zoe had stayed with Jack.

"I figured we needed to talk about some stuff. It actually worked out, with what happened tonight."

"What do we need to talk about?" A new kind of fear set in. Was he about to ask her to move out? Was it that he and the woman were officially dating? This would go on record as one of the worst days ever if either were the case.

"It's not important now," Oliver said, shaking his head. "Not with you upset."

"I think it is if you have Zoe at your dad's. You never send her there. I'm going to worry more about it if you don't tell me."

He sighed. "Riley . . ."

"Oliver . . ." she parroted back. She mentally prepared herself for bad news.

"I wanted to talk about the things that happened recently."

"Right, okay." She took a deep breath. "We can do that."

"I don't really think now is the time."

"We never will if we don't do it now," Riley said. "Just tell me, please."

"That night, when Zoe asked you to be her mom . . . I wanted to make sure you were . . ." Oliver paused. "Still sober."

"Oh," Riley said.

"There isn't any judgment here if not," he said. "It was such a bad night for you, and I handled it so poorly that I-I wanted to know how much it affected you."

"Well, it was a close call," she admitted. "But honestly, no, I'm still sober and fine. Camilla now knows I don't drink, so she gave me a place to sleep and talk."

Oliver nodded. "Okay."

She stared at him for a long moment, and he stared back. He gently moved a piece of hair from her face. It was moments like this when Riley wondered if he truly had no feelings for her. With the way he was looking at her, she could swear she saw love in his eyes.

Riley wanted to ask him why he slept with her at Christmas, and she was almost brave enough to do it, but as she opened her mouth, no words came out.

The emotional exhaustion of the day hit her instead, and she knew there was no way she could do anything else difficult. She was done for the day.

"I'm gonna go to sleep. Goodnight, Oliver."

"Night," he said, nodding slowly.

Riley went upstairs to her bedroom. She brushed her teeth to get any remaining scent of David off of her before she laid down. She was exhausted, and her nerves were shaken at the events of the day, but she knew she was most unnerved at the idea of asking Oliver what happened at Christmas.

Deep down, she knew she was afraid of her worst fears being confirmed. She was afraid he was going to tell her he didn't see her that way and she wasn't good enough for him. That, coupled with the disaster that was her life, gave Oliver plenty of reason to look away.

And she couldn't even blame him.

Chapter Twenty-Four

Riley

Riley definitely had her fair share of hangovers, but usually they involved alcohol. They were awful and they never seemed to stop.

Somehow, emotional hangovers were worse.

She groaned and rubbed her hand over her eyes and cheeks. She didn't want to get up and face the day, but work was calling her name and that was a call she had to answer.

Slowly, she rolled out of bed and threw on jeans and a T-shirt. She paused at her door, not wanting to see Oliver. She knew he was up, since he always had been an early riser, but seeing him after how she was last night—that was going to be awkward.

She sighed and opened her door. She had to face him head on and deal with it.

She came down the stairs only to find Oliver had a cup of coffee ready for her. The gesture was small, and almost normal at this point, but it meant a lot after her terrible night.

"Thanks," Riley said.

"I know you're about to go to work where there is coffee but . . . I figured you would like some before you had to head in."

"I would. Thanks for always making me coffee."

"It's no problem," he said, and then he added, "How are you feeling?"

"Hungover, actually," Riley said. "Even if I didn't have anything to drink."

Oliver didn't seem to know what to say to that, but he looked at her with an intensity she hadn't felt in a long time. She had no clue what it meant.

"Do you think you might not go in, then?" he asked.

"I don't know," Riley said, sighing. "I don't have a closer."

"I'm actually worried about you going in."

"The shop needs me. He's not a big guy or anything. I can fend him off."

"You shouldn't have to," he said softly.

"But I do," she told him. "And unfortunately, I can't miss work, and even if I did, there's no telling if I would lose my mind being here all day. I need to do what I do best, and that's being busy."

Oliver sighed. "I can't talk you out of it?"

She shook her head.

"Fine," He said. "But please be safe. For me, okay?"

Riley nodded, shocked by the intensity of his words. Before she could leave, he swept her up in a hug, pressing her entire body to his. Her traitorous brain flashed back to what he felt like on top of her, but she forced that out of her head and focused on hugging him back.

She pulled away with a smile before her phone buzzed. She pulled it out, only to find David had called her. That sent a chill down her spine, but she ignored it and left for work.

Driving in, she tried not to think of everything going on. When she got to the shop, she did her normal opening routine, up until about noon, when Sarah walked in.

She seemed down, and as much as Riley wanted to tell her to leave, she couldn't. She was still angry for what Sarah did, but this was still the woman who brushed Riley's hair for prom. This was the same woman who had cried to Riley after dropping out of college, scared of what her mother would say. They shared many years of being friends, and it wasn't possible to forget any of them.

But they were still tainted.

"Hey," Riley said, sitting down.

"Hey, how are you?"

"I'm fine," Riley replied with a sigh. The conversation already felt stilted. "What's wrong?"

Sarah shook her head. "What happened . . . was a mistake."

"You and David."

She nodded.

For a while, Riley couldn't think about how what happened *did* happen. It was burning a hole in her, and somehow, she assumed it was her fault. Maybe if she had been a better girlfriend, maybe if she gave David more attention, or hung out with Sarah more, then this would have never happened.

But there was a story there, and maybe it was time to hear it.

"What actually happened?" Riley asked. It was a sore spot, like a bruise that was forever tender, but she needed to know.

Sarah sighed. "Are you sure you want to know? You always said you didn't."

"I am," Riley said.

"Well, you know that I never really liked David," she started. "And I thought he was a bad influence on you. I mean, you started working at a bar instead of an office job, and then you started drinking more. I was worried, but you seemed happy and so I didn't say anything else. But then, you kept drinking, and Jane called me, so I went to go off on David—about how bad he was and how he treated you.

"And the thing was, he *knew* he wasn't good for you, and in that moment, I saw him as a real person and not this loser my friend was dating. So, we talked, and he told me about his family, and his life. I felt for him, you know?"

Riley crossed her arms and tried to keep her emotions in cheek. Hearing this was way harder than she imagined.

Sarah sighed and continued. "The first time we kissed, I felt so bad. I felt like an awful friend, and that I betrayed you, and then it kept happening. David kept saying he would talk to you, though he never did. And I knew you would want to hear it from him, so I kept it to myself. I made a lot of mistakes, and I thought it was because he had this sob story, that I could fix him. And I was wrong."

"You're right about one thing," Riley said. "David wasn't right for me. I guess I was so happy to have an adult boyfriend I let a lot of myself go. And deep down, I knew I wasn't happy. But that still doesn't make it okay that you did what you did. I mean, I would have rather heard it right when it began instead of finding out like I did."

"And now I know that. David made it sound like you guys were so unhappy."

"We were, but I didn't know that then."

"I am sorry. I know it's going to take a lot more than that for us to be friends again, but I am. I regret it."

"So, I do need to confess something," Riley said. "I did know you and David broke up."

"How?"

"David came to see me after work yesterday," she explained.

"Oh, why?"

"He said he wanted to get back together," Riley said. "And he kissed me."

"I'm sorry . . . what?" Sarah asked, her voice sharp. "You're back together with him?"

"I'm not."

"Was this some sort of revenge tactic?" Without waiting for an answer, she added, "God, that would be something you would do because you can't let something go."

"Okay," Riley said, keeping her voice level. She should have seen this coming. "You cheated with him first, and I never wanted to kiss him or be with him again. I was telling you so you knew. I was being upfront with you, unlike either of you were ever with me."

"Whatever," Sarah said. "I know when you're lying, and you wanted to get revenge because you're still mad. But two wrongs don't make a right."

"I didn't—"

"This will come back and bite you in the ass. And to think I apologized to you! God, you are so much like David, it's not funny. Just remember when you're old and drunk and he leaves you for someone hotter."

With that, Sarah stormed out of the coffee shop.

"What the hell just happened?" Riley muttered to herself. She should have known Sarah would jump to conclusions. She should have known this whole conversation was going to go south, and it did.

Hearing how Sarah and David got together hurt, but it was nothing like being accused of getting revenge. That was what Sarah thought of her, that was what she probably would have done, if it hadn't been for how her life had changed. Was she really that bad of a person back then? So much so her best friend genuinely thought she would want revenge in such a horrible way?

Of course, Sarah was probably hurt too, and unstable after the breakup. She had never handled her emotions well, and breakups always made it so much worse.

It still hurt, though. The fact that Sarah assumed Riley would want revenge was tough to bear. But what was even harder was the fact that at a certain point in her life, that would have been something she would have considered.

Oliver

"You didn't talk to her?" Jack asked while Oliver was picking up Zoe from her sleepover.

"No, something else happened," Oliver said. "I got through the talk about her sobriety, but not about the . . . other thing."

Jack sighed. "It's true you can't plan these things, but don't let this get away from you."

"Her ex is trying to get back together with her. She doesn't want to, but it's an issue."

Jack nodded. "That is unfortunate. I guess it would be best to give her time."

"That's what I was thinking," he replied, sighing.

"Don't worry too much," Jack said. "You will talk to her when she's ready."

Oliver nodded, but then Zoe wanted to leave. Jack gave him a small smile as he left.

As he drove home, Zoe asked about Riley and what she was up to. He told her Riley was at work, but that only made her want to see Riley *at* work.

He had never been to the shop before, and it was incredibly out of the way, but he needed to be sure she was okay. After the previous night, he wished she'd stayed at home where she was safe.

But she was at work, and both he and Zoe wanted to check up on her.

He decided to take them there. It was a nice place. The classic Nashville wood tones were throughout, and the shop had people almost to the door. It was homey, and he could see why Riley loved it.

Oliver planned on getting in and out. He didn't want to corner her in her workplace, especially after she had been so many times.

But then again, after the events of the previous night, he also wanted to make sure she was okay.

They got to the counter, where a woman with tan skin and dark hair was taking orders. Oliver ordered a latte for himself and a cinnamon roll for Zoe. As they were waiting for their food, Riley came around the corner. He hoped he could get out of the shop without her seeing them, but Zoe had other plans.

"Mommy!" she called.

Oliver saw Riley nearly jump out of her skin, and he felt bad for even bringing Zoe here. However, she put on a smile when she saw the girl, which looked tired, even to him.

"Hey, kid," Riley said. "What brings you two here?"

"Sorry," he said. "She wanted to see where you work."

"Wait, is this Oliver?" the woman from the register asked, walking over. A guy was manning the line now.

"Yeah," Riley said.

"Oh, hi! I'm Camilla." She reached her hand across the counter to shake Oliver's. "It's so nice to finally meet you."

"You too," he said, returning the gesture. He took a second look at her, now knowing she was Riley's close friend, and someone Riley spent a lot of her time with.

"Here, I'll bring the food out if you guys go grab a table," Riley offered, and she grabbed Oliver's drink and Zoe's food. He picked a table and got Zoe settled in.

"Is everything okay?" he asked.

"Yep," she answered. "He called me, but Dustin said he would stay late, so I won't be alone."

Oliver felt something loosen in his chest.

"Please talk to me about anything other than David."

"There's the scheduling for next week," Oliver said. Riley looked relieved. She glanced at Camilla, who gestured for her to stay where she was. Oliver was grateful—after last night, they didn't have much time to talk.

"Okay, what's up?"

"So, I'm at the office for a full week," Oliver said. "Are you working here at all during the day?"

"Actually, I'm here most days. I was going to mention it, but I can't watch Zoe."

"I can watch myself," Zoe offered.

Riley shook her head. "Not yet, kid."

He sighed. "It's really getting hard to schedule things around our jobs."

"I can ask for time off, I guess."

"No, I don't want you putting things in jeopardy here. You like this job."

"I do," Riley said. "I mean, what I would suggest is maybe putting Zoe in an early learning center. She's old enough and isn't far away from school."

"She wouldn't like that," he replied. "She hated daycare."

"Well, it would be a bit different than a daycare. It's technically school."

"I want to go!" Zoe insisted and Oliver turned to his daughter, shocked.

"You do?" Riley asked.

"Yeah, I wanna learn to read like you!"

"Well, Zoe, school would be with other kids," Oliver explained. "And not at home."

"That sounds fun!" Zoe said with a bright smile.

Oliver never thought he would see the day where Zoe willingly wanted to be out of the house. He turned to Riley, who shrugged.

"I think it's worth a shot," she said. "My mom's already been looking."

"Of course she has," he retorted.

"Landon goes to one," Riley said. "And Amanda says he likes it. They spend most of their time outside playing."

"I wanna do that!" Zoe exclaimed.

"Okay, fine." Oliver sighed. "We'll give it a shot."

Riley nodded and then turned to see the line growing again. "We'll talk later. I have to get back to work."

He nodded and watched her walk away, feeling conflicted. He had always known Zoe would eventually be more independent, but nothing was like the day where it actually happened. It hurt, but he was happy at the same time, and he didn't know what to feel about it.

The next morning, Riley provided a few names for early learning centers. Oliver knew he wasn't going to be able to get off work to go look at them, so he let her pick out whichever one Zoe liked the most.

His personal phone rang later that day while he was at work, and he was surprised to see Jane's name on the caller ID.

"Hello?" Oliver answered. "Jane?"

"Oliver! So glad you answered. I wasn't sure you had my number."

"Riley gave it to me when we started the adoption process. Is everything okay?"

"Have you heard from Riley today?" Jane asked, her voice tense.

"Uh, not since this morning, why?" He was suddenly worried something happened. Images of her getting into a car wreck with Zoe, or something worse flashed into his mind.

"David called me and said he and Riley were getting back together."

Something did not compute. "What?"

"Yes!" Jane said. "This would be a huge mistake. She told me you two weren't in a romantic relationship, but I am asking you to talk to her and try to get her to see sense."

"She's—Riley isn't with David. She's with Zoe right now."

"But do you know if she's been in contact with David?"

He sighed. "She has."

"See? This could be a horrible mistake—"

"Jane, she said she hated him. And he's not exactly the cream of the crop."

"It's not like she has you, though, does she?" Jane insisted.

He felt himself get frustrated, but it wasn't worth losing his patience at Jane. She was right—they weren't dating.

"I don't think she would go back to him," he said. "They had a huge disagreement the other night."

"Oliver, I'm not stupid. I know you have feelings for her."

"I'm not going to bring this up to her while she's dealing with her ex," he said, shaking his head at how to-the-point Jane could be sometimes. "I'm giving her time."

"And if you give her too much, that man will manipulate her and have her right back at his side."

"What do you mean?"

"David is manipulative. More so than Riley ever told you. He manipulated Riley into that bar job so she would be dependent on him. He manipulated Sarah into a relationship behind Riley's back. Why do you think I kept her on

Facebook? I knew what was happening. I don't know what he has said to her but if he senses any insecurity in Riley, he will expose it and take advantage of it."

Oliver didn't want to believe it, but he could see it happening. If he had been manipulated into a relationship with Sophie, who's to say Riley couldn't be manipulated back into a relationship with David?

"I'll call her," he said quietly.

"Thank you," Jane said. "I don't want her to go back to someone like him."

"Me either."

Jane hung up and he immediately dialed Riley. Her phone rang once, and then went straight to voicemail. That did nothing to cure his anxiety about the situation. He checked her location, which she had shared with him for when she was with Zoe, and there was no luck there, either. In fact, her phone didn't even pop up.

On one hand, Oliver knew her phone could have died. She had an older model that didn't hold its battery life. On the other hand, she could have ignored his calls.

Riley was supposed to be out with Zoe either way, so he couldn't know anything until he got home. His anxiety high, he had no idea how he was going to make it through the remainder of the day now that he was worried about Riley.

Chapter Twenty-Five

Riley

It was the afternoon when Riley finally decided which center was going to be best for Zoe. The place was near home, the kids spent most of their time outdoors, and had flexible scheduling. Plus, while Riley was talking to the enrollment counselor, Zoe already made a friend.

Tuition was expensive and Riley hoped Oliver would cover some of the cost. If not, then it was going to take up way more of her income than she wanted, but she would do it if she needed to.

She came home at five, right when Oliver would be done with his day too. She tried to text him, only to find her phone died at some point, which was frustrating. Depending on how much Oliver was willing to cover for tuition, Riley was going to have to consider getting a new phone. She put hers on the charger as soon as she got inside.

Oliver came in a little later. Zoe ran to hug him, but Riley immediately noticed he looked tense. She wondered if she should even bring up the center.

"Mommy found a very fun school!" Zoe said, and Riley immediately knew she was going to have to explain. "Can I go?"

"We'll talk about it later, Zoe," Oliver said. Zoe seemed appeased and ran to play in the living room.

"Everything okay?" Riley asked.

"Were you really looking at schools all day?"

She was a little offended at the question. "Yeah. Since when do you care where I am?"

Oliver sighed. "Your mom called today."

"She called you? Why?"

"David called her and made it sound like you guys were back together," he explained. "And you didn't answer your phone all day."

"Wait, excuse me? He did *what*?" Riley said. "And you believed I would do that?"

"I don't know. Your mom made it sound like he's manipulative and—"

"He is, but that doesn't mean I want to be with him," Riley said. "God, I can't believe you would think that."

"It's not like it's impossible!" he said. "And if you were with him, then I would have to consider the fact my daughter would be around him."

"Our daughter," Riley reminded him. "And I wouldn't do that to her."

She shook her head, trying to make sense of the situation. She was frustrated with Oliver, but mostly frustrated with David. Why would he bring Jane into this? He called *her*, sure, but she never thought he would go far enough to call her mom. Unless he was trying to pressure her into a relationship.

"I've had enough of this," Riley said to herself. "I need to go see David."

"Why?"

"I need to put an end to this. He needs to stop bothering me at work, bothering my family, and thinking I want to be with him. He's not good with confrontation so I'm gonna go do exactly what he hates."

"Are you sure?"

"No, but it's better than sitting around and doing nothing."

"Okay," he replied, but he grabbed her arm gently. "Just come back, please."

A moment passed where neither of them said anything. Riley wasn't sure what made him say what he did, but it felt intimate in a way she wasn't used to. She stared at him for a long moment, taking in his worried expression, wondering what could be going through his mind.

She said gently, "I'll always come back." It was true—she never wanted to leave.

Oliver nodded and she was grateful he didn't try to argue. She walked out of the house and climbed into her car. She drove down familiar roadways until she arrived at the apartment she used to live in.

The last time he was here, she was a different woman. She drank every night, worked at a shitty bar, and had no plans for her future. She was in a bad relationship and she didn't even know it.

Things changed. There was a sense of nostalgia, walking up to the old place, but not a fond one. It was a reminder of where she had been, but not something she wanted to come back to.

Riley knocked on the door and was surprised when Sarah opened it.

"Where's David?" Riley demanded, ignoring her surprise.

"Why are you here?" Sarah said.

"Why are *you* here?" Riley asked.

"I came to talk to David. He said he wanted us to get back together."

It occurred to Riley then what an absolute piece of shit David was. Riley refused to be with him, so he went back to Sarah like he never said any of those things to her.

"Let me guess, you're here to get him back too?" Sarah said with obvious disdain.

"No, actually. I'm here to tell that little shitweasel to stay the fuck away me," Riley snapped.

Sarah looked shocked at her tone, but Riley saw David come out of the hallway.

"Riley?" David said. "What are you doing here?"

She pointed at him. "Listen, you need to leave me alone. Seriously, or I *will* get a restraining order."

"I haven't even talked to you."

"Oh, so my mom is lying when you called her today? Or the cameras at the coffee shop for when you forced me to kiss you?" Riley barked. Sarah looked in between them with wide eyes, but Riley was on a roll. "I like my life right now, you asshole. I have a daughter and a steady fucking job using my degree. I don't have time for your drama. I don't have time for your manipulation. Leave me the fuck alone."

Both David and Sarah were stunned by her outburst, and it gave Riley a sense of satisfaction she hadn't felt in a long time.

"You're lying," David said. "None of that is true. It's not on your Facebook."

"I don't use Facebook," Riley said, rolling her eyes. "And you know what?" She took out her phone and deleted her profile. She had been meaning to do it for a while and knew exactly where to go. "It's gone. I don't need social media to tell you guys I'm happy now. So leave me alone."

"You're so pathetic it isn't even funny, Riley," he said. "You come here acting like you have it all together, but you don't. You can say what you want, but I know you work at a shitty coffee shop with someone from high school and bought a fancy car to make it look like you have it together, but you never will. You're a failure."

Those words could have easily hurt, but Riley wouldn't let them. She was done feeling bad about what she had.

"That's fine if that's what you want to believe," she said, shrugging, "And if you do think that, then you should have no problem staying the hell away. I'm serious. I have a lawyer. I can easily pull the video footage from the night you camped out by my car, drunk, and kissed me against my consent. I will put you through the ringer, and I'm not afraid to do it."

"Did you really do that?" Sarah asked David, her voice quiet. It was the first thing she had said in a while.

"She's lying," David repeated, but Riley could tell his voice was wavering. He didn't like being threatened.

"Try me," Riley said. "You two have a nice life. I'm done."

She left it at that. Neither of them followed her, so she took it as a good sign. She didn't bother to think about what would happen with Sarah and David after that because, frankly, she didn't care. If he wanted to flip-flop between the two of them, then David could have Sarah, because she was the only one who would put up with it.

Riley drove home, and when she was back in her own driveway, she took a deep breath to calm herself before going inside. It was past dark, and Zoe was in bed, but Oliver was awake. He had been waiting on her.

"Hey," he called as she walked in. "How did it go?"

"I called him a shitweasel and threatened him with a restraining order," she said. "Sarah was also there, so I have a feeling he's done talking to me for a while."

"Thank God." Oliver let out a breath of relief. Riley smiled and walked over to sit next to him on the couch. "I really don't like that guy."

"Neither do I," Riley said. "And you," she added, pointing at him, "I'm not getting back together with a person like that, ever."

"I get it," he said. "I'm sorry I was worried. It's just that . . . after Zoe's mom left—"

"I'm not her," Riley reminded him, "and I don't want to be."

Oliver stared at her, as if he were waiting for her to take back what she said. She knew she wasn't going to. Meeting Zoe had been exactly what she needed to get her life on track, and now that it was, she refused to go back.

"I guess I should count myself lucky I've met someone so willing to be here for Zoe," Oliver said.

"Are you kidding? I'm the lucky one. You could have easily told me I was too close to Zoe and there would have been nothing I could do about it. So . . . thank you for giving me a chance to be her mom, Oliver."

They were sitting so close, either of them could have easily leaned in in that moment, but everything felt heavier than it used to. Now there was a child between then, and neither of them could afford to mess up Zoe in the hopes of starting a relationship.

Oliver had never admitted to liking her romantically, either.

And despite this, she knew what he felt like. She knew what it was like to be held by him, and what it was like to wake up next to him. She wanted that more than anything else. But it wasn't going to happen, not when she was second-best. And she still didn't have an answer on what he had with that date of his. Maybe this new woman was amazing, and he really liked her.

Plus, she had only just gotten rid of David. Her ex was a wound that hadn't healed.

Riley leaned away from him, breaking their eye contact. It was a sore reminder that she wasn't what he wanted or needed.

"I'm gonna go do dishes," she said before getting up. He let her, which she figured was an answer all on its own.

"Wait, I'll help," Oliver said. "We need to discuss Zoe anyway."

Riley nodded, and they walked into the kitchen to discuss what to do about the school Zoe wanted to go to.

In the end, they decided Oliver would cover the costs of daycare since that was an expense he was used to covering. Riley was adamant she could cover some of it, but he insisted, and she knew eventually she may have to move out, so she agreed to let him do it.

Riley

Riley spent the next day at work, busy as usual. Even though the shop wasn't packed, she was plenty busy preparing for payday and getting everything ready for a new employee that they were hiring.

She sat at a back table working when she felt eyes boring into her. She looked up and groaned when she saw it was Sarah.

"I was serious about the restraining order," Riley said.

"I'm not here to yell at you," she admitted. "But I knew you wouldn't answer if I called."

Riley crossed her arms. "Would you blame me?"

"I want to talk. I can go, though."

Knowing she couldn't deny someone when they wanted to talk, Riley sighed. "Fine, but it can't be forever. I do have work to do."

Sarah nodded quickly and sat down. She was so tense, Riley thought maybe she would run if there were any loud noises.

"I wanted to apologize for how I've been acting," she said. "I don't have an explanation but . . . I think David got in my head, and you coming and yelling at him . . . it woke me up. You don't yell like that very often."

"I know. But he called my mom and said we were together. I couldn't let that go on."

Sarah nodded. "You shouldn't have. But by the way, he was messaging me all that time too. I think he was seeing who would come back first."

"Dirtbag." Riley rolled her eyes.

"I still love him," Sarah said.

She felt a bubble of anger, but pushed it down. "It doesn't last."

"Really?"

Riley shook her head. "No, manipulation doesn't last. The hurt does, though."

Sarah looked down, obviously feeling guilty. "I know, and I had a part in that."

"You did," Riley said.

Sarah sighed. "I made a huge mistake. You know the story, but I wanted to really say how sorry I am."

Riley nodded. "Apology accepted, I guess. But that trust is gone."

"I know, and I'm not expecting it to be back. I only want to move forward."

"I do too."

Sarah's tone changed, and she said, "So, I decided to go back to school. It's out of town. I had applied when David and I broke up, and I almost went back on it yesterday, but I should go, right?"

"If you want to."

"I do. I'm twenty-six and still live with my mom. I've only worked dead-end jobs. I need more out of life, and not just what David wants me to be."

"I understand that," Riley said.

"I guess I'm sort of inspired by you," she replied. "All of that stuff about your job and adopting a child . . . is that true?"

Riley nodded again. "It is."

"Your mom posted a photo of you with her at Christmas. You must be close if she met your mom. Was that her dad in the photos?"

She bristled at the mention of Oliver. "Yes."

"He's cute."

"We're friends," Riley said. "He's . . . seeing someone."

"And he let you adopt her?"

"Yep. I'm really grateful for it."

Sarah nodded and got a look on her face as if she were about to give Riley advice.

"Anyway, I'm really happy with the arrangement," Riley cut her off.

Sarah blinked, and the reality of their ruined friendship settled in. Sarah looked down and cleared her throat. "Well, anyway—I didn't want to leave on a bad note."

Riley nodded. "I'm glad you didn't."

Sarah smiled. "I'll leave you alone now. Thanks for talking to me."

"I'm glad we settled things. Good luck out there."

And then she was gone. Riley watched her go. She knew deep down Sarah wasn't going to be her friend anymore, but she still hoped Sarah found herself on a better path than she had been on.

"Everything okay?" a voice asked. Riley was jostled out of her thoughts by Camilla, who had walked up to her.

"Yeah, everything's fine," she said. "Just burying the hatchet with my old best friend."

"Sarah?"

"Yeah, but it's all good. I think all of it is officially over."

Camilla gave her a relieved smile. "That's great, Riley."

"So, what's up?"

"I need to head to the bank," Camilla said. "I'm finally going to ask about opening a new location."

"Yes! I'm so excited for you!" Riley cheered. That had been something Camilla wanted to do for a while, but before Riley, she had no clue if she had enough money to manage it.

Riley had been able to assure her a second location would be profitable, and she had most of the money to open it.

"Let's hope it goes well."

"Do you have the bank statements I gave you?"

"I do, and the profit reports you made. What would I do without you?"

"Be behind on taxes." Riley smirked.

Camilla laughed. "You're right. So, are you okay to man the fort?"

"Sure," Riley said. "You go charm some bankers."

Camilla laughed and left the store. Riley collected her work and moved to the counter where she made sure they weren't behind on anything and helped where she could. The day flew by, and Camilla came in an hour before closing.

"Hey," Riley said. "How did it go?"

"Oh, uh, it went okay."

Riley frowned. "That doesn't sound like good news."

Camilla gestured to a table and Riley abandoned her station to sit down.

"So, they agree it's best to open a new location, but they aren't willing to finance it."

"Why not?"

"They said the financial risk is too great, but *I* know it would go well. Especially with you at the helm of it."

"I mean I only run the numbers . . ."

Camilla gave her a look that told Riley she did way more than she knew. Riley decided not to argue the point.

"Basically, they said I need to find an investor for about ten thousand dollars. Someone okay with high risk—higher than what they can deal with. Where am I going to find someone I trust enough to invest? How will I split the profits, and how can I guarantee they won't screw me over?"

Riley's mind was turning, crunching numbers to figure out exactly how much she had saved. She knew she had a lot, and when she bought her car, something told her not to spend all of her savings on a down payment. Maybe this was it.

"How much did you say you needed again?"

"Ten thousand, if I want to get a location in East Nashville, which would be *perfect*."

"It would be," Riley agreed. "*I* could invest."

"Wait, seriously?" Camilla asked.

"Yeah, I have that much saved up. I didn't spend it all on my car like I thought I might. I elected to finance it because I felt like I needed to. Maybe this is what I needed to do."

"Wait, are you serious? You have that much money saved up?"

"I was planning on moving out eventually, but I can put it back a bit."

Camilla shook her head. "I don't want to ask you to do that."

"Why not? Things with Oliver are fine. I could always room with you if it gets too bad."

Camilla broke out into a wide smile. "I would totally let you! Plus, since you're an investor, I would share the profits with you, and if it's anything like this location, then it should be pretty good. You'd have your money back in no time."

Riley nodded. She knew how much Camilla was making. It was a smart move—if the new location worked out.

"I'd wanna talk about the new location and your plans for it if I'm investing."

"Of course," Camilla said. "I should have a contract drawn up. I've got so much to do before we settle. Are you sure you're in?"

Riley considered it for a moment longer and made sure she was okay with her decision. It felt right. She was pretty sure this was the only time she was going to have an opportunity like this.

"I am. Let's have a contract drawn up."

Chapter Twenty-Six

Oliver

Being in love was weird. Oliver felt like he was in limbo whenever he saw Riley, and he wasn't sure what to do about it. He knew eventually they were going to have to talk, but there always seemed to be something that came up that interrupted them.

First, it was Zoe wanting to call Riley mom, and then it was finding an early learning center for Zoe. He was fine with the distraction. He was waiting for either her to bring up their relationship, or for him to finally get the courage to possibly get rejected.

Again.

And waiting was fine, he decided. They had to tread carefully, especially where Zoe was concerned. Plus, Riley's ex had thrown a wrench in the plans too.

Oliver took it day by day. It was all he could do.

"Hey, can I talk to you about something?" Riley asked after she got home from the coffee shop.

He nodded. "Yeah, what's up?"

"You're cool with me living here for a while, right?"

Oliver blinked, confused. "Why do you ask?"

"Camilla is going to open a second coffee shop, and I was considering investing in it."

"Wow, that's a really smart business move."

"I'm hoping so, but it's going to wipe out my savings." She sighed. "It's a good idea, but I moved in when I was still a nanny, so I guess I'm asking if it's still okay I stay here."

Oliver hadn't exactly thought of Riley moving out because he enjoyed her living with him. He imagined any empty house, where it was him and no one else. He didn't really want to go back.

"Yeah, of course you can."

"Are you sure? I know it's sort of weird I'm here when I'm not your employee anymore."

"I like having you here," he said.

"You do?" she asked, as if she were genuinely surprised by that. "I mean, it's your house, and I'm not even paying rent."

"I've been alone for four years now," Oliver explained. "It's nice having someone else around."

"Okay, but you'll tell me if I'm overstaying my welcome, right?"

"I don't think you could."

Riley laughed. "You say that now, but you never know."

He shrugged. He didn't know how to tell her he could never imagine getting tired of her, that he wanted to wake up with her next to him every day.

"Thank you though . . . for letting me stay," Riley said. "Wiping out my entire savings is scary, but I think it'll be good for me. I'll get a good return."

"If it's as busy as I saw the other day, then you will."

Riley nodded. She turned away from him, mentioning something about some work she needed to do, and he could only watch her walk away. She had come such a long way from the woman he met a few months ago.

Riley Emerson never ceased to surprise him.

Chapter Twenty-Seven

Riley

When Jane called Riley to ask if Zoe could spend the night, she was shocked—so shocked she could only say sure and didn't even question it. When the night came, and Zoe seemed excited to spend a night away from home, Riley brought her over to Jane's house.

"Don't look so worried," Jane assured her. "I need to get to know my granddaughter."

"I'm surprised you're not saying it's weird I adopted a kid."

"She's a good one, and besides, since when do I stop you from doing anything?"

"True."

Riley couldn't believe Zoe was so comfortable around her mother, and her mother was so kind to the little girl. Zoe could truly warm the heart of anyone around her.

When Zoe was ready to be left alone with Jane, Riley decided it was time for her to go. Zoe gave her a kiss before telling her adoptive mother goodbye. Jane looked excited to play with her granddaughter—a look Riley hadn't seen in a long time.

She decided to visit Camilla that night. They discussed business logistics until Camilla's wife demanded they do something fun. It was a weekend, so they wound up going shopping to try to fill the time. It was a great night, and Riley felt way better than she had when she was drinking.

She came home in a good mood and ran into Oliver as he was heading to bed. They exchanged a short conversation before he excused himself to get some sleep.

There was only one other thing she wanted in her life, and he was the same man living with her. The same one who had made a million mistakes but been there when it counted.

Riley shook the thought out of her head and went to bed. She wasn't ready for that kind of commitment anyway.

The next morning, she headed to pick up Zoe. She hadn't heard from the girl or her mother, so she hoped everything was fine. When Riley walked in, she found both of them eating breakfast and Zoe in a good mood.

"Mommy!" Zoe yelled, abandoning her breakfast and running to Riley. She jumped into Riley's arms to get a tight hug.

"Hey, kiddo," Riley said, smiling. "How did it go?"

"I had so much fun! I want to come back soon."

"Okay, well maybe we can work something out, unless your Gran had *too* much fun." Riley looked at Jane who was cleaning up toys Riley didn't recognize.

"Don't you dare insinuate that," Jane said. "She is my first granddaughter and the *only* grandchild who doesn't terrorize my house. Now, did you and Oliver talk?"

"Talk about what?"

"Oh, come on. You know what."

"Mom . . ." Riley said. "I don't . . . we don't—"

"Riley, don't lie to me."

Riley sighed. "We didn't talk."

"You need to," Jane said. "No good relationships start with secrets."

Zoe glanced at them, and Riley asked the little girl to get her bag, leaving Riley and Jane alone.

"Can we not talk about this in front of her? I don't want her getting ideas."

"Fine," Jane said. "I admire you not putting everything in front of your child, but you and Oliver must talk so I can have more grandkids."

Riley's jaw dropped and Jane only gave her a knowing look.

"Time to change the subject," Riley muttered. "I have news."

"If you're telling me you're adopting another child, I must ask that you at least let me have coffee first."

"It's not another child. It's about work. I'm going to invest in Camilla's new coffee location."

"Really?"

"Yes," she replied. "I know it's going to do well, and she needs the extra investment money in order to get a better location. I know it's not the best idea, considering the circumstances—"

"I think it's a great idea, Riley," Jane said. Her voice was sincere, but Riley stared at her mother anyway. It had been a long time since she heard any word of praise from her mom.

"What?"

"You don't have to pay rent, and your new car was discounted. I know how busy Camilla's coffee shop is. If she's opening another location, then it would be unwise not to invest."

"But . . . I thought you'd hate the idea."

"Now why would I do that?"

"Because I need to find a place of my own and I'm spending my savings on a coffee shop."

Jane shook her head. "No, you're investing it in something you believe you will get a profit on. It's a smart move. And besides, shouldn't Zoe's parents be together?"

"Not together as in . . . dating," Riley said, feeling nervous. "But it's best that we live together, yes."

"Then you'll be fine," Jane said, smiling. "I'm proud of you, Riley."

Riley stopped. "You wha—?" she asked in disbelief.

"I said I'm proud of you. Why wouldn't I be?"

"Because you seem to have a problem with everything I do, mom. And no problems with anything Amanda ever does."

There. Riley said it. She said the one thing that had bothered her for years. In the time she imagined this conversation, Riley always thought her mom would fight her on it or be defensive of her point of view. Instead, Jane's expression grew into something even more surprising: guilt.

"I've been too hard on you, Riley," she said.

Hearing that was a shock, to say the least.

"What?"

"I said I have been too hard on you. You've always been a smart woman and when you were with David, I saw a lot of your father in you. That scared me. And then I let my fears get in the way of everything. I wound up pushing you away instead of bringing you closer. So, for that . . . I'm sorry."

Riley could have cried right on the spot from relief. Finally, *finally*, her mom said it. Maybe Jane wasn't as stubborn as Riley always thought.

"Thank you," she said, hugging her mom tightly. "I really needed to hear that. And I'm sorry . . . for even being with David in the first place."

"I realize I was playing favorites for a long time. It's that . . . you look so much like your father. It hurts sometimes."

Riley looked down, feeling guilty for something that wasn't even her fault.

"But that's my issue as your mother, and I should have never let it affect you," Jane said, shaking her head. "I want us to be better from now on."

"I do too." Riley's voice was thick. Somehow, this time, she believed it was possible.

Riley drove home with tears in her eyes. She felt both raw and healed at the same time. The conversation with Jane was more than needed, but it was bittersweet at the same time. Riley finally felt she and her mom were on solid ground, and that was all she wanted for years.

She pulled into her driveway and got Zoe inside, her mind on dinner. Her thoughts were all over the place, so she felt like this was a night that justified going out. She was nowhere near up for cooking.

When Oliver arrived home, Riley broached the topic, wondering if he would be interested. Apparently, his day hadn't been easy either so he was more than happy to get food from somewhere else. Riley had been willing to go get it and bring it home, but Zoe was antsy and tired of being in the house, so they all piled into Oliver's car and went to a nearby Mexican restaurant.

It was a busy night, and Zoe made it all the more hectic. She loved going out to eat, but she also made a huge mess that Riley had to clean up. Oliver wound up paying for the meal, and they drove home after Zoe's bedtime.

It was his turn to put her to bed, and Riley laid on the couch while he did so. She was emotionally exhausted from the day and was more than ready to go to sleep, but her mind wouldn't turn off.

Oliver came downstairs looking just as tired. She almost wanted to run away from him, but she didn't want to be alone.

"Hey," he said, sitting next to her.

"Hey. Did Zoe go to sleep okay?"

"She was exhausted, so yes," he said. "How did it go at your mom's? Zoe seemed happy."

"It went well," Riley said. "She and my mom get along great. Who would have thought?"

"I sure didn't, but I'm happy they do. Your mom didn't say anything to you that upset you, right?"

"No," Riley said softly. "We actually had a good conversation for once about how hard she is on me. I think we're on the road to healing."

"That's great, Riley." His tone was gentle. "I'm really happy for you."

"Me too. It seems like everything is working out for once," Riley told him. "Unless the coffee shop goes under, then I'm fucked."

"I doubt that will happen," he said, shaking his head. "You and Camilla have done the research and it's going to work out."

"I hope so," she said. She looked at him for a long moment. Deep down, she wished more than anything that a relationship with him had worked out, that they could have been together. While other things were fixing themselves, Oliver and Riley had been at a definite standstill. "And thank you for letting me stay here longer. If you ever need me to move out—"

"Why would I need you to?"

Riley opened her mouth to say, *in case you found someone else.* But she couldn't. The idea broke her in more ways than one.

"I don't know. I think I'm expecting something to go wrong. Things are too good right now."

Oliver nodded, looking relieved. "I don't think that's going to happen. You deserve good things, Riley."

Her mouth went dry. A silence fell over them as she worked out what to say. In that time, Oliver brushed a piece of hair out of her face and smiled.

"Get some sleep. Zoe will probably be up before dawn and it's your turn to take her to school."

Riley nodded, trying and failing to put all thoughts of Oliver out of her mind. He walked to his own room, and Riley found herself wishing she followed him.

Chapter Twenty-Eight

Oliver

"Daddy," Zoe said, her voice teasing. Oliver didn't expect to hear anything exciting from his daughter, but he listened anyway.

It was the afternoon and he was the one who was picking her up from school.

"What, Zoe?" he replied, glancing at her in the rearview mirror. They were on their way home. Usually she was quiet, needing some time to herself after playing with other kids all day.

"You love Mommy, right?"

Oliver's eyes shot to the road. How the hell did he answer *that*? "Wh-what?"

"You love Mommy, right?"

"You mean like you love Mommy?"

Zoe shook her head. "No, like a Daddy loves a Mommy."

Oliver's face was on fire. It was one thing to be called out by a member of his family, but his daughter? This was a new low.

"Yes, I do," he said.

"Gran says you two are being dumb. What does that mean?"

Oliver sighed. "Wait, when did you hear that?"

"Gran told me when I was over there. She said Mommy loves Daddy and Mommy and Daddy are being dumb."

"Wait, she said Mommy loves Daddy?"

Zoe rolled her eyes and nodded.

"That's not true, Zoe."

"Yes, it is."

"No, it isn't."

"Did you ask Mommy?" Zoe asked.

Oliver didn't have an answer for her.

"See? Dumb."

"You're really smart, you know that?"

Zoe nodded emphatically "Yes, Mommy says that all the time."

There was nothing more stirring than your own child calling you out. Though he had been avoiding it, he knew he needed to talk to Riley. Even if she wasn't ready, more than enough time had passed from their miscommunication. It was time for him to come clean about his feelings. He was never good at romance, but he wanted to make this special, even if he got turned down.

When he got home, his mind was still trying to come up with a way to admit his feelings to Riley. His phone buzzed. He picked it up, realizing he had a friend request from Camilla. He quickly accepted it and an idea popped into his head. He glanced at Zoe, who was playing with a doll, and decided to message Camilla.

This may not end with them together, but he had to at least tell her the truth.

Chapter Twenty-Nine

Riley

The next day, Riley was behind the counter when a delivery came in. It was a man with a bouquet of flowers. Her first thought was Camilla's wife was being sweet again.

"Delivery for Riley Emerson," the man said.

She blinked. "I'm sorry, what?"

"The name says Riley. Does she work here?"

"Um, I'm Riley," she said, and she took the bouquet. The guy gave her a quick smile before leaving. She held the flowers, feeling like she was dreaming. Since when was she the kind of woman who got flowers? And who would even send them to her?

What if they were from David? She held her breath as she checked for an attached card. She plucked it out, hoping to get some answers.

For my favorite coffee investor.

That didn't tell her much.

"Ooh, what is that?" Camilla asked, coming around the corner.

"I got flowers," Riley replied.

"I can see that." She peeked over Riley's shoulder. "Wow, no signature, huh?"

"Why don't you sound more surprised?" Riley said, turning on her friend. "Usually you would be all over this."

Camilla put her hands up. "I know nothing."

"You know something."

"Nope," Camilla said. "Nothing."

"But—"

"You're still on to close the shop, right?" Camilla asked, and normally, Riley would be offended she was interrupted, but Camilla winked as she said it. It was obvious she knew something, but Riley wasn't going to get any answers.

"I am. Is something happening tonight?"

"Nope. Bye!" Camilla said, darting away.

Riley could only watch her friend leave, confused. What could it be? Was it her mom throwing a surprise party? Was Amanda about to ambush her?

It puzzled Riley until closing time. Dustin asked to leave early which only left her with Camilla.

She heard Camilla bumping around, but then was confused when the door shut. Ever since David cornered her in the parking lot, Camilla refused to let Riley close alone.

She walked to the seating area, only to find there was a lit candle on a single table, and the rest had been pushed to the side. Soft music played in the background and the golden glow of the candle gave everything a romantic vibe.

Camilla had to be playing a prank on her. There was no other explanation.

But then she saw Oliver. He came around the corner from the dining room, dressed in fancy clothes like he was out on a date. He looked nervous. Riley's brain shut off.

"Oliver?" she asked, blinking. "Where's Zoe?"

"At your mom's."

"What?" Riley shook her head. "Where's Camilla?"

"She left."

"Why?"

"I asked her to."

She looked around. "None of these answers are making sense."

"I'm trying to make a gesture here," he said. His voice wavered, his nervousness showing through.

"What?" Riley said, turning back to him. "I don't . . . Wait, did *you* send the flowers?"

"Yeah," Oliver said, chuckling.

"You didn't sign them."

"I thought you would know."

"I had no clue it was you," Riley said. "First rule of flowers, you have to sign them. And what were they for anyway? Is it a congrats for the investment?"

Oliver looked around him. "Uh, sort of. But I figured all of this would explain it."

"All of what?" Riley said.

He gestured to the table which had plated food on it. She still didn't get it. Was he wanting to eat with her? Couldn't they do that at home?

But then reality hit.

The flowers, the candlelit dinner, everything—it was all starting to come together.

"Is this . . ." Riley turned around again to make sure she wasn't hallucinating. Her face grew warm. "Is this a date?"

"Maybe," he said. "If you want it to be."

Riley didn't know what to think.

"Okay, um . . . just to be clear, are you expecting . . . someone else or is this for me?"

Oliver stepped closer until there was less than a foot of space between them. "It's for you, Riley. Always for you."

She stared at him, her heart racing. She had long since accepted they were only friends, but this wasn't what friends did. Friends didn't send flowers or set up a night alone in a coffee shop with music playing.

"How did you do all of this?"

"I worked with Camilla."

"And planned a date in the coffee shop?"

"Zoe called us both out for being dumb. We need to talk, and I figured this would be the best place for it. And I also got delivery from your favorite Italian place." He gestured to the table. Riley stared at them for a moment.

"Well, you sure know how to treat a girl."

"Is this decent? Because I'm not really good at this romance thing."

"Is that what you're doing—romancing me?"

"Yes. I'm trying to, anyway."

Riley couldn't help the excited giggle that burst out of her mouth, but it dulled when her mind caught up. "Wait, me? What about the woman you were dating?"

"I only went on one date with her," Oliver said, shaking his head. "And that was a dumb move on my part."

"Yeah, probably," she said. "Why did you do it?"

"I thought you'd say something if you were interested in me, but I should have asked you."

"It would have saved a lot of time if you had."

He sighed. "Yeah, it would have. And I meant to talk to you after our date, but things kept happening, and I could never do it."

"And now?"

"Now we have dinner."

Riley nodded, her mind trying to catch up to what was happening. It felt like a dream, being the center of attention for a guy she liked, with no secrets or misunderstandings. She didn't know what to do.

She felt filled with hope—a dangerous hope that could consume her. She wanted this. She needed this. And she didn't know what to do about that.

"So, what now?" she asked, her body warm.

Oliver smiled and put his hand on the small of her back, leading her to her chair. He pulled it out for her, and she watched him with a smile on her face. They sat across from one another, still for a short moment, before Riley was reaching out for the food and happily digging in. She was starving.

"So," she said, swallowing a bite. "You really aren't dating her?"

"No. That was a one-time thing. I told my dad I didn't want to be set up anymore after that."

"And when was this?"

"The night Zoe asked you to be her mom."

"Oh, right. That entire night was a dumpster fire."

"Yeah, it was. And I've been meaning to talk to you about this for so long, but things kept coming up."

"So . . . what does this mean for us?" she asked. She wanted to believe this when he admitted he had feelings for her, but a dark voice in the back of her mind was telling her she was making it all up.

"I don't know. I don't think saying I like you is enough," he said. "But I can say you mean everything to me, and I'd spend the rest of my life with you if I could."

"Well, I signed adoption papers, so I am with you for the rest of your life anyway."

"Riley, I'm in love with you. Romantically. Physically. Emotionally. It's all there."

She stared at him, wondering if she was dreaming. "Why?" she asked softly. "I've done nothing to deserve this."

"That's not true," he said, shaking his head. "You've done so much, not just for Zoe but for me. If you don't feel the same way, that's okay, but I hope you do."

"I thought you were looking for someone else."

"I'm not. I'm really not."

Riley stared at him, trying to find any hint of a lie, but there was none. And yet, she still didn't believe him, as if it were too good to be true. But maybe that dark part of her brain wasn't right, and maybe Oliver did love her in the way he was saying.

She was willing to risk it.

"So, what do you say?" he asked. "If you need time, especially after everything that's happened, I'll understand."

She knew she wasn't over what happened with David. She knew she had a lot of pain to overcome, but she couldn't resist his warm eyes and that kissable mouth.

She was terrified, but not nearly as much as she wanted this.

"I say fuck it," she replied. "I love you too."

"Not the answer I was expecting. But it's very on par for you."

She laughed. "I'm probably never going to do what you expect."

"I know," he said, smiling. "It's one of the things I love about you."

She stood up and pulled Oliver into a kiss over the table before she could talk herself out of it. He reciprocated immediately and she could feel him smile against her lips.

The kiss was far from perfect, and later, Riley would tease him for picking garlicky Italian food for their first date, but it didn't matter, because when they pulled apart, and for the first time, they were seeing eye to eye.

Oliver and Riley's story will continue in:

Under Any Conditions

Acknowledgments

This was a tough book. It was one of the first I wrote with the intent to publish, and it went through so many edits to get where it is today. With the help of Kasey Kubica, the kindest soul in the world, this was edited even further to bring it to this point. I owe her a lot.

To my husband, who graciously helped with housework and childcare: I appreciate everything you do. Having help with daily chores made this possible and I am so grateful I was able to do this while also wrangling our child.

To my friends: Cisco, Jewels, Lizzie, and Aislinn: thank you for your support. I needed someone to cheer me on through the self-doubt, and you all were there for me. I can't thank my support group enough.

About the Author

Elle Rivers was born and raised in Nashville, Tennessee, where she still resides with her son, husband, and six cats. In addition to writing, Elle loves reading, dancing, biking, and watching nerdy TV shows with her friends. Her Twitter handle can be found at @ellewrites.

Printed in Great Britain
by Amazon

31752758R00185